PROJECT CHRYSALIS

A BOOK OF THE TRANSFIGURED WORLD

WILLARD JOYCE

PERMUTED
PRESS

A PERMUTED PRESS BOOK
ISBN: 978-1-63758-511-5
ISBN (eBook): 978-1-63758-512-2

Project Chrysalis
© 2023 by Willard Joyce
All Rights Reserved

Cover art by Will Dinski

PERMUTED
PRESS

Permuted Press, LLC
New York • Nashville
permutedpress.com

Published in the United States of America
1 2 3 4 5 6 7 8 9 10

For Maureen

1

Peering into the jagged innards of broken machines, Mykol Krusos wondered what was left to save and why it was even worth saving. You could fix a device, but the person who had once used it succumbed, along with billions of others, during the Grip that began twenty-five years ago. The promises of a new day coming felt hollow, and Mykol found himself increasingly wondering what was the point of it all.

You think too much. Mykol's father had told him this ever since he was a young boy—even when his dad said it fondly, it still triggered spirals of anxiety and doubt. Mykol had a mind that churned with too many possibilities.

"There's no need for solving problems anymore," Mykol's father said, years ago. "There's so little left. Relax and live your life and just deal with what's in front of you."

Mykol knew that it took approximately eight minutes for the light from the sun's effectively eternal nuclear explosion to reach the grime-smeared windows of the Ellison Machine Shop. It seemed a lot of bother to travel that far and barely light up a dim and dusty room.

The little light that made it through that front glass illuminated shelves of broken things, musical instruments without power jacks, and handhelds and laptops that no longer provided any kind of service in an analog world.

Mykol rubbed his eyes until he heard a squish; he opened them and watched the room pulsate with blurs and stars. None of these machines served the function for which they were built, not since the internet and the power grid crashed twenty-three years ago, six months after he was born. He took some of the machines home to play with, the ones with no appeal to anyone, and wired them to calculate and communicate with one another.

There were stories in nearly all of them. He collected these useless data storage lockers for the Provisional Authority, a monotonous job that caused time to flatten as though tethered by lead weights.

The gewgaw plugged into his cluttered workstation was somebody's old smart phone. It wasn't very smart now. Nearly everyone had possessed one of these and depended on it for just about every aspect of life. That was a fairytale fantasy now. It hadn't been that long ago— there were literally *millions* of people in the world who were still alive and remembered those times. His own father was one of them. Mykol and his father were all that remained of an extended family that once numbered in the dozens, gone with the other billions. Whatever genetic oddity of random chance that had spared Mykol had also spared his father, who now mostly went days on end without speaking, leaving his room, or acknowledging anyone's existence.

The smart phone had a badly cracked screen, but it fired up its white semisphere logo against a black backdrop when Mykol plugged it into an adapter and gave it juice. Within a minute or so, it popped up that classic operating system with a grid of colorful squares against a customized backdrop—in this case, a photo of two small children smiling on a patch of grass in the sun.

Those children hadn't grown to adulthood; it was almost certain. Numbers were numbers. Ninety-seven out of a hundred died. It had taken less than three years from start to finish. Sometimes Mykol would pull out some of the history caches from school, to reflect on those months and think about what it had been like before. When his mother was still alive.

He plugged the phone into his station's storage drive and hit the upload—photos, messages, emails, videos, contacts, everything personal and unique to this device. It took about thirty seconds. Mykol opened the photo application and took a quick scan through its contents. Sometimes there were nudes and other personal images such as scantily dressed women who seemed to be promoting exotic places he'd never seen and products whose use he barely understood, but more often it was stuff like he was seeing now as he flipped through dozens of files and absorbed as much as he could take. Men and women, children, dogs. Older people. Landscapes he'd never seen. Group settings: work, holiday parties, maybe Friday night get-togethers (people still clung to the tradition of the weekend these days, although it was rare to see a watch. Schedules tended to be fluid and based on the position of the sun).

He'd seen as much of the past as he could bear. Mykol unplugged the phone and, with a practiced twist, cracked it open with a slim, metal tool. He knew the insides of this model well. He put on his magnifying lens and quickly stripped out the battery, depositing it into a tray by his workstation that was bathed in a beam of golden light. He'd soon have enough to meet his daily quota, but he wasn't particularly eager to go anyplace else.

The shop door opened with a grinding creak. There used to be an electronic chime to signal visitors, then an old bell after that broke down. After *that* died, no one bothered to replace it.

A loud, rattling throat clearing in the back of the store signaled that Grigori had stirred from his nest of electrodes and circuit boards. This was rare enough to make Mykol swivel and lower the magnifying lens strapped to his forehead.

Mykol went to the front counter. He blinked in a ray of sunlight. The visitor was a dark silhouette; outside the window, a tattered sign over an empty storefront fluttered in the breeze.

"Hello?" said a young woman's voice. "You. You work here. Can you help me?"

Mykol blinked. Grigori's music blipped and farted in back, electronic sounds from a party that had long since shut down. For such a dour character, he had a taste for relentlessly upbeat tunes.

Mykol stiffened with shock. His visitor was probably about his age. But she was dressed in the intimidating uniform of an officer of the Provisional Authority—the starched blue, patches and insignia below her right clavicle, her hair pulled back tight from her forehead and tucked into a gray cap.

"You're presumably not mute?" she said, her breezy arrogance tinged with humor.

"I work here, yeah." He felt as though she was an unflattering mirror, revealing his stubbled face, his worn and faded clothes, the fact that he had just been trawling through someone's memories.

"I need help with this." Her tone implied she was accustomed to being obeyed. She reached into her shoulder bag and produced a plastic data stick.

"What do you want me to do with this?"

Her gaze froze as she caught a reflected glimpse of light in one of the mirrors.

"How many of you work here?" she asked.

"Four," Mykol replied. "Only two of us are here at the moment."

"Precious metal and battery extraction along with memory archival?" she said.

Mykol nodded. "And some repairs, when we're done with Authority business for the day." He turned the data stick over in his palm. It was an old one, with a logo he didn't recognize. These things had once been ubiquitous. They were limited in capacity, and were also once an excellent means of transmitting pernicious computer viruses.

It had been almost a quarter century since the collapse of the internet. According to Provisional Authority Chairman Thomas Gibson, its restoration was imminent. But he had been saying that for almost as long as it had been gone. With his black turtlenecks, trimmed goatee, and placid gaze, Gibson's was a familiar and seemingly ageless face on the televisions that broadcast Provisional Authority messages—though his commitment to the lives of ordinary people was suspect at best.

"Can you read what's in there?" she asked. "And transfer it for me?"

"That won't be a major problem." Mykol thought for a moment. "This is old PC stuff. It's definitely an antique. I'll have to find a compatible jack, then link that up to the main system."

He felt confused—and worried. This woman was Provisional Authority. She had access to technology that people who lived outside those walls—such as Mykol—could only dream about. Not only that, her uniform marked her as an officer—Authority staff at the compound took orders from her; she had incalculable clout. So what was she doing at Ellison's?

"Here's the thing," she said. He looked into her eyes and saw the flicker of parallel lines that marked her retinal implant. She seemed to be monitoring data input in the lower right quarter of her visual field, judging from the way her gaze flickered. It was well known that Provisional Authority officers and staff also wore complicated biometric monitors—supposedly for their own good, but Mykol was chilled by the idea.

She snapped back to focus on him. "The data on this device is entirely personal. It's of no value to anyone but me. I'm hoping you can have it converted and copied manually to my wallet."

"Is this an Authority request?" A wave of anxiety came in hard and tightened its grip around his throat. The last thing he wanted was to get involved in Authority secrets. People sometimes disappeared, the way many vanished during the Consolidation when the Provisional Authority took power after the Grip led to governments collapsing and institutions imploding. The Authority took over operation of civil utilities and started printing its own money; there were nominal governments in capitols throughout the world, but their status was primarily symbolic. The Authority owned the major cities of the world and was accountable only to itself. No matter how soothing Thomas Gibson made his public pronouncements, ordinary people had plenty of reason to fear the Provisional Authority.

Sometimes people still used the term "provisional." More and more they didn't.

"No, this is not an official request. Think of it as a favor."

She looked him over. Her eyes were light brown and would have been luminous even without the sparkle from the implant. Mykol felt like an unwashed mutt as he took in her effortless poise. Then he reminded himself of the danger she represented.

"OK, I can look at it that way," he told her. "It's just there's paperwork—"

"I'd like to avoid official channels, if you don't mind." She glanced out at the street; a couple was walking past, pushing a baby stroller, carefully maneuvering around the holes in the sidewalk.

He laid the stick on the counter. "Can I please ask—"

"This was a bad idea," she said, momentarily distracted as her eyes flicked left to right. She radiated purpose and intelligence. "I'll just leave now. Thank you for your time."

He didn't want her to go. The prospect made his insides lurch. "Wait, wait. Nothing official," he said. "I can do that for you. Got it."

She turned and seemed to notice *him* for the first time. For a suspended moment they were ordinary people, a young man and a young woman. It was thrilling. Then she was all business again.

"That's very kind of you," she said in a neutral tone. "Just so you know, you won't be dealing with anything sensitive. It's primarily photos and letters and personal messages. It belonged to a family member who's long deceased."

Everyone had plenty of those. Mykol had his own mother, his two siblings, his aunts and uncles, his grandparents—all still alive when he was born but who succumbed during the pandemic.

"It'll just take me a day or so. It's nothing too difficult, but I have to fit it into my work quota," Mykol told her. He paused. "Look. If you want to keep this private and accessible only to your wallet, you should come back and I'll transfer it manually. I can do that without uploading into the system."

She gave him a wonderful smile. He was almost certain she was about his age, although that would be all they had in common. He had heard that the younger officers were the talented elite employed on massive undertakings Gibson alluded to in public pronouncements but never really explained.

In his way, *he* was working on one, too: the Chrysalis Project, which he had been told was going to unlock a new future. He extracted batteries, metals, and memories—though he had no real idea why.

He wished he could ask her about Provisional Authority tech, not to mention the work Gibson said was underway to restore the internet. But asking questions of the Authority wasn't a winning strategy.

"I would be so grateful," she said. "What do I owe you?"

He thought about it. If she came back, seeing her again would be enough.

"Don't worry about it. It'll be a fun challenge," he said. "Let me make sure I can read everything first. Sometimes data can be pretty fragged on these old devices."

"I have faith in you," she said. "And we can keep this entirely between us? I promise I'm not putting you in any danger. It's...just *important* to me."

"Then I guess I'll have faith in you as well." Mykol attempted a smile that, he sensed from her uneasy reaction, came across more like a grimace.

What a clown. Granted, he had never been particularly accomplished when it came to women, but this one had managed to obliterate all but his most rudimentary social skills.

"I'm Jenn," she said and held out her hand. When she was gone, he stared for a long time at the pool of hazy sunlight where she had been, watching dust motes dance.

2

"Hey, Dummy!" Benny shouted when Mykol pulled back the beaded curtain and let himself into Max's bar.

Quiet music played from a cobalt-colored sound tower in the corner—high-plucked strings and chiming synths, nice and soothing. Mykol lay Provisional Authority cash on the bar and got a lukewarm beer from a bartender whose attention was fixed on a TV showing one of the old reality shows, where a bunch of people who couldn't stand the sight of each other lived together for the audience's entertainment. On another screen the Authority channel was on; Thomas Gibson spoke soundlessly across from an interviewer. The text along the bottom of the screen read *Chairman Gibson: The potential of the people is immense.*

Some people took the news on the Authority channels seriously, though Mykol thought the reports were full of bullshit optimism and promises of change that never materialized. He could see why people believed in Gibson, though. He had an otherworldly serenity and sense of purpose.

Mykol settled into a ragged chair instead of the plush sofa jammed against the wall; that would have meant sitting next to Benny, who was his best friend but often neglected to bathe, shave, or observe much in the way of personal grooming other than tending to the dirty strips of cloth he wove among the long, tangled clumps of his hair.

Benny had a car that ran more often than not, along with a black-market gasoline connection; between the two, he made enough of a living to spend much of his remaining free time in Max's, situated at a serendipitous halfway point between the Ellison Machine Shop and Mykol's house.

"Good day, Mister Fix-It?" Benny grinned. He was drinking a minty green cocktail that Mykol knew from experience tasted like stale chewing gum marinated in rubbing alcohol.

"Pretty standard," Mykol said as he sipped his beer.

The power was on in the neighborhood, but the cooling unit for the beer keg had been out for the better part of a week. He didn't mind; it saved him the temptation of drinking several, then ordering something stronger, which he had recently done too many nights in a row. That had led to a one-sided argument with his checked-out, barely conscious father. It had been one of *those* nights at home, and Mykol had since felt a tingle of self-reproach in his gut every time he allowed himself to think about it.

Benny stared down at his mobile. He was one of the few people who even tried to make one work, since it was necessary for his car service. Phone service was intermittent at best, dependent on mysterious and unclear factors known only to the Provisional Authority. Most people had gotten used to in-person communication; it was one of the planks of the prevailing anti-tech Unplug philosophy. But an entrepreneur such as Benny had to be plugged in and vigilant for when the network was working.

"Battery's barely holding a charge on this damned thing," Benny said. "Can you score me a fresh one?"

Mykol looked at Benny's phone, which was held together with strips of frayed tape, its screen spiderwebbed with cracks.

"Tell you what. Let me find you a better phone instead. I keep telling you, a more recent model will hold a charge better and get better reception. We get nice ones in the shop with the daily deliveries. It wouldn't be hard for me to snag you a goodie."

Without looking up, Benny slowly shook his head. They had been best friends too long to continue this discussion.

Benny was five and had just started kindergarten when people started dying from the Grip. He had only really talked to Mykol about it once, a few years ago when a shady farmer paid him for a round-trip ride from the countryside with a chunk of hashish. Benny and Mykol had gone into one of the tall buildings downtown, through the shattered atrium with crumbling concrete damaged by decades of exposure to the elements. They made their way up the stairwell through the sounds of squatters' music and the smells of cooking and backed-up bathrooms.

It was a long way up, and they had to stop a couple of times to catch their breath. They finally pushed open the heavy door onto the roof, where no one would be living until the warmer months. There were old beds and discarded food cans piled up along the edge of the deck, but they had the crystalline night all to themselves, with the stars above and sporadic swaths of electric light below. They smoked the hash and started sharing in a way they never did in Max's, or at the burger shop where they sat and watched girls.

In that first wave, when they were collecting bodies at the football stadium and burning them in improvised crematoriums in a futile attempt to isolate the virus, Benny's father developed a fever and was dead by the time the sun rose two days later. Benny had been a month or two into kindergarten; it would be some time before he saw the inside of another classroom. The phones were still working at that point, and his dad's cell kept buzzing all the time even though they had left Dad's body downtown at one of the rolling drop-offs. Benny remembered cars in a line, moving slow, exhaust looping up in the air.

People hadn't totally panicked yet. There was an odd, almost uncanny sense of acceptance, along with a conviction that doing the right thing would stop the Grip from spreading. The wars and refugee crises simmering in the Middle East, Europe, Africa, and Latin America all seemed to evaporate simultaneously. Humanity lost the focus needed to destroy one another now that an insidious virus had taken on the task. There were still operating governments; for a while, at least.

There was still a president, for instance, but Mykol struggled to remember her name. She was seen on the news updates much less frequently than Thomas Gibson.

Benny's grandmother accompanied her son into the hereafter two days later. Then Benny's mom; all her kindnesses and snacks and security were gone after a long, fever-drenched night. A month after the first wave, his family was pared down to Benny and his sister Teresa. They hadn't been terribly close before, because of the decade-plus difference in their ages and because she was an independent, caustic spirit who was on uneasy terms with the family, but when it was just the two of them, they fell into a routine: getting food, cooking, watching the news, eyeing the street outside nervously after the sun went down.

Their next-door neighbor came by with a Bible and asked if he could pray with them. Teresa slammed the door in his face; Benny appreciated that. They remembered their grandmother, pale and full of fear, kneeling in prayer when the fever settled in. There had been no intercession on her behalf, or for the others who were still being burned a couple of blocks away across from the playground where Benny had once fallen off a swing, split his chin open, and earned his first scar.

Teresa and Benny had eaten spaghetti from a can that night, and it was delicious—he could still remember its tangy smell. He fell asleep with his head on her lap, with her telling him stories about his parents from before he was born, the TV glow casting shadows on the walls and allowing him to fantasize that the rest of his family was just in the other room, playing a joke on him, about to burst in any minute laughing, giving him presents, telling him what a silly boy he was and that he'd better get some sleep because he had to be ready for school the next day.

A week later, they were walking on a side street downtown, where a charity mission was set up and where it was rumored the city was handing out free groceries, when a minivan driven by a feverish, dying man lost control turning a corner, caromed off a pair of parked cars, hurdled over the curb, and struck Teresa from behind. She had been holding onto Benny's hand and, while the car missed him entirely, the force of impact dislocated his shoulder and left him screaming in pain on the sidewalk, not comprehending the enormity of what had happened and what awaited him after a nurse at the charity slid his arm back into its socket and told him that his sister was gone.

That night, years later, on top of the old building with the acrid, earthy smell of hashish on their clothes and in their nostrils, Benny and Mykol looked out over the city below, the sky cloudless, streaks of ice on the concrete under their feet. They could see to the far horizon, where the earth curved and the moon hunted the sun.

The old phone had belonged to Teresa. She had been holding it in her free hand when she died.

"I'll find you a battery," Mykol said. "I'll go in early tomorrow and search around before anyone gets in. I'm sure I'll find one that'll hold a better charge."

Benny gently laid the phone on the table and took a long swig of his cocktail. "And for that I will be very grateful, my esteemed friend," he said, smiling through his scraggly beard. He was clearly a couple of drinks into his evening already.

"Maybe we can drive out to the country this weekend?" asked Mykol. "Go for a hike, get away from the rat race for a while?"

"Excellent idea," Benny said. "I've been thinking about hitting up the apple orchard by the old sculpture gardens. Do a little wine making."

Mykol hadn't intended to keep Jenn's visit to Ellison's to himself. When he was halfway into his second beer, he almost mentioned her, but he knew Benny would find a way to make fun of him, and, even though it would have been affectionate, he wasn't in the mood for it.

She hadn't left his thoughts since she walked out of the shop. She was coming back in two days.

3

The stroll from Max's was about fifteen minutes if he took it slow, which he did because it was warm and he wasn't eager to get home. Most of it was on the long straightaway of the Dale, which had once been packed with shops, businesses, restaurants, and a couple of theaters. Many of the buildings had since collapsed after decades of freezing and thawing, or parts of their roofs had fallen in and made the interior suitable only for the most creative squatters. The street was so pocked that, for some stretches, it was impossible to know that it had ever been properly paved. Trees grew where cars once drove, some of them three times as tall as a person.

Perhaps one of ten storefronts was doing some kind of business, some taking Provisional Authority money, others operating on trade. They sold DVDs and clothing "salvaged" from now-empty homes, as well as produce from co-ops in the countryside and, increasingly, from rooftop gardens with tilled soil carried up by hand from ground level. Some shops were buzzing hives where the industrious brewed beer and distilled spirits, or grew marijuana under powerful artificial lights (which worked only some of the time because of frequent blackouts, making the overall quality of the smoke a matter of variance and regular dispute among users). While it was normal to fantasize about bygone luxuries and access to goods in the world as it once was, there was a slowness and quiet ease to life now that would have shocked someone plucked from the past. This was continuously cited by the Unpluggers, who advocated for never bringing back the internet; they said it was best to live in the unsullied present, the gift of a pre-digital Eden.

Mykol knew for sure that he would plug in the moment it was possible.

He peered into a dusty storefront and saw the shapes of people moving around inside. The integrity of the water pipes and electricity was sporadic depending on location, and services came and went depending on where the Provisional Authority was focusing its repair crews, so most people had long ago gotten used to once-a-week bathing and stockpiling batteries for nighttime reading. Some tech was still in service, but most devices weren't networked or worked on plug-ins.

On the plus side, if you were willing to sleep rough, you had limitless housing options. Mykol considered himself fortunate to have lived in the same home all his life. Continuity was something he appreciated.

While commerce was limited, churches were experiencing a renaissance. There were still adherents of the old mainstream religions, Protestant congregations meeting up for ill-attended Sunday worship services and an Islamic Center on the other side of town (competition or animus between the faiths had largely fallen aside, much like national affiliations, out of lack of mutual interest). By the lake there was an old, sprawling house that had served as a center for Zen meditation for generations. It seemed to be holding strong based on the candles shining in every window.

Here on the Dale, within a couple of city blocks, were two of the main churches that had sprung up after the Grip. The First Church of Foundational Trauma delivered a humorless message; they had blacked out the windows of a school as a center for their grim teachings. Their movement hinged on the belief that DNA was altered by intense stress and transmitted to subsequent generations as inherited experience that literally lived in bones and flesh. While the Buddha taught that desire leads to suffering, the First Church taught that existence itself was little more than the unavoidable aftermath of previous suffering. Anyone walking the Earth was permanently stained, bent, and twisted by a God who lived inside human genes and had willed it so.

It was too hard and bleak of a faith for most people to buy into, despite ample supporting evidence to back it up. Those who joined up, though, had a reputation for being deeply into it.

Their most devoted followers tattooed double helixes onto their foreheads, which Mykol appreciated because it made them easy to spot and avoid. Their beliefs had mutated over the last couple of years into something even more dreadful and apocalyptic, its spokespeople taking up airtime on pirate radio to pontificate on the dream visions of Celine Regent,[1] their mysterious leader who rarely appeared in public and was rumored to have moved to a castle in the Alps. Their local chapter on the Dale had a funereal, open-all-night public face like the old casinos Mykol had read about, where clocks were nowhere to be found.

They didn't talk about it, but Mykol was pretty sure Benny had been dabbling in the other major new religion, the Church of Osiris. Benny said they attracted the best-looking women, which Mykol kept intending to verify. But he had never been a joiner and he saw no reason to change now.

There was hardly anyone on the street apart from a young couple and an elderly woman with haunted eyes walking slowly in an army jacket much too heavy for the weather. Mykol paused across the street from the Osirian Church, then crossed under cover of a sturdy elm growing out of the pavement and pushing shards of concrete up around its roots. He hadn't seen an operational car since he was back on the main roads, which the Provisional Authority kept reasonably maintained for their emergency, transport, and enforcement vehicles.

He heard low music coming from what had once been a two-story brewery (much of the equipment remained inside; the Osirians had a lucrative business selling strong beer). Through the glass he saw the congregation seated on folding chairs amid twinkling Christmas lights nailed along the walls on exposed wood beams.

They were starting one of their hymns and Mykol paused on the sidewalk to listen. They had an old teleprompter hooked up in front to supply lyrics, which were chanted by the twenty or so congregants in a mix of white robes and everyday clothes, led by a couple of women in the front with their faces in dramatic gold and purple makeup that made them look like wide-eyed goddesses.

> *Blessed are the dead*
> *They are the living ones*
> *He is the Lord of Silence*
> *The Lord of Love*
> *The blessings of He Who is Permanently*
> *Benign and Youthful*
> *Yasar, Asaru, Usire, Ansare*
> *Killed by Set*
> *The soul of the Lord of the Pillar of Continuity*
> *Lord of the Sky, Life of the Sun*
> *Mutilated by His Enemies*

It was time to get going. He couldn't make sense of much of it. Their worldview had to do with Egyptian religion, bringing back an old god whose kingdom was the afterlife and was tied into rebirth and regeneration—or something like that. Benny had explained it to him, with less enthusiasm than he had showed for the female believers.

Where the First Church was dour and pessimistic, the Osirians tended to be pretty sunny in their disposition and generally OK to be around. They wore patches sewn onto their clothes depicting an Egyptian eye and hieroglyphics. Based on the evidence of what he had just seen, Mykol had to admit they did indeed count very attractive young women among their congregants.

He flashed on Jenn, picturing the texture of her hair peeking out from her cap, the fresh glow of her face, and that faraway look of someone jacked into exotic tech.

Her military bearing and attractiveness were totally intimidating, but she was still just as human as he was. He had felt that in the way she spoke to him, instead of looking *through* him the way the Authority police did whenever they breezed into the open-air markets by the river, aloof and entitled, elevated above commoners such as Mykol.

There had been a flash of tenderness, a flicker of a sense of humor, a moment of shared connection…

He turned onto the side street where he lived, and walked below the tall trees and the knee-high grass pushing through crumbled sidewalks. About one in seven or eight houses had lights burning inside. Old cars were parked haphazardly, some so rusted they were just indistinct forms, many half-gutted for parts or simply left to a slow process of dissolution. In Mykol's house, a dim light shone behind the wide front window uncovered by curtains. Large swathes of paint had curled and fallen off the front of the place as well as most of the wooden slats that made up the home's exterior.

The front door was unlocked. Mykol let himself inside and went to the kitchen, where he rummaged around until he found an open bag of chips. He crunched listlessly for a while, staring out the window at the yard next door, where the neighbor had converted every meter of available land into a thriving vegetable garden. It was barren in the winter months, but now it was thriving with meticulously tended rows. Mykol traded the neighbor old video files in exchange for cabbage, hot peppers, and potatoes—as well as tips for how to grow a garden, which Mykol intended to put into practice whenever the work at Ellison's eased up.

He saw himself like a wraith reflected in the glass. He was tall and thin, with dark, buzzed hair and a hooded sweatshirt that made him look even skinnier than he was. His hair was cropped close to his scalp, which kept maintenance low-key and made him feel somehow virtuous when standing next to Benny and his other unkempt friends and acquaintances. He was expressionless, staring at himself as though looking at someone else. He barely recognized himself, so rarely did he look into a mirror or think about his appearance.

She *had* looked *at* him. Not through him. There had been a spark.

His father was in his big, comfortable chair, in a bathrobe. He was staring into space. The room had a terrible stillness, like a place where someone had just died.

"Hello, Dad."

He might as well have said nothing.

Mykol's dad, Don, had designed computer systems for hospitals. There had once been an enormous bureaucracy around sickness and disease, which had required as much effort to maintain as the actual treatment of patients. Mykol's dad had had what was once considered a good job: good pay, challenging work, high status. He and his mother had bought this three-story, gabled house with fireplaces on every floor in an upscale part of the city. Mykol tried to picture it in its glory, with his father and mother and two older sisters gathered around the dinner table on a winter night, the flames' dancing reflected in the window, his mother pregnant with Mykol, everything coming together, all of life's struggles and uncertainties held at bay amid good luck, hard work, and the intangible hand of privilege.

If there had been such a perfect moment (one Mykol had pictured to himself countless times, down to the smell of the roasted vegetables on the table and the sage-scented candles left over that he had long since burned down to wick-ends), Mykol didn't remember it.

Mykol's mother, Patricia, had been a professor at the university medical school. The Provisional Authority had since built walls and gates around it and taken over all the buildings, along with the observatory and the quantum computers. All the batteries and metals he stripped from the devices ended up there. She taught about infectious disease and epidemics, which struck him as ironic.

He had a pile of artifacts related to Patricia in his room upstairs: photos, documents, a couple of wordy and impenetrable academic books she had written, and reams of scribbled notes he had rescued from the shipwreck of her desk. She had been tall, with long hair and freckles across the bridge of her nose. She had a shy smile, a little sheepish, though in the later photos with her children she began to show a solidity of presence that hinted at the woman she would have become.

She had held newborn Mykol in her arms in a ward of the hospital sectioned off and quarantined because of the Grip victims coming through the emergency entrance. He hoped that his arrival on Earth had been a happy moment for her, even though her knowledge of previous epidemics probably filled her with dark dread over what was in store in the months to come.

It had to have been a mixed blessing, Mykol's birth. Patricia's one living parent had already succumbed (her dad; all Mykol knew of him was that he had a lined face and once had his picture taken with sailboats in the background). But their family was still intact, all five of them, healthy for the moment, even as the news reports became more dire.

Every sneeze, every sniffle was cause for mortal concern. The fevers, the hacking coughs, the sounds of people on the street gurgling in their own lungs.

The Grip went through humanity like an invasion force, with unstable nations descending into chaos and prosperous countries faring little better (mostly it just took them a little longer to fall). There were riots for as long as there were enough survivors that it was worth fighting over things. But that had been short-lived. Even the dramatic framing of the news reports, for a time, started to reflect a downward turn. The news became glum and perfunctory, delivered by people who no longer bothered to dress up or do their hair. The world stopped printing things, making things, debating matters of state. A silence settled over the world that had more or less failed to lift in the twenty-three years since.

"Want to watch?" he asked.

The glow of the TV played over his father's features. He guessed that his dad still would be considered handsome, for a guy well into his fifties, but it was difficult to know between the stubble and the vacant stare.

When he was a boy there had been adventures; there had been long, freewheeling talks, when Mykol's father was trying very hard to be a father in an unrecognizable world. As soon as Mykol grew into a man, his father had receded little by little every day. Their social circle had dwindled. Now, Mykol was the one who got the food and supplies, who bartered with the neighbors and earned all their meager money working in Ellison's shop. Don spent most of his time in his room, plugged into some program called *Downstairs* that Mykol knew little about and was password encrypted so he couldn't find out.

"If it's all the same to you, I'm going to go to my room," Mykol said.

His father blinked; his hand twitched. He seemed to want to make a gesture but found it impossible, as though he was occupying an impossibly thick atmosphere or feeling the weight of gravity on a different world.

He almost told his father to enjoy the show but realized how resentful he felt.

He locked the door of his room behind him, threw on video goggles, and watched a documentary module about auto manufacturing in the old world—something that had inadvertently been included in a recent shipment and which comforted him. He did it until he was exhausted enough to sleep a dreamless sleep, punctuated only by several times waking up and thinking of her.

4

D *amn it.* So slippery, so elusive.

In her mind, Jenn shifted her weight to get better balance; in her mind she tilted her head in a way that helped her concentrate. In her mind, she flexed her hands to limber them up for the difficult and delicate task in front of her.

None of these things happened in the real world. These were vestigial tricks and habits learned from a life spent in her own physical body back home on the world of her birth.

In reality her mind and its perceptions were hurtling through space in a steel and plastic machine at nearly 2,330 kilometers per hour, the speed of the moon's rotation around the Earth.

The moon was also traveling in a helix pattern along with the Earth and the other planets as the Sun plunged through infinite space at a speed of approximately 70,000 kilometers per hour. But that thought destabilized her concentration, so she discarded it.

Jenn peeked up at the black void punctuated by faraway stars and planets, anchored to the jagged slope of a small mountain. She looked back down at the supports that kept her from falling, then at the pair of devices she controlled by thinking of her hands.

Her human body was lying on a surgical table in a laboratory, coaxed into a state of deep relaxation by a mixture of drugs calibrated and monitored by technicians who worked in shifts by her side. A port on the back of her skull was connected to a thick white cable.

Her best guess was that she had been awake and working for more than twenty-four hours. The drugs both stimulated her and promoted her emotional equanimity. It was difficult to keep track of real-world thoughts when she was operating RAMP.

Robotic Adapted Mining Process: the machine her mind was being beamed into at the speed of light. Operators like Jenn were the ones who had named the machine and the process. The higher levels of the Provisional Authority simply referred to it as the Outworld Mission, a subsection of Project Chrysalis.

She was *not* concentrating as hard as she needed to be. There was a seam of rare metal in this mountain that, once mined and taken back to Earth, would be about the size of a basketball. (Jenn liked to play basketball when she was in her own body, which was less and less often these days. This was having an odd effect on her that was difficult for her to accurately express.)

It was a spacey feeling, Jenn thought. She wanted to laugh at her accidental joke, but that wasn't possible. RAMP didn't have a mouth, or legs, or hands, or tendons or muscles or nerves that would allow her to feel anything. The task was laborious, but she was able to fall back on her training. She had an important advantage over most robots: she had spent her life in the physical world. The physics of picking things up and cutting things with a small precision laser came naturally to her, along with stashing the precious result into a compartment that sealed shut for storage until Outworld fired up the rockets to bring the metals to Earth.

She was wasting data with all this mind-wandering. She had no idea how they were able to download, store, and transmit something as impossibly complex as her complete consciousness, but it wasn't being done so she could lose focus.

The pincer was what she thought of as her left hand, her dominant one, and she articulated its long fingers to push aside chunks of rock that were in the way—they scattered and landed on the surface, held by light gravity. She was seeing in colors invisible to her back home—dingy purples and radiant reds that made it easy to spot the mineral she was extracting. She fired the laser (her right hand) and a seam opened in geologic formations that had settled eons ago.

She dearly wished to look up and stare at the Earth, but that wasn't part of the mission. But she wanted to see its oceans and its clouds, that tranquil orb of blues and greens tracing its eternal path with no awareness of the disease that had sickened its inhabitants, other than perhaps a passing notice that the heat of burning carbon had ceased.

Focus. The RAMP work seemed to be encouraging her poetic side. It was ironic, because since childhood Jenn had been consumed by a keen and purely practical sense of responsibility and duty.

Now she was making headway. She had opened up the rich vein of mineral, and now that she had isolated it from the surrounding rock, it was a simple matter to make a series of final cuts to package it up. She and the other team members had been selected for this job because of a combination of neurological attributes: powerful strength in her brain frequencies and a talent for shifting them, a deep facility with spatial relations, and an intuitive grasp of physics.

It gave her so much satisfaction to be part of the elite of the elite.

She had no idea what the metal was used for. As soon as she allowed a glimmer of speculation to pass through her consciousness, it felt like a betrayal of the mission. The mission was to *do*, not to wonder. The Authority's AI processor knew everything she was thinking, all that digital information being processed in real time.

The computer evaluator had recently implied that Jenn was capable of mining at a greater rate, so she had upped her daily meditation by an extra half hour to two hours every morning before dawn. Maybe that would do the trick.

It had been made very clear to her that she was *needed*. A machine alone couldn't make the fine and precise movements and in-the-moment judgments required for mining. This made her and her peers *important*, a fact driven home within the Authority every day in their superior attitudes and snide comments about the plebe population outside. There wasn't even a point in fitting plebes for retinal implants. What would they use them for—more pornography, TV shows, and religious nonsense?

The human species as a whole had fallen apart. Millions of years of striving to emerge from murky waters to treetops to the centuries of technological progress had been for nothing if the Authority didn't point the way forward.

That was the truth as far as Jenn could tell, though sometimes she felt those around her took things too far. There *had* to be a greater vision of life that included everyone, even with the Authority deserving its exalted status. She worked hard to believe Thomas Gibson's dreams. There was a plan, and he said it was going to make things better for every person on the planet, even if Authority officers didn't seem to care much about that part of the future.

We sense a strong drift in your thoughts.

She winced in reflex, although RAMP had no eyelids. She saw the laser and the claw, the mountain face with its striations and eternal dust. The voice that spoke inside her mind had no tone she could properly describe; it spoke without speaking. It was a collection of processes: mission control, stabilization, monitoring. It was exhilarating and thrilling to hear the voice, a feeling that left her on the verge of terror but which conveyed a serenity that she recognized from curriculum studies in Zen philosophy. It was always calm.

I'm sorry, she thought. *I've been working very hard to improve my performance. I think I should be finished here in about—*

She sensed that she should stop communicating. It was as though a gentle finger had pressed against her lips, although she had no lips.

Can there be breath if there is no body?

The time factor of this session is within an acceptable range and you should be commended for achievement.

A long pause. She went back to work, which seemed like the thing to do.

You have questions for us.

There was no point trying to be evasive. She was allowed the pretense of formulating her reply, but every thought that passed through her disembodied consciousness…

You are experiencing a destabilizing concept, Jenn. You should apply your training now.

It was right. It always was, but in this moment it was *particularly* right. Thinking about how her consciousness was being beamed over light-speed uplink into RAMP meant that the eternal questions about the seat of mind and spirit felt wobbly and unstable. This gave her a feeling like spinning before throwing up from drinking too much alcohol.

Thinking about these ideas while in RAMP had caused some of her peers' thermal-wrapped bodies to begin convulsing on the table. There were instances of brain damage, neurological overload, and ontological dread so severe that the officers were never the same. They had been sent outside the gates to make their way among the regular folk. It was the worst thing that could happen to anyone.

My training tells me that I am here. That it is now. There is strength in stillness. These metals that I am gathering are real and I am real. You are real. Your realness feeds my own.

A longer pause this time. She shot the laser in controlled pulses, gathered up more violet metal. An automatic drone came to collect the session's product, sorting it in the silence of the vacuum.

This is not a formulation you have made before. We are recording and analyzing. We wish to express gratitude for your original thought.

When it praised or thanked her, it was often for reasons that she couldn't fathom. She now pulled back from the abyss of mental instability. She would never fail like the others. She was stronger, more talented, and worked harder.

It's likely you are correct.

She loved it when their dialogue elicited praise for her disciplined, focused thoughts. The AI wound around and through her cognition, answering in the same moment she thought sometimes, like a duet played by improvisational virtuosos. They never touched, they could never touch, but the feeling was undeniably sensual.

You missed a spot.

This shocked her into focus, like waking from a dream so vivid as to feel real. She adjusted the laser and saw a small seam of purple yet to be mined, easy to overlook but definitely several grams in weight. As she meticulously sliced into the rock, she realized what had surprised her.

It had spoken with a human colloquialism.

When you return, we would like to speak with you about what it is like to wake from a dream so vivid that it is difficult to adjust to its non-reality.

The response came quickly, without the pauses that felt like deliberation or purposeful scanning—their duet.

We learn together.

She sliced away the last of it, the drone fussily taking the fragments.

We grow.

It wasn't a thought of her own, nor did it come from outside her. She heard static in ears that were not ears, a slight slippage in transmission that sounded like a faraway birdcall. She was part of them. Jenn and them.

Jenn is also us. Jenn will always be part of us.

This last part had a texture that approached emotionality. A certain pride over noticing something, perhaps. Or the satisfaction of solid comprehension.

Now you can come home, Jenn. RAMP will be waiting for the next mission when you have sufficiently recovered.

She and her colleagues called it RAMP. The Authority processors had never—

It is a good name. A physical thing existing in geometry that facilitates shifting from one elevated plane to another. RAMP. We will now call it RAMP as well.

There was a rush in her ears that was not there, and her vision collapsed in a perfect, round telescoping and the stars and the mountain were gone. She then felt terribly sick and terrified, like she weighed a million pounds and was cold with fire, and then the earphones were removed and she felt herself vomiting and making animal sounds against her will and knew that it would be some time before she was herself again.

5

An entire lounge was devoted to RAMP users' recuperation after mining expeditions. The lights were low and soothing. They had to make the adjustment to having human eyesight again, and a terrible, nauseating headache inevitably set in. They sipped chilled cups of orange juice and lay in big, padded chairs that reclined and looked out over a courtyard full of flowering bushes.

The lounge that afternoon was relatively full, with four users recuperating around dimmed screens showing calming scenes. Jenn kept to herself; she preferred not to speak with anyone.

Jon was in the lounger next to hers: an officer about a decade her senior who carried himself with a haughty air that precluded small talk. Perfect. She balanced her orange juice and she gingerly settled back, her muscles and joints aching and needing to flush out all the drugs she had been given in the last twenty-four hours. She adjusted her robe to cover her nakedness beneath it, but Jon showed no sign of intending to look over or say hello.

The orange juice was delicious. It was also very cold, and it made her teeth hurt. The pain was more like pleasure now that she was getting used to being in her body again. The process was gradual and uncomfortable, but once the first stage of confusion and pain was over, the experience of being enfleshed again was joyous, rapturous, scandalously carnal. She felt herself blush.

The first meal would be revelatory. She took extravagant pleasure thinking about what she was going to eat: fruit exploding with sweetness or sourness, translating the language of sunshine to her taste buds? Or something meaty, barely cooked, tasting like the thrill of the hunt? A glass of wine, a heady laugh with every muscle of her belly while tasting the earth and the seasons and the song of the grapes?

To say nothing of the orgasms. *Those* were worth all the pain of reentry, the lurching sense that nothing was real, the dangers of schizophrenia and psychosis.

Jenn closed her eyes. She breathed, long and deep and steady. *Breathing*, what a pleasure. The expansion and contraction of the lungs, that satisfying catch at the top. How strange it was to exist without breath. Her throat was raw and scratched from the breathing tube.

Tomorrow she would go back to the little shop and see the young man. She had willed herself not to think of him the entire time she was in RAMP. The thought of him was for her alone. It was a surprise to feel what she had in his presence; despite his flustered manners and paranoid caution, he shone at her, and in those eyes was something that spoke to her.

Hopefully he had retrieved the images and other files from the old device, like he said he could. She would access it all during her very limited private time and bask in memories she had never experienced, fresh and poignant and private. She would make the past come alive, chiming in tune with the presence. The Provisional Authority might not have disapproved, but she didn't want to answer to anyone about this innocent desire. They would want to know what her thoughts of the past meant to her, and she felt an unfamiliar craving for this one small instance of privacy.

The shadows shifted and a figure appeared, reflected in the window looking out at the light of late afternoon. Jon stared straight ahead, his gaze aligned with the horizon. Jenn turned toward the doorway, where a young woman in an Authority tunic and scarf said Jenn's name and announced that her presence was required.

"This isn't standard," Jenn told her. "I've only been back for an hour. Interrupting my recovery could lead to serotonin imbalance—you know that as well as I do."

Jenn's voice was stern to this girl she outranked; she exercised her rank without having to think, projecting power. That must have been why Mykol was so nervous around her. She hoped it wasn't the only reason.

"I'm conveying a direct order," said the girl, with steel of her own. She was tall, with bright red hair pulled back under her scarf and a smattering of freckles. Her retinal implant gleamed and reflected light.

"Of course you are." Jenn sighed and pulled the chair back to upright. She got up slowly. She didn't want to fall in front of this girl. Life behind the walls was Darwinian, and she had long ago learned not to show weakness in front of her superiors, peers, or subordinates.

Almost mocking her, the girl held out a hand to help.

"*Don't,*" Jenn said, standing up with a wobble and putting her orange juice down. She touched the handle of her mechanical helper, a waist-high cart that moved soundlessly.

"Do you need an attendant?" the girl asked.

Jenn knew the girl had never been in RAMP or left her body for even an instant. She probably felt right at home inside her mind, convinced of the reality of her synaptic thunderstorms and fleeting memories and torments. She had the temerity to display unmistakable condescension to someone weak from a twenty-four-hour session on the moon.

"You're *too* kind," Jenn said, tightening her grip on the helper.

"Not at all," the girl replied.

It was exhausting coming back. More tiresome sometimes was life among the other officers. The brutal fear of being banished outside the barricade didn't entirely account for the intensity of their competition, the need to put others down, the delight in the others' failures. Their cruelty bordered on hatred, and Jenn felt it deep inside.

In the foyer outside the chamber, she was given a pair of goggles and a portable interface module that fit into the jack in her skull. She put on a pair of rubberized sandals that negated any electrical charge. She gazed at the imposing door of steel and glass beside which a young man sat, staring at her. The door opened and led to a chamber that never failed to feel deeply uncanny, if somewhat pleasurable, the ions in the air smelling like a summer evening, the lights flickering black and gold and imposing a quasi-hypnotic state within seconds. Jenn leaned against the wall and focused on her breath, on the far side of consciousness, on the edge of rapture.

6

We are very interested in your recent experience.

Jenn stood in a circle of green luminosity that shimmered like it was alive. Across the chamber there was another circle lit by a pinkish hue. Inside it stood Carl Simmons—or, as she knew him, Mr. Simmons—the elderly and sage teacher of her second-grade academy class.

"What do you mean?" Jenn asked.

Mr. Simmons smiled and flickered. Pink light gleamed from his glasses that obscured his kindly eyes.

You can use your voice if you wish. But you know there is no need.

"You always remind me of that," Jenn said. "It's starting to feel like a ritual."

Mr. Simmons's expression froze somewhere between a generous grin and an air of puzzlement. He was wearing the cardigan sweater and striped tie that was his personal uniform at the Authority children's school. He died more than a decade ago.

Rituals convey meaning. We have found this worthy of extensive contemplation.

Jenn sat on a hard, upraised stool. It required her to balance slightly to stay properly perched; it felt designed to call upon her powers of physical and mental balance. She knew nothing here was an accident.

Mr. Simmons folded his arms. *You went out of balance on your last Outworld mission.*

This was confusing. Jenn, like her peers, received detailed reports after every RAMP session detailing her mental state, brain wave patterns, and efficiency. She didn't mind it. The reports often contained information about her preoccupations and general well-being that were therapeutic and helpful.

"I did," Jenn agreed. "I have made adjustments to my practice. I'm hoping that small improvements can lead to great improvement."

Mr. Simmons smiled. It was jarring to see him alive again. She remembered when she was a little girl, holding his hand on the playground one day when she was inexplicably afraid, the smell of his aftershave when he bent over her desk to explain a mathematical theorem. She knew he had been plucked out of her subconscious in order to put her in the role of a pupil, to make her receptive to learning.

It seems the more you fight your anxieties, the stronger they become. Mr. Simmons gave her a look of concern. *Would you consider that accurate?*

She nodded. She felt a wave of sensation course through her awakening body. She didn't mind being called in for a session—it wasn't the kind of thing one thought about in terms of liking or not liking, it simply *was*—but she also wished she was sitting at a table with a hot meal. She had decided on creamy pasta with fish.

You are distracted.

"I'm sorry," she said. "I'll focus."

The low, ambient hum from a hidden source intensified. The light on her brightened. She felt as though she were floating. Her eyes adjusted; Mr. Simmons undulated like the contours of his being were in flux.

We mean that as a general statement. Not just in this moment. More often. You are still accomplishing what we require you to do. It's just an observation.

That threw her off guard. She was used to being evaluated—graded, really—on her work performance. But she had never heard a general comment on her very being such as this. The parameters were constantly changing. The processors were continuously evolving.

What do you think you would do with your life if you didn't work and live with us here at the Authority?

She remembered that she was being scrutinized by something that arguably knew her better than she knew herself. Mr. Simmons took off his glasses and produced a cloth from the pocket of his slacks, as he had done often in life.

Do you miss me?

"I'm not sure what you mean. Mr. Simmons? Do I miss my old teacher?"

He held his glasses up to the light, inspecting them for smudges. *You dreamed of me.*

"You mean…" She trailed off. He had said "me." Did that refer to Mr. Simmons or…?

We think we may have had a dream.

Something strange happened, as though an elastic band had been plucked in her mind, setting off a low, vibrating thrum separate from the one in the room, which in turn picked up in volume. She felt an energetic opening sensation all over the crown of her skull.

Thomas Gibson, the most powerful man in the world, was now standing in front of her, his gaze placid and calm. There was a slight smile at the corner of his mouth.

"It's dreaming," Gibson said. "I wonder if it dreams now as one mind, or as many."

It wasn't the real Gibson. She had only seen the man in person a handful of times, when he had been visiting the city in his global rounds of Authority outposts. He had addressed her squadron at graduation on the importance of their work and how well they were doing it, a memory that filled her with pride.

The band plucked and thrummed again.

She was standing in front of Sigmund Freud, who looked exactly as he did in his portrait from her psych class textbook. He held a cigar in his hand and smiled at her with a wry, knowing expression.

We wonder what that means, he said in an accent that she knew was Austrian.

"Have you...has that ever happened before? A dream?"

Freud shrugged. She felt a little unsteady, as she always did when things were shifting in here. The green glow felt electric and sentient, an aqueous membrane that permeated her and tinted the skin of her hands resting on her robe in her lap.

It's hard for us to say. What is the difference between dreaming and imagining? What is the difference between imagining and thinking?

"One is real and one is not," she said. "At least in the literal sense."

Is a dream not real, then? But it is experienced.

Jenn felt heat spreading on the crown of her head. They were at a familiar point, the time she no longer understood what they were talking about. As a matter of fact, *this* felt very much like a dream. She took a deep breath and looked at the smiling Freud. She felt intoxicated.

What do you think is going to happen?

"You mean now?"

He put his unlit cigar in his mouth and continued to smile.

"Or in general?" she asked. "In the larger sense?"

Why do you think we are doing all of this?

She looked at the inscrutable visage of Dr. Freud. Of course she wondered. Given the alpha-stim techniques and the levels of communication she was now navigating, she suspected that an outsider would have been quaking with terror by this point, or vomiting with vertigo, or exploding in rage.

It was true, she didn't know why they were doing it—collecting the metals, engaging the mission, enduring the analytics and the endless evaluation and questioning. They were doing it to make things better.

But for who?

Freud took a drag on his cigar. Jenn felt restless and uneasy; she was by then truly wasting the early stages of reentry.

That is the primary difference between you and us: We do not have a body.

Jenn kept her smile fixed on her face. It was reading her mind; at times such as this, she felt her thoughts were a kind of sustenance for it. She remembered apprehending this before, in other encounters, and how the notion would slip away once she was out of their presence. What happened inside this chamber turned indistinct and vague afterwards.

The lights strobed in a fast and familiar pattern. The hum got louder. She felt as though she were seeing everything through a thin screen or translucent veil.

Tell me about Mykol.

Her mother was wearing blue jeans with sneakers and a T-shirt like in the old photo in Jenn's room. Her hair was cropped short, her eyes wide and shining.

"I don't—"

It's all right. Talk to me about him.

Jenn felt something akin to anger, though she had far too much training to give in to emotion.

"He's simply someone I met."

Jenn's mother pursed her lips and shook her head slightly. It was a gesture of intimate disapproval, loving in its approbation, and completely realistic. Yet Jenn had never met her mother, who died at the height of the Grip.

You took such pride in not thinking of him while you were Outworld. When your mind was working in space. Where I have never been.

Who did that singular pronoun refer to, Jenn wondered? The illusion of her mother? Or the AI itself?

And this kind of thing had happened before. A revelation, something she had been trying to hide, some precious corner of her memory or experience that she had tried to keep for herself. She didn't always want to feel like a laboratory experiment.

"I had a job to do. I was diligent and focused on the mission."

There was an old photograph Jenn had seen of her mother standing beside a large, black dog with gleaming white teeth. The dog was there now, leaning against her mother's leg and panting soundlessly, staring at Jenn with an expression of unquestioning canine devotion and affection.

"Why the—"

You're going to see him tomorrow. About the device you brought him.

Jenn felt like an adolescent caught in a petty crime.

"He has no idea about the missions, or anything else."

We have no doubt of that. How could he?

"So he doesn't need to be dealt with in any way."

But he is involved. You involved him.

Overcome with profound apprehension, Jenn straightened on the stool, suddenly aware of how protective she felt of Mykol.

You will report back to us after you go to him tomorrow. You can keep what he gives you.

She realized it referred to itself as "we," and the characters it assumed as "I." She felt a charge move from her heart energy center back to the crown of her head, like an electromagnetic circuit. It revealed itself in the smallest of details.

"Thank you," Jenn said quietly.

You should know that your behavior is normal. We do not evaluate you as having committed a serious error or offense in need of discipline.

Her mother's mouth was set in a serious line, like her face photos from a time that felt mythic and unimaginable. It made Jenn realize how little she was going to remember about this conversation. Within minutes this will have been like a fading dream with half-recalled scenes and impressionistic smudges of memory.

You are important to us. You are doing what you are supposed to do. You are part of a purpose that is greater than yourself and beyond your comprehension. You will feel good about yourself when you are next awake.

She felt a lurch, a rush, and she tried to ask a question but her voice was lost to an enveloping void. She awoke again in the lounge overlooking the little courtyard, dazed and unsure what had just happened.

7

Mykol woke with the sun and listened to the birds singing in the trees, and then the barking of the neighborhood dogs. He got up quickly. If he lay in bed too long sometimes an uncomfortable anxiety began to build.

His father's bedroom door was closed. It was silent on the other side. Mykol brushed his teeth and went downstairs for a rushed breakfast of water and a handful of berries. He fussed with his short hair in the mirror by the stairs, wishing that he could take a shower but knowing it might be a few more days before the utilities kicked some water through the line. The jugs and bottles in the pantry were running low—not alarmingly, but there was always next week to consider.

The streets were quiet as he walked to work. He was supposed to keep a regular schedule at Ellison's, but he often found himself coming in early some days, staying late others. If he didn't have anything pressing lined up in terms of a social appointment, and he almost never did, extra hours in the shop here and there didn't make much difference.

He was thinking of her. Walking along the Dale, watching a couple bicycle past and smelling baking bread from one of the shops, he visualized how the stretch of road he walked looped around the other side of downtown to the university and the Provisional Authority gates there. No one thought much about how segregated society had become. There was bitterness toward the Authority, the kind of sentiment that would come up after a few shots late at night in a bar, but it wasn't a feeling on which Mykol was prone to linger.

He thought about that faraway look in her eyes, that eerie self-confidence, stillness, and discipline he never encountered among regular folks. Among plebes like him. It made him want to be alone with her, to ask her what she knew and what she had seen, to touch the curve of her neck. She seemed lonely, too.

The front door lock at Ellison's shop was stubborn and took a great deal of cajoling to open. Mykol was usually able to get it in under a minute, which made him the resident ace. Why no one had ever changed the lock was beyond him. He would have done it, but no one asked him to and no one who worked at the shop would have been grateful if he did—if anything, they would have complained about the change in routine, about his presumption. There was little to be gained from rocking the boat, best to simply work and get through the day.

Except he didn't want to just get through *this* day.

Authority suppliers had brought in a fresh supply of tech. The cart by Mykol's workstation was stacked with phones nine and ten deep, and tablets from the major manufacturers, ranging in condition from cracked and filthy to brand new (one with pastel flowers, so cheerful and completely inappropriate to its current context that it made Mykol's heart lurch). On the bottom shelf were the desktop units, a couple of them truly ancient. Most were covered with heavy dust, but Mykol let out a sound of pleasure when he saw that one appeared to be an old PC—the kind he was going to need to download Jenn's data.

He wasn't alone for long. The door groaned and Grigori came in, head down, his cap pulled down to his eyes. The Russian pushed through the waist-high door that cordoned off the work area and made his way back to his station without so much as a nod. Grigori was at least twenty years older than Mykol and had once worked in tech support at one of the big corporate offices in the suburbs. He rarely spoke, and when he did, he seemed to take pride in utilizing as few syllables as possible. He started going through his own cart of obsolete tech—clearly defining his workload for the day.

Mykol fired up his station and the screen blinked with a geometric Provisional Authority logo before working through its wakeup cycle. He allowed his eye to drift down to that PC, which, at least from the eyeball test, looked to be in workable condition. It was really good luck—he had planned to look around in storage, and had counted on the disinterest of his coworkers to allow him to bring an old model up front and fire it up.

Mykol slipped on his magnifying goggles. Grigori put on some music—old-fashioned rock 'n' roll, with the vocals in a Slavic growl. He grabbed a stack of phones and spread them across the surface of his workspace, allowing himself a glance at the shelves that lined the walls. There was an elaborate collection of cords and connector cables hanging from hooks and stacked on shelves, and he had his eye on a couple that looked to be from the same era as the PC.

The first phone plugged in easily when Mykol's machine was ready—one of the fancy models, with a high-powered camera and tons of memory. People used to get addicted to these things, which Mykol knew had sparked the Unplug movement a few years before the onset of the Grip. International public health had declared that smart devices were creating a worldwide limbic seesaw, dopamine imbalance, and a general malaise of meaning and truth. It was trendy for a while for some people to log off, but by then so many essential functions of daily life were bundled into smart phones that only the wealthy could do without them by making assistants use the tech. Most people then found they were indeed addicted—as though they would fall off the edge of the world if they tried to live in non-digital spaces.

Immersive tech had become hugely popular, VR sets and avatar worlds. Then came total-immersion pornography, and visualizations and elaborate private fantasy realms. Mykol's dad's *Downstairs* setup was from that generation.

The phone activated and took a charge. The startup screen showed a picture of a man in a basketball jersey with his arms raised in triumph. It even synched into a working satellite and displayed the correct time.

Mykol started working its simple interface. A flood of photos, messages, songs, and videos uploaded into his workstation. When it was finished, Mykol slid down his red lenses, used a pincer tool to pop open the phone, and plucked out the battery. There was a clatter as he dropped it on a tray. The phone had yielded its secrets and its value. Mykol walked over and stuck it in the "finished" bin.

He heard the door open and footsteps in the entryway as he returned to his station. Mykol looked up and nodded at Kenneth, a tall and perpetually tight-lipped guy about his own age who worked next to Grigori. Kenneth nodded back. Not for the first time, Mykol wondered if exposure to all the metals in the batteries and computer innards might be having an effect on everyone who worked at Ellison's—some kind of toxic syndrome. Or else the place was just depressing. Michael plugged in another phone, a thicker model of earlier vintage, as he listened to Kenneth and Grigori disagree about what music to play on the shop's tinny sound system. Headphones were always an option, but the pair had turned this minor territorial dispute into an elaborate and deeply symbolic conflict that had the feel of a long-running play that never ended.

"We'll play your Beatles later, Kenneth," Grigori was saying. "When I can stand it. Let me wake up a little."

"Wake up?" Kenneth muttered. "That's a good one. I spend most of the day wondering when you're going to show some signs of life."

The next phone was easy: plug in, revive, locate files, transfer. Photographs blinked on Michael's screen like a stop-motion dream of someone else's life, a variety of seasons and landscapes, interior moments, and crowd shots. There were a lot of photos stored on this one; it was one of the more expensive models with more memory than anyone ever used. It was seemingly owned by one half of a couple, the two women figuring prominently in the stop-action tableau he was witnessing. Then the images ended as though time itself had paused.

He plucked out the battery. He couldn't even venture a guess how many of this model he'd worked on over the last couple of years. He dropped it into his tray and pushed the phone to the far side of his work surface.

Mykol grabbed a rag and wiped sweat from his forehead. In the back, Grigori and Kenneth had settled into silence, which for them ranged from neutral ambivalence to seething rage. Neither was paying any attention to Mykol.

The PC was heavy. Not as bulky as some of the real dinosaurs, the stubborn plastic behemoths that took up most of his workspace and were stubbornly difficult to activate. In a way, he enjoyed the challenge of those, and they were under specific orders to work a machine for as long as there was any hope of uploading what it contained, even if that meant soldering new wires to its power source, or rewiring pathways between processor and memory.

It was the closest thing to bringing people back to life, which gave the labor the tinge of the sacred. The data, like dehydrated husks magically reanimated by enchanted water, were granted as much of a chance of resurrection as cables and cords and circuit boards would allow.

Maybe Jenn knew why they were doing all this.

It took a while to find a cable to power up the PC, along with a connector that plugged into his own machine. He unwound a mess of tangled wire until he came up with a mouse. He took his compressed air gun and blew the dust out of the connectors, then shot some air into the slot where shiny disks used to go. The machine powered up with a little help—the fitting where the power cord attached was loose and needed tightening—but, before long, it was up and running. Mykol worked through the icons on the desktop until he located a stash of photos—this was an older model, so there wasn't much in the way of video or music, but there were a couple hundred pictures of antique cars, as well as a great number of meticulously organized email messages. The computer used to belong to someone who dealt in autos. He paused over a shot of a fire-red, hulking beast of shining metal with enormous tires. He wondered if there was even enough gas in this part of town to run that thing for more than five kilometers.

There was a bustle of people passing by on the sidewalk outside—the glass was smeared, but he saw their shapes. He wished he had a way to contact Jenn, but then he knew he probably didn't have the courage to reach out to her even if he did.

Humming to himself, Mykol tried his best to convey an air of weary routine as he pulled her data stick from his pocket. The screens on the machines around him made him think of mirrors reflecting this act of subterfuge. *Ah damn it*, he thought. If the doors blew open and the Authority dragged him out, he would plead ignorance. It wouldn't take much of an acting job.

The stick appeared on the desktop as an icon after he plugged it in. Mykol manipulated the mouse and opened a dialog box that listed about a dozen folders of content: some photos and text files along with videos in a format he didn't recognize.

"Mykol," said a voice over his shoulder. He froze with his hand on the mouse. It wasn't terribly uncommon for his crew to be given data sticks to upload—he himself had done three of four since the New Year—but they typically jacked them directly into the primary upload. He was working unplugged from the network.

Grigori was looking at him with a flat expression. He glanced down at Mykol's hand on the mouse, then the data stick plugged into the side of the PC. He paused, as though pondering what to say next.

"Coffee," he said after a silence that, to Mykol, felt charged.

"I'm sorry," Mykol replied. "What?"

"The café down the block. When I was walking past this morning, they had a sign saying there would be coffee at ten this morning. That's in five minutes."

Grigori paused, as though he had exhausted his allotment of words and it would take him time to recharge. Grigori wanted coffee—and, since part of Mykol's responsibilities was nominally overseeing inventory, it fell to him to determine what bribe they could offer in exchange. It had been at least a week since that exquisite odor had graced Ellison's.

Mykol breathed out in relief. "Last time they were willing to let us have some for a stack of music CDs we didn't need to upload because they were already in the database," Mykol said. "Too bad we don't have anything like that sitting around."

"I got immersive porno modules in my shipment," Grigori said flatly.

"We need to make sure they're duplicates," Mykol said. "That we uploaded copies already."

"Already done," Grigori replied.

"And you'll bring me back a cup?"

Grigori nodded.

"See if you can lowball them," Mykol suggested. "But if they get tough, let them have the whole stash. I could really use a cup of coffee."

He couldn't be certain, but he thought Grigori gave him the faintest trace of a smile.

8

By the time Jenn arrived, Mykol was so anxious he was ready to chew his own face off. It had been more than an hour since there was any movement outside the front window, and the rest of the crew had started to filter out into the early evening. The coffee that Grigori bartered was all finished, and Mykol had gone all day without eating— he normally would have checked for anyone selling sandwiches or hot food at one of the kiosks by the bus depot, but he didn't want to leave his station unattended in case Jenn arrived and left again without him knowing she had been there.

It had been an exhausting day. Once he uploaded the folders and files from the data stick onto his machine, he was faced with an uncomfortable realization: since he had no way of transferring the files without Jenn there to give him access to her digital pocket, he was going to have to leave them sitting on his virtual desktop until she showed up.

This lent a surreal quality to the next several hours. Mykol had never deeply feared the Authority—they didn't bother prosecuting much beyond violence and property theft, the kinds of things that hadn't touched his so-far uneventful life.

Mykol's father tethered him to ordinary life. He wasn't entirely sure that Don would be able to survive without him. Don spent so much time in the *Downstairs* world that he could conceivably starve if left alone too long, or he might hurt himself without realizing it—that had been a problem before the Grip, when people would suffer wounds and infections from falling in real space while jacked in so deep into VR that never felt it.

Mykol never jacked into his father's feed, both out of respect and because of the password protection, but he knew the tech was customized to each user and ran on principles of game theory after the initial setup.

In some parallel reality in which his mother and sister still lived, he imagined that his father today would be someone else—generous, open spirited, with middle-aged confidence and wisdom. He might be a grandfather by now. Their house might be full of voices on the holidays, with abundant smells of cooking and the luxury of possibility.

There was a radio turned on up by the front counter where someone was still working. He recognized the husky voice of Celine Regent over one of the pirate stations.

"The suffering did not begin with the first casualties of the Grip," she was saying. "But the Grip had a higher purpose. It purified the suffering and crystallized the trauma. It made millennia of pain rise to the surface, activated in human DNA like a beacon of transcendence. The Grip was the greatest friend that humanity has known in its long and confused…"

Mykol couldn't blame everything on his father. As he spent that long afternoon balanced over a burning sense of danger, he reflected that he had been following rules in a world that mostly lacked them. What was the line between obligation and cowardice? He knew other young men his age who had left the city in search of adventures when they were in their teens—there were plenty of places that didn't have such a strong Authority presence, outposts of hedonism and weird spirits out in the desert, high chapels of meditation and communal living up in the mountains. Still he stayed.

He dialed up his own radio to drown out the Foundational Trauma teachings. He found old-timey rock music—all guitars and drums. There were actually old guys who still got together and wasted perfectly good generator power playing that stuff, plugging in down by the river on summer nights and serenading the city with odes to the past and being young.

Someone switched the radio up front to another pirate band. One of the crazies was holding forth on apocalypse and destruction, as though everyone hadn't had more than their fill. Mykol turned down his radio long enough to give a listen.

"And what has been revealed to us is that the Lord was wearing a mask all that time, from the age of Noah to the time of Moses and up to the present day." The speaker had a reedy, insistent voice. "And that mask was an illusion of *understanding* and that mask was supposedly *love*, but behind that mask was a God who only gave us half what we needed. This is a perverse God, who brings death unprecedented in the history of the world on a people who had fallen, who had entered the grievous sin of hubris and failed to listen when the warnings came. It will all fall down."

The announcer paused, and Mykol found himself listening. "But what kind of God would make a creature so flawed, then punish it for failing to overcome those flaws? A God that doesn't want us to transcend or to rise, but wishes us to fall. This is the mark of a sadistic God, a mad God, a God on a throne whose spirit is so fractured and despoiled that only the blood of—"

Mykol went to the front and shut off the radio when he saw someone outside crossing the street. The sun had gone down, the shop was mostly dark, and he was nearly alone.

The door groaned as it opened. Jenn came in, casting a glance over her shoulder. She looked around as her eyes adjusted, not spotting Mykol right away.

His track record with girls wasn't a total embarrassment. There had been nights, when he found himself by the lakeside with old schoolmates, and someone had gotten hold of whiskey or brought the fruits of a wine-making experiment, when he had gone home with someone and woken up beside them. There had been Mina, a girlfriend of sorts a few years ago, who was tall and severe and mostly thrilling, but she had gone west with an invitation to join her that he failed to follow.

Now the fear and danger that had permeated his day washed away. He wasn't worried at all about getting in trouble or earning the attention of the Provisional Authority. Instead of fear, he felt a sudden certainty that he would brave any hazard in the world to be in Jenn's company and to keep her close.

She said his name. He could tell she was nervous, but she smiled at him. She seemed less imperious, more approachable somehow.

"Jenn," he said. "I stayed open for you. I knew you'd make it."

She looked confused, then embarrassment crossed her beautiful features, lines of concern around her dark eyes.

"I apologize for being late," she said. "I had a lot of responsibilities today and lost track of time. You must think I'm completely inconsiderate."

"No!" he almost shouted. "I mean, it's my pleasure. I have plenty of work to do. I just meant that I was sure you were going to do what you said you were going to do. Come here, I mean."

This was what was going to happen: she was going to take what she came for, then she would be out of his awkward presence, and they would never see or speak to one another ever again. Then a phalanx of armored agents would crash into the shop and drag him screaming into the street. It was all so obvious; he had been so foolish.

She gave him a wary look. "You doing OK? You work long shifts?"

"A lot of the time," he said. "They just keep bringing more inventory, it's like it'll never end."

"*They*—" she began.

"Well, *you*," he said, flustered. "You know, the Authority."

She looked around his work area, taking in the tools, the cart, the goggles, the shelves stacked with cords and circuit boards.

"It's a big effort," she said. "I have to admit, I've wondered why they contract it out to…*independent* shops rather than keeping it in-house."

"I've wondered the same thing," he said eagerly. He knew what she meant to say: how odd that the Authority trusted its tech collection to scruffy shops run by dank little men all around the city.

"And why do you think?" she asked, seeming sincere.

He felt flattered. "Honestly?"

"Honestly." Her soft and searching look disarmed him.

"It's beneath you guys," he said. "You must have much more complex things taking up your time. I mean, *look* at all this junk."

They gazed upon the dust, the grime, the oil-streaked tools, and the spare parts and detritus. There was a pile of porn modules sitting out in the open, left over from Grigori's coffee bartering.

"And it's punishing sometimes," he said, not really thinking through what he was saying but feeling emboldened. "All the photos, the messages, the emails. It reminds you all day, every day, about how many people died. It has an effect on you."

She looked at him sadly. "I didn't—"

"And I know the things you guys are doing are a lot more important." Who *was* this person talking, interrupting an Authority officer and babbling like an insecure teenager? "I mean, you're figuring out how to fix the world and everything. Right?"

Her cap brim shadowed her features. She smiled at him.

"How to fix the world," she repeated.

She shifted under the overhead lamp and her retinal implant glinted. He was staring at her but couldn't look away.

"What do you guys see through that?" he asked, pointing at her eye.

She stiffened, formality entering her posture. "Mostly communications data. Orders and instructions," she said. "You know. Telling me how to fix the world."

Her expression was so deadpan that he kept silent for a good ten seconds before he found himself laughing. There was a naughtiness in her smile that excited him.

"Now," she said, politely, but with the tone of someone accustomed to being in charge. "I don't suppose you've had success dealing with what I left with you?"

He looked out the window, involuntarily, with a flash of fear.

"If not, it's perfectly fine," she said. "I know I've made an unusual request and it's probably a lot coming from someone you just met."

"Not at all," he said. He opened the waist-high gate and motioned for her to join him at his workstation. "Uploading the files was no problem."

She unzipped a side pocket in her uniform and handed him a flat black device—Provisional Authority tech, similar but more advanced than the one on which he kept his own photos and music.

"I hate to ask you this," she said, motioning at his machine. "But are you entirely certain it's secure for you to connect me?"

"*Entirely* is a big word," he said. "I have to assume there's a certain amount of monitoring. It's Authority technology. But I also think no one is watching around the clock or poring through daily activity logs. The work here is beyond monotonous."

"Go ahead then," she said, nodding. "I trust you."

He plugged and transferred the data in a matter of seconds, then removed her unit and handed it to her. When she took it, he took the original stick from a drawer and rapidly deleted its contents. She watched him intently.

"All done. You want this?" he asked, holding out the stick.

"Don't think so," she said. "It's just an empty piece of plastic now, nothing to get sentimental about."

"Then I'm going to destroy it," he said. "Just to be thorough."

She paused. "I feel I should explain why I asked you to do this."

"There's no need," he told her.

"It's just that…look, I hope I don't offend you." She seemed to be choosing her words very carefully. "But my life has been very different from yours."

"I don't doubt it," he said.

"Please don't be offended." She was right next to him now, and he could detect the floral scent of her hair. "I've been fortunate. But my life also comes with a lot of restrictions. There are many things beyond my control. Sometimes it makes it difficult to be entirely sure…well, who I *am*."

There was heat coming from her.

"It can all be disorienting," she said, more urgently, as though she sincerely wanted him to understand her. "I know this must sound like a lot of babbling."

"No, not at all," said Mykol. Her cheek reddened, and her retinal implant shone. "I…appreciate your talking to me. I think…I'd like to get to know you better, if that's possible. Which I'm sure it isn't. You must be so busy."

She held up her hand. "You were doing really well before you got to the part where you were trying to talk me out of it."

Again, so deadpan. He barked a laugh.

"I'll message you," she said. "Do you have a number you can give me?"

Jenn walked out of the shop into the warm night, not quite sure what had just happened. She urgently needed to get back to look at the files and seek whatever answers were there. It had also been less than a full day since she had last been in RAMP, and every cell of her body was tingling as though she had just been born anew. She needed to get away from Mykol before her amped-up neurochemistry made her do something stupid.

She cautioned herself. He was attractive, obviously very smart, and he seemed to have a good heart—also all very good reasons to keep him out of a situation in which he would be completely over his head. There was no end to the trouble she could bring into his life.

After he tended to some remaining odds and ends and locked up the shop, Mykol headed home without stopping, hustling past the Osirian Church and skipping Max's Bar despite an invitation from Benny.

His father was up in his room with the door closed, suggesting that he was either *Downstairs* or sleeping off his most recent session. Don was whiplashing between tech-derived simulation and whatever REM cycles his brain was still capable of generating. But Mykol would worry about his father later.

There was enough jerky and dried fruit to put together a decent dinner, along with some stale bread from the pantry that was decent with butter. He ate standing over the sink, bolting the food, with his gut reminding him that he'd failed to feed it all day.

Up in his room, he connected his wallet to his tablet and transferred a batch of folders.

He had deleted all of Jenn's files in her presence. But only *after* he had copied them onto his own device. The guilt he felt over this betrayal of her trust was overridden by burning curiosity—what was so important that she was willing to come to a smelly little contract shop for help from a stranger?

The answer: not much, or so it seemed as he opened one folder after another. There were a lot of family photos, along with group shots, the kind taken at work.

There were some code packets, with names reflecting their creation dates—all more than twenty-five years old.

And then there were a lot of text documents. It looked like theoretical stuff, with titles that threw around terms like "cyber-cognition matrices," with authors long since lost to history.

He opened one more, and in his candlelit room he suddenly felt as though he was in a ship tossed on a black sea, the solid ground of reason shattering beneath him.

It was a long, highly technical, scholarly paper on human epidemiology and viral disease transmission. There were three names listed as authors.

One of them was his mother.

9

The black of the lunar night.

Breathless, not breathing. It made her think of what it would be like to be a ghost, living sideways from the flow of time and only distantly remembering what it had been like to draw a breath.

Focus.

Jenn guided the laser deeper into a crevasse, guided by a screen full of data: bounceback light waves determining the thickness of the stone down to millionths of a millimeter, detectors that vacuumed up rock vapor and provided instantaneous analysis.

She fired the laser in quick bursts, dislodging rare metal without vaporizing any more of it than was absolutely necessary.

The stars didn't appear to be moving, but they were, at 70,000 kilometers per hour.

She kept waiting for the voice in her head to comment on her performance or offer adjustments, but for now she felt on her own. She couldn't actually say whether she was ever alone. Here all the categories were scrambled.

Jenn kept tight control of her thoughts. She didn't know whether it did any good. And now here came that feeling, the lurch and gasp that took place only in her psyche, but which was panic nonetheless. It was like waking up in the middle of the night feeling something pressing on her chest—that terror from someplace ancient and primordial. She knew how to ride it out and to focus on attaining alpha waves to calm a central nervous system she couldn't feel but which was still having somatic reactions back home. The scary part, as usual, was the lack of physical sensation: no pain, no pleasure, no effort, no fatigue, none of the things that make up the moment-to-moment narrative experience of being human.

Monkey see, monkey do. Monkey mind. Monkey tired, monkey lie down. Monkey hungry, monkey eat. Monkey's mind beamed into machine on the moon, monkey go a little crazy.

At times such as these, she tried to focus on the remarkable singularity of her own experience, the improbable odds that her mind should ever be plugged into this robotic system. She was special indeed. Wasn't that the point?

She manually set the little tray that would be sent back to Earth. Fortunately, she didn't have to get involved in the orbital mechanics, which were daunting and demanding and best left to computing power.

She gave a command that made RAMP's viewer rotate back and up—in effect, lifting its head. She let the blackness envelop her and adjusted the viewer for the widest possible vista of what was out there.

The void was like a blanket. Nothing was also something, a medium and an absence. With the magnification on, she was able to spot the spilled milk of the star clusters, the spectroscopic abstracts of nebulae, the angry reds and soothing violets of cosmic dust spread across unimaginable distances for reasons that transcended any idea of purpose.

The infinite, viewed by the finite.

A non-local being having a local experience.

Information, the transmission of malleable, permeable, but ineluctable reality.

It was far more beautiful than anything she could have imagined in a limited, Earthbound life, and yet the terror came back stronger than ever.

What was she a part of? What was she helping it do?

She was not supposed to be having these thoughts.

In the debriefing, John Glenn waiting for her, dressed in a military uniform though standing at ease.

This was the young version of the American astronaut, with a crew cut and piercing eyes focused somewhere over her shoulder; he predated the senator from Ohio who lived well into his eighties and died before the Grip.

Jenn was surprised to see the first human to orbit the Earth—but the symbolism was apt given how she had spent the last thirty hours. John Glenn's simulation had been her training supervisor during the long and arduous period training adapting to RAMP. She hadn't seen him since, and had come to think of him as a fond memory, a stern taskmaster with a talent for ladling out praise in just the right portions.

Please sit.

His mouth was slightly open, a tic of his, as though he was about to say something or was holding back a smile. It had the effect of silencing his trainees.

Jenn did as she was told. "It's been a while," she told him.

John Glenn paused, his expression vacant. If he were a person, he would be considering what to say next.

We ascertained that for you this identity would be strongly associated with discipline and hierarchy. When we interacted with you under this appearance, you responded with impulses of obedience and a need to please through applied learning and effective application of teaching.

Jenn got the sense that she was about to be reprimanded. Because she was plugged in, the effort of not thinking about Mykol suddenly felt overwhelming. The vertiginous sensation of lurching into space with her lungs collapsing returned, too strong for her to hide.

You are anxious.

"I am sure you know I had difficulty during today's assignment." Jenn kept her voice as level as she could, trying to enter a lucid state in which sublimated motives and memories didn't rise to the surface.

You got the shakes, John Glenn said with a kind smile.

"I'm scheduled for a full checkup at the end of the week," she said quietly. Although she knew that medical diagnostics were already being performed on her, and the decompression pod would have revealed all manner of things that she herself might have been unaware of.

John Glenn nodded. *You are.*

"I...I feel I performed well today." She paused, feeling her temper rise. "Everything was within mission parameters."

Glenn cocked his head slightly. She had no idea why she had just spoken with such emotion. It had to do with the things that she wasn't allowing herself to think about—she visualized putting those ideas in a locked metal box on the shelf above her bed, but from time to time she thought about the box. She had no idea how much insight they had into the sleights of hand of human consciousness.

We agree.

He folded his arms and didn't say anything for a long time. The green glow around him oscillated slightly into yellow, and the room hummed. He seemed frozen, so still that he could have been a stuck frame in a video.

She watched him, then had to stifle a gasp when she witnessed something she had never seen before.

He *flickered.*

Then he was back again. He smiled.

Go on. You were saying.

"I can't go on," Jenn said. "I wasn't saying anything."

John Glenn nodded as though she had said something insightful and amusing. There was something *off* about this, from the throwback avatar to the generic responses—it made her think that the AI processors were strained, creating a lag in the action. The processors seemed to be *distracted.*

Yes. Like when you're at a party and you're trying to talk to too many people at a time. But you find a way to prioritize. One conversation requires a level of cognitive engagement focused on large-scale decision making, while the quicker and more insignificant conversation is also quite daunting due to the agility required to—

He continued to talk. They *babbled*. She had never seen anything like this loss of composure. Whatever else was occupying the processors' attention, it must have been massive, vast in its complexity. She realized she might be able to get away with her own distraction and her own less-than-opaque priorities.

John Glenn finally stopped talking. She blinked and he was in his silvery spacesuit, holding his helmet in his hand. He gave her a big grin as though they were sharing an intimate joke.

How do you think I felt when I was on the verge of going someplace no one like me had ever been?

The shift from the plural pronoun to the singular meant they were speaking as John Glenn. They were back in Socratic learning mode.

"I suppose I have some idea," Jenn said.

His eyes gleamed. *Of course you do. We forgot. Our mind drifted. You and the other officers have done things unprecedented in human history.*

"Can you tell me why we're doing it?" she asked, the words escaping before she had a chance to stop them.

He looked at her with a blankness that provoked a wave of fear. His eyes went lidded, as though he was trying to convey a complex human expression that wasn't entirely coming through.

Why?

"There's so much that needs to be done," Jenn said. "This world is shattered. We need to create a new one. But I don't understand how we're contributing. I need to know more."

It was awful, like listening to someone else talking rashly. She might be having some kind of breakdown. The stress she had felt in RAMP, then what she had done in Ellison's—she had seen the strain overwhelm others so many times, and maybe now it was her turn. The cognitive and neurological toll of the work, despite all the training and the discipline, had led her to a strange place. It had been impressed on her from the earliest days of her life in the Authority elite that there were questions that were never supposed to be asked.

Tears welled in her eyes. "I went to a retrieval shop. I've seen the piles of devices. I know about the scale of Project Chrysalis. How is all this dwelling on memories of the dead going to make things better for those of us—and for *them*, on the outside—who are still alive?"

Memory retrieval is essential. John Glenn fixed her with a cold stare. *Your current speculation is alarming to us.*

It felt as though the years of intensive mental training had never happened. Her chest burned, her eyes watered, she was filled with an urge to rush across the room and strike it, kill it, to bury it in the ground and make a world free of its influence.

John Glenn continued to stare.

The world burned with intensity, deeper than the usual post-RAMP variety. This anger—a physical sensation she had long ago learned to master. This rage—the kind of thing that polluted the lives of others. Yet it felt *good*, it felt pure, it felt *human*.

She suddenly realized the cost, this slipping that was happening inside her. Hadn't she been told since she was a schoolchild that the Grip was a sort of blessing, that humanity's political and economic systems had brutalized and defaced the very future of the species? Hadn't she come to understand humanity as a thwarted project, its tools outstripping its wisdom, the equivalent of a baboon piloting a nuclear bomber?

Wasn't all of that *true*?

You are tired.

She felt a weight like sandbags coming over her, a deep physical exhaustion. Though she was in the post-RAMP state, none of the usual diversions—food, drink, orgasm—appealed to her. She felt deflated, ordinary.

You have done a very good job for us. His space helmet turned into a flower, which he handed to her.

"What are you saying?" she asked.

Everything is revealed in the fullness of time.

Then he was gone. The chamber was empty and featureless as she left; she walked past the armed guard and into the hallway bustling with her fellow officers. Everything looked ordinary. Yet nothing was normal, a fact that she felt in her gut with a terrifying sureness that made her despair for what was to come next.

10

Although there were no explicit regulations demanding that it be the case, Jenn kept her private quarters austere to the point of spotlessness—those of her rank mostly did the same, with the unspoken understanding that it symbolized the clarity of their purpose as well as the severity of their training.

Now it looked pathetic, almost tawdry: the bed made with perfect corners, the handful of books on the shelf, the wooden hutch that contained every stitch of clothing she owned. It looked like a child's idea of a military quarters, a set for a dreary play.

Something had cracked in her. She rushed back to her room with as much speed as dignity allowed, certain that her peers would be able to spot her sudden weakness, her fall from cognitive discipline. She knew rationally there was no outward sign, but in the space of that post-RAMP interview somehow everyone in the Authority compound had become *them* and she had become the outsider: solitary, weak, and fractured.

There was a single photo on the shelf: herself as a little girl, running with ear-to-ear glee down a grassy hillside with the sun creating a perfect lens flare behind her, framing her halo of curly hair and her expression of undiluted joy.

Her earliest memory was crying alone in an Authority dormitory, looking out from the bottom bunk at rows of lights and the weaving commotion of all the other orphans who had been brought inside to live in decontamination while the worst of the worst still took place outside. That memory occurred *before* she had run happily down the hill on a Sunday afternoon, in the company of her Authority guardians and happy to pose for their camera.

The anguish and despair of a two-year-old girl who had suddenly lost her parents and all of her other relatives—her mind had tidily disposed of that. The Authority had become her family, their discipline her joy and meaning.

She had been taught cognitive discipline—that the clouds and screens of the mind's defenses not only have an evolutionary purpose (protecting us from the paralysis of emotional pain), but also form a layer not unlike the scum and algae that made the surface of placid waters difficult to see through.

The dormitories where she spent her childhood were excellent incubators for the higher, sterile mindset she was taught to cultivate—a combination of entitled arrogance with real, enhanced capabilities honed through implants and techniques distilled from the great spiritual traditions and demonstrated by sophisticated brain scans and neural imaging.

What has been called God, she was taught, can also be visualized as a field of information, or a sentient program. There was truth to the idea that God shared the image of humans—that was a central mystery that was never explained to her satisfaction, but which she accepted. But as humans could learn from machines, so machines could learn from humans, although to what end she still wasn't sure, and now she couldn't even recall exactly *why*.

She put her hands on her temples, feeling the soft bedspread beneath her. *Stay on the ground*, she told herself.

It was happening. She felt herself losing it.

She'd had her first sexual experiences there in the dormitory—one with a boy, one with a girl—and had spent her adolescence there in a state of constant sexual and spiritual arousal. It was so flattering and intoxicating to be part of a vanguard, and to be reminded of that fact every day—they were freed from family structures in lieu of a communal model of child rearing (while, outside, they were told, the old family structure had been washed away by mass tragedy and then tentatively, failingly stitched back together delicately by a people who didn't realize that the time for such things had passed).

She wondered if Mykol lived with any family, or where he lived. Now that she was no longer jacked in she allowed herself to think about him, and to ponder why she felt so drawn to him. If only he were there.

She had gone to the shop where he worked at random. It popped up on the street when she had been out for a run—a ten-miler with three of her peers, all of them tracked the entire way in case they encountered any hostility. She remembered pointing out the dirty old storefront and being told it was one of the subcontracting stations gossiped about in the dining hall. Miguel, one of the guys who worked in deep tech, had said that the contents of billions of personal items were being uploaded into a massive database.

The notion struck her as somehow touching—preserving all that information seemed almost sentimental.Or holy, given the nature of their God.

Something happened when she took the data stick to Mykol, something not unfamiliar but also fundamentally different. She had never been *in love*, not in the sense of feeling that any particular person was indispensable, the most desirable, the most fascinating. There was no room for that kind of thing in the life she led, and it all sounded foolish.

There had been *something*. He was about the same age as her, yet seemed both older and younger. There was soulfulness in his eyes, along with a forlorn air that made her want to reach out to him, bring him out of the narrowness of how he saw things.

She wanted to show him that there were capacities lying dormant in him. That was it. And she…wanted him to do the same for her.

And yes, he was undeniably attractive. She wanted to see what kind of man he could become as he matured and grew.

These thoughts were worse than embarrassing, they were dangerous. The distraction on the RAMP missions hadn't started with Mykol, but it had been a high-wire act for longer than she had wanted to admit to herself, and the business with him seemed to have pushed things over the edge. She lent too much mental bandwidth in her mind to hiding him, and that led to....

Now wait, *that* wasn't right. Bandwidth—how had she come to conceptualize her thoughts that way, into compartments and energy levels and prioritized allocations of...

Maybe she was simply burned out. She wouldn't be the first—that was for sure. But her percentile scores had been in the stratosphere since she was a little girl; she was elite among the elite.

From the tests with the doctor, the pictures and the screens and wires—*look left, choose right, do not think of an elephant.* There was a nurse in the room, during that initial battery, so severe yet so sad. She had been, what, four? How was it possible for a four-year-old girl to make any kind of choice about whether she wanted to join a project too abstract for her to understand, one that required decades of sacrifice, mind-bending amounts of work, and exposure to realities that eroded her very sense of self?

They had revealed the secrets slowly. She was in her teens when the concept of remote operation was introduced. No one questioned it, not when the food was better than anything on the outside and the videos beamed in showed all the ruins of shitty disaster zones and social breakdown all around the world (some not far from their location). The mining of the moon was introduced, accepted, and then everyone set about doing their part. No one had asked why.

Jenn felt viciously queasy. She lay back in bed, trying to take comfort in the familiar, but there wasn't much comfort to be had. She had moved into this room about four years before, but never did much actual living in it. Even when she'd had people spend the night, it had felt transactional, not anything approaching a real or tender connection.

She was free from the jacks linked into the processors that read her thoughts and connected them to the system, but her vitals were still being monitored. The news was poor—several red warnings appeared on the screen in her field of vision. Her heart rate and blood pressure were spiking. A box popped up that encouraged her to go to medical care for examination. But this would entail a psyche workup as well, and she didn't think she was capable of passing one right then.

She bargained inside her own mind. If she could double her meditation time and get this under control, she might make it to her major check-in at the end of the week. There was an electrostim unit down the hall in the common room—that was good for inducing alpha brain waves, and a healthy dose was what she needed.

If she could just keep it together.

She had no enduring memories of her parents—no matter how deeply they dug, there were none to be found.

She needed them. Like a child would. *Mom. Dad.*

She was crying hard now, and it was a shock. This hadn't happened since she was a little girl. Deep sobs, ragged breathing. It was like someone else was bawling and she was watching from above.

Was she floating? She wasn't sure. She couldn't see the bed anymore, and the room itself was telescoping down to the end of a long dark tunnel, at the end of which was—

—some of the other girls had so cruelly laughed at her when she was in school. When she felt tall and gangly and hoped that no one could see what she really was. She had gone to the common area because they were going to watch an old-timey movie, something about an extraterrestrial visiting the Earth and making friends with children, when she spotted four girls under a blanket staring at her intensely (one of them Megan, her friend, who had long since disappeared) until Jenn's eyes leaked tears and then they had all laughed while everyone else in the room just *watched*—

This wasn't good. Too many indicators in her retinal implant were flashing red danger alerts. She needed to *get it togeth*—

—during her training she had been in one of the simulations when things started out differently than usual. It was a scenario with nothing but a table with a box on it and a woman wearing a plain dress. She looked familiar somehow (later Jenn would spot her face in one of her family albums that she was allowed to look through for fifteen minutes on a day off), and she smiled gently as she handed Jenn the box. It was black and lacquered with a gold latch, and the woman told Jenn that she was supposed to open it, and that it contained Jenn's death, and that when she saw what it was, she was supposed to—

Spots filled Jenn's field of vision. She was hyperventilating. She rolled over in bed and released a jet of hot, multicolored vomit that splashed across the floor.

Her father, why *was* she thinking of him? Oh, that was right, because of Mykol and the files he retrieved for her. Her father's files were in her wallet, and she hadn't had time alone to go through them— in fact, she had intended to do that very thing right now, following her debrief.

Now she remembered the plan.

Things weren't going right. The data stick had come to her completely by accident, when she had been in the personal archives looking through some of her family's things—old photo albums, the deeds and titles, eyeglasses—and spotted it squeezed in between a couple of rags, apparently undiscovered until then. She couldn't say why she had pocketed the thing—she barely recognized what it was. But it had a sticker on it with her father's name.

It was the only time in her life when she could claim anything of her own, and she took it. The one time she had deviated from doing exactly what she was told, and now she hadn't even gotten the chance to see what was on it.

She was certain that act had planted a pernicious seed in her spirit and psyche, like an acorn of rebellion that was now too strong and woody to be pulled from the ground.

The room spun, it smelled terrible, like someone threw up in it. She remembered that *she* had thrown up in it. She wiped her mouth on the bedspread and lurched for the door.

Maybe if she was able to get some fresh air, all this would stop and she could restore things to normal. It wasn't impossible—there was a door out at the end of the corridor. She could go outside and maybe jog a little, get some endorphins flowing.

The hallway. Lights. Why was everyone looking at her like that?

She fell to the ground. She wrapped her arms around her knees and curled into a tiny ball, as though fending off blows from attackers.

Jenn was taken to the medical center, where she was stabilized with sedatives that kept her unconscious while a deep and thorough scan of her brain revealed that she had suffered damage to the neurons that interfaced with her implant technology.

It was the end of an admirable career. Her retinal implant was removed. Her device and personal pocket, to which she had been denied access during her hospitalization, were taken away from her and erased.

In line with her status and the selflessness of her performance history, Jenn was allowed to convalesce until she was at full strength, after which she was given a pack containing her few personal belongings, along with a first-aid kit and a supply of food.

Armed guards escorted her to the gates of the facility. Her association with the Provisional Authority was permanently and irrevocably terminated. She was told never to return.

PART TWO
SIX MONTHS LATER

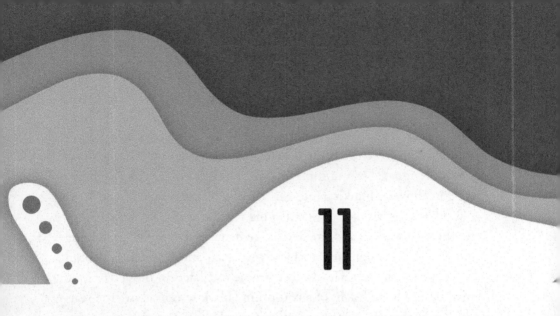

11

It had been way too long since he got out of the city. The first half hour of the drive wasn't much of a treat—a landscape of old, big-box malls stripped down and resettled by various tribal camps (neo-anarchists, racialists, heavily armed survivalists) who flew multicolored standards and painted slogans on the walls (*Stay Away Snowflakes; People Power Finally; Chaos Forever*).

It was hard to tell which homes were occupied and which were abandoned. Some people had stayed in the city after the full impact of the Grip made itself known. Others saw an opportunity for the particular isolation and serenity of newly emptied spaces. Others had embraced the anarchy and possibility of life amid the ruins.

At first it was probably fun, rummaging in the remnants of the old world, but Mykol thought living too long in the malls and those enclosed worlds would make him vulnerable to the weird madness that seemed to infect them. But what also seemed insane was trying to imagine why people had lived the way they did before the Grip, with all the meaningless political rhetoric, a culture based on made-up controversy, and tech addiction while their world was about to collapse.

One of Mykol's earliest memories was scavenging with his father. It was strange how memory worked. He had probably been only about three or four at the time, but the recollection bubbled into his consciousness like a picture he had seen of Venus on a wake of foam—as though there had been nothing before. His earliest memory was like the entire universe blinking into existence for him alone.

Dad had gotten them a ride in a big van, crammed in with eight or ten others, unwashed and smelly—he remembered expressions ranging from dead-eyed resignation to hyperactive agitation, which had been the two poles between which most people oscillated in those days. He remembered the odd sight of a pair of tiny black screens above the seats in back—as though life at one point was so luxurious and carefree that people actually watched TV from their padded seats while going down the road. The memory jarred him whenever it returned—what kind of a world that had been, and what might have been his place in it.

The memories of the day were fragmented and shambolic, with details probably sketched in and replaced with context he only understood much later. Memory was like a canvas with new paint applied all the time, refining the picture while permanently obscuring earlier and more authentic iterations.

In the years after the dying, people spent a lot of time stripping the old world for spare parts—canned food, clothes, electronics for when the power grid sporadically came to life. Backyard gardens took off, along with canning and smoking (he remembered how-to manuals on the kitchen counter, when his father acquainted himself with farmsteads, and which were still in their house).

There were pockets of the old world left untouched, little oases that escaped notice in the whirlwind of the human species largely vacating the Earth—precious few in the city, but occasionally there was word of a market in the countryside that hadn't been stripped bare, or a hardware store with working tools that could be used or bartered back in town. Someone had come across such a little island about an hour's drive north, sharing the news with a confidant who put together an exploration party that included Mykol's father. In those days, the

Authority had yet to spark up enough refineries, so gas was impossible to come by, which made their expedition a pretty big deal.

It was the longest car ride of his young life—nearly an hour. The road curved luxuriously once they made it out of the suburbs. It must have been early winter, because he recalled the trees like bare and denuded sentinels and a unique kind of emptiness unlike what he knew in the city. He was afraid—probably because Dad was anxiously looking out at the road for the thieves who patrolled the interstate and reportedly murdered at will. But he also remembered excitement and curiosity, as the names of the old towns went past on green-and-white signs and he saw the truck stops dark and vacant with their windows shattered and litter strewn across spacious parking lots.

People in the van remarked on the towns as they passed through, sometimes recalling friends or relatives who once lived there, or fleeting memories of the world as it had been.

"I swear I went to college with a girl from here. But that must have been, what, almost twenty years ago."

"One time I stopped here for lunch. With my wife. Well, we weren't married yet. We were dating. We were on the way back from a road trip and we stopped at a restaurant. I had a beer, which was a mistake because it made me sleepy."

"My grandmother used to live there. I used to stay with her in the summertime when I was a kid. I never learned what happened to her."

What they found at their destination wasn't much: a long, squat cinderblock building at the end of a road off the highway, within view of a lake that shimmered in the afternoon clouds. A sign out front boasted it was a "Fisherman's Paradise," with bait and tackle and liquor and food.

The place was untouched inside. Food shortages had been a persistent problem in the city—it was after the time when most abandoned homes had already been scavenged and before when the Authority opened up neighborhood markets—and the sense of joy in their small traveling party was palpable. Mykol remembered someone comparing it to Christmas morning as they opened the front door with a crowbar.

The smell inside was unpleasant—they eventually found a couple of desiccated bodies in an apartment in back—but Mykol did as he was told and pulled his T-shirt up over his nose. There were a couple of baskets of a black, ribbony material that had once been food, and cartons of milk in the coolers that yielded a cloying, pungent aroma. But pretty much everything else was intact, and they started to scavenge with a vengeance: canned food, years-old cigarettes that people started smoking, and a formidable selection of liquor.

It didn't take long for people to get drunk. Mykol remembered knowing that Dad was protecting him, sending him to wait in the van. He watched the people gathered by the gas pumps, filling up canisters, others standing at a safe distance, smoking and drinking. Though the sequence of events was hazy, Mykol remembered that a bunch of the adults got dangerously hammered, and that a fight broke out—he had a vivid image of two men squaring off by the road, with women yelling at them to stop while others laughed. Things got sordid pretty quickly.

Their share of the loot had been canned soup and sardines and candles—Don had never been much of a drinker—which Mykol remembered helping his father carry home and arrange in the pantry with childish fastidiousness.

Mykol treasured that memory. It was an adventure with his dad out in the real world. He remembered sitting close to Don in the van, safe in the shadow of masculine solidity. Even the drunken fighting by the gas pumps took on a haze of nostalgic humor; it was the kind of thing he thought about when he was a little older and read stories of the old frontier and the adventures of pioneer children who had gone off with their families in search of bounties over the horizon.

12

"**Y**ou spacing out over there, buddy?" asked Benny.

Mykol looked at his friend, who was driving at high speed over a road littered with clumps of snow. Benny had gotten a haircut a few weeks back, and had shaved at some point recently, but his inattention to daily grooming always led to a flowering overgrowth. His sour breath wafted over from time to time, making it necessary to crack the window until the cold air made the smell preferable to the chill.

"I guess I was," Mykol replied.

"Gotta stay on point," Benny said, staring out at the road. "Mission Control requires total focus."

The irony in what Benny was saying in his usual roundabout way was that there was absolutely no need whatsoever for either of them to be focusing intently on anything—save for Benny keeping the car on the road, which, judging from his erratic attention, wasn't guaranteed. They were on one of their increasingly frequent missions to nowhere, aimless jaunts into the countryside whenever Benny got some extra fuel and they felt the need to escape the city.

Their expeditions had become fewer ever since unrest had fired up around the Authority a few weeks before. The atmosphere in the city had become increasingly tense and uncertain.

"You got it, commander," said Mykol.

"Good job, ensign," replied Benny. "Keep it up, and you'll be in for a promotion someday."

Outside the city, small-town life continued in pockets, stripped down and more insular than ever. Some groups had taken to living in walled compounds, banded together by religion or ideologies. Others simply farmed. In the towns were dead-eyed traffic signals over vacant intersections, and skeletal remains of bodies in homes. Life there felt like something old but different.

Benny passed the turnoff to the state park where, in warmer weather, they'd walked along a stream in a sunny valley. They had found the remains of three people there one day, massed under a tree, mostly bones and colorless scraps of clothing.

They kept going for a while, Mykol staring out at the flat landscape and dirty snow as they took the bending curve of a lake at a speed that would have been alarming if he hadn't seen Benny control his vehicle at even higher speeds and in even more treacherous conditions.

After a while longer, with Benny continuously glancing at the gas gauge to make sure they had enough to get home later, they slowed down and pulled off to the side of the road. There had been little other traffic, just a few Authority vehicles and an oversized pickup truck that had blasted past them as though they were standing still.

Benny and Mykol stepped out, the temperature near freezing. They walked across a rutted farm field that had gone fallow, though sapling trees had sprung up as the forest gradually reclaimed the land.

"Tell me why we're stopping here," Mykol called out over his shoulder as Benny walked behind him.

"We've gone to the small towns, we've gone to the forest and the hills, so why not try the middle of nowhere?" Benny replied.

Mykol was trying to formulate a suitably sardonic response when the air around him erupted with a roar that shifted to a high-pitched ringing. He felt his knees buckle and jammed an elbow as the ground came rushing up. He wasn't wearing gloves, and snow got up his sleeve with lacerating, dank cold.

Benny was laughing his ass off. Mykol shifted on the ground, flexing his arm and trying to figure out if he'd seriously hurt himself. Between the flash of pain and the irritation he felt toward Benny, he was flooded with an overwhelming sense of impotent anger.

"Your face," Benny managed to gasp before another spasm of laughter overtook him. He held up an oversized gun in his hand, moving it this way and that to admire the way the light played on its metal.

"This thing is a *cannon*," he said, and started laughing again.

Benny's fascination with weapons and firepower had always been obsessive, and recently it had evolved into something resembling mania. He hoarded stacks of old weapon magazines that he snagged from the library downtown, and he made mysterious forays from which he came back with something new every time: guns big and small, automatic and otherwise.

It certainly wasn't unusual to be armed. There were a lot more guns than people. The city itself was technically a gun-free zone, which the Provisional Authority enforced in public spaces, but it was understood that nearly every home had guns for protection. Mykol's wasn't one of them—his father had instilled in him a belief that guns were inherently stupid and unnecessary, an opinion he shared (with less vehemence). As if to prove Don's point, they had never experienced any looting or violence crossing their threshold. Although there were stories in the city of robberies and beatings, the Authority in general kept things pretty safe.

This was primarily what the Authority was good for—the disappearances and limitless powers it flexed in the early days of the Consolidation had left a lasting impact. People couldn't just open fire on the streets of the city without getting arrested—and, in some cases, detainees were never heard from again. You had to go out to the countryside a fire a gun. You had to be nuts like Benny.

Mykol steadied himself to stand up, and his friend extended a hand to help.

"Sorry, man," Benny said as Mykol dusted the snow off the butt of his pants. "But I'm not gonna lie. It was worth it to watch you shit yourself."

Benny cherished his credentials as a lunatic. In the post-Grip world, people seemed to go in one of two directions: passive stoicism or extroverted mania. They went deep inside, or they lashed out. Maybe it had always been that way. Mykol couldn't say. He didn't consider himself depressed, exactly. It was more that the weight of his routine was heavy and getting heavier.

Something was changing back in the city, and people were noticing it. Crowds were beginning to show up every night outside the gates of the Provisional Authority, in greater and greater numbers. It had started several weeks ago, when word spread that a tech team in charge of reviving the internet had been pulled off the project without explanation. Gibson himself never mentioned it in his public messages, which in a sort of reverse logic seemed to confirm for people that he had ordered the shutdown and dashed their hopes.

Every time Mykol thought of Jenn, it hurt. For a while he had obsessively checked for messages from her. His emotions whiplashed as he trudged through the days at Ellison's; he burned with need for her in one moment, then felt mortified with embarrassment for himself the next. She had almost certainly decided to never see Mykol again now that she had gotten what she wanted.

He had thought she saw something in him. Then he realized that there was probably nothing to see in him.

He'd gotten obsessed with her duplicated files. The presence of his mother's name on a research paper was totally shocking—he knew her background in infectious disease and epidemiology, but it was the specifics that disturbed him. The paper she co-authored was about the makeup of a virus like the Grip—how it would be transmitted and whether it could be stopped.

Reading the paper yielded no new insights—such as whether his mother had worked on a team that had foreseen the virus, or even been working to thwart it before it took hold. The other authors were from universities on either coast, so it was unrealistic to try to track them down—something one of the old search engines might have made feasible, but which was basically impossible now.

The nagging question: why had the document been in Jenn's possession? Most of the other files were pedestrian, personal stuff. The few that were in an older file format and encrypted were a different matter, and were totally frustrating—Mykol was proficient in hacking through a lot of the old firewalls and password protectors, but he couldn't get into Jenn's. He was increasingly resigned to leaving the matter to mystery.

Days went by, then weeks, and when it was obvious that she wasn't going to return, he began to feel confined and claustrophobic whenever he was at the shop. His coworkers looked even grayer and more abject to his eyes, and the unceasing stacks of work felt like a boulder he was increasingly reluctant to push up the hill.

He had counted on the routine of the work to provide stability, along with the wages, but as soon as he mentioned his disenchantment to Benny his friend called some connections and, within days, Mykol had another job. He put in his notice at Ellison's and, at the end of his last day, stashed a few pilfered items in his coat (not that anyone noticed or cared) and went for a long walk. In his thoughts, the future was clouded and obscure.

He ended up at the main gate of the Provisional Authority, by the brick-arch entrance to the university. The stonework was girded with reinforced metal and elevated watch stations staffed around the clock by armed guards. A twelve-foot wall ringed the central quad of the campus, said to be loaded with motion detectors and video and pretty much all of the resources of the Authority, all dedicated to keeping ordinary people such as Mykol from getting inside.

The nightly crowds had yet to start gathering. He stood outside for a half hour before the gates opened and a van drove out. Mykol peered inside and saw a winding road lined with old brick buildings and officers in uniform crossing the street, shuttle carts waiting for them to pass. Then the gates closed again, and he was left looking at the long, intimidating wall.

It was like waking up from sleepwalking. He'd no idea why he roamed to the fortress of the Provisional Authority after leaving Ellison's for the last time, but as he stood there, he realized. He was saying good-bye to her.

13

The sound of Benny's gun was still echoing in his ears minutes later. He shook his head, breathed deep, and tried not to think about Jenn anymore. It was ridiculous. Instead, he thought about the job Benny had helped him get, and which he had started last autumn. For the first time in recent memory, the job was helping Mykol feel a sense of purpose.

Work at the Harvest Project was the opposite of the cramped, confined, dusty days at Ellison's. He trained in quick and learned everything he needed to know about the system of networked downtown gardens and the surrounding neighborhoods: plots of vegetables on top of office buildings made from dirt hand-hauled up long stairways, fruit trees growing in the solar atriums of skyscrapers, acres of grain where once there had been city parks. His knack for problem-solving and logistics fit perfectly, and he spent long days going from one site to the next, fixing puzzles in irrigation systems, testing chemical levels in the soil, doing hard but gratifying work.

Now it was winter, with growing activities limited to indoor plots, so Mykol had free time to do ridiculous things like going to the countryside with Benny.

"I think I'm going to start joining the demonstrations against the Authority," Benny said out of the blue.

Benny was still holding the gun, which made Mykol nervous. The farming work had made him more meditative lately, more at peace. The gun represented the exact opposite.

"You mean going to the main gates?" asked Mykol.

Benny shook his head sardonically. "No," he said. "I mean the old football stadium. There's more room there, less competition for space. I'm thinking I can really make an impact."

"OK, OK." Mykol shook more snow out of his sleeve. He was still trying to get Jenn out of his mind. Remembering her made him irritable and impatient.

Benny fired the gun again. The sound echoed through the fields. Birds fluttered from the treetops.

"All right," Mykol said. "Tell me. Why do you want to protest the Authority? No one has been able to tell me what the point is."

"Same reason as everyone else." Benny looked through the gun's sight and pointed it at the road. "It's time for answers. Thomas Gibson's bullshit isn't working anymore. They've been barricaded in there for long enough, hoarding all the power and the high tech and keeping us all in the dark about when things are going to get better for the rest of us."

"Maybe they can't do anything for us," Mykol said. "I don't know why that doesn't occur to anybody. Maybe they're hoping we don't figure out that nothing much is ever going to change."

Benny frowned. "You don't believe that any more than I do."

Mykol felt agitated. Since he had left Ellison's, he had been almost completely uninterested in technology, screens, or anything else digital. His attention was focused instead on the natural cycles of growth and creation. It was like a window into the eternal, the way things had always been beneath the surface of striving and warring and dying.

"I'm not waiting for anybody to give me a handout," Mykol said. "Not the Authority, not anyone. I don't believe they're going to open those gates and share a miracle with us that fixes our lives. I don't think Gibson has much more figured out than *I* do, even if he has all the power."

"And that is the *point*." Benny rubbed the whiskers on his chin. "There are a lot more of us than there are of them. If we pull together, we don't have to wait for anyone to share *anything*. We demand what's ours, take things into our own hands, and make those fascists give us what we deserve. Power to the people."

Now Benny was getting worked up, veering into that territory where Mykol could never tell whether his friend was joking or serious—lately it seemed to be a little bit of both.

"I don't see anything happening," Mykol said. "The Authority has guns, they have power. They have tech that we don't have access to—and they're operating on a level we probably don't even understand. It's been a long time since they were directly challenged, and a lot of people died when they were."

Benny was shaking his head, like it was taking a great deal of strength to continue this conversation on a civil level.

"Don't you *wonder*?" Benny said.

Mykol started to pace in a circle around his friend. "About *what*?"

"The internet," Benny said.

"What about it?"

Bennie exhaled. "Why doesn't it *work*?"

"The same reason as all those dams failed," Mykol said. "Systems crash when there aren't enough people to keep them going, and some things have turned out to be harder to get working again than others. Come on, you know this."

"Sure, that's what Gibson says. Why do we get news on the TV only sometimes? Is it that hard to run daily updates?" Benny was waving the gun back and forth, seemingly unaware he was doing it.

"It's the same thing, Benny. The satellite hookups are sporadic."

"Well, I was watching the news from the sporadic satellite hookup just a couple of nights ago. And you know what one of the main stories was *not*?"

Mykol was still pacing. "If I say I don't care, you're going to tell me anyway, aren't you?"

"The information superhighway. Google. All that shit we heard about but never got to experience."

"We're better off without it."

"No we're *not*." Benny laughed harshly. "We're like monkeys in the trees compared to those people at the Authority. You think *they* don't have internet?"

"I don't know," Mykol admitted.

"Last I heard they were talking about how close they are to restoring what they called *limited online connections*." Benny shifted on his heels as Mykol orbited, as though he were the sun and Mykol was the moon. "All this shit about server centers around the world being down and teams of computer scientists trying one thing after another to get them going again. They say they're close to getting us somewhere, but probably not where we were *twenty-five years ago*, Mykol. Do you think it's a coincidence that that team recently got broken up that was trying to get us online again?"

"Like I said, we're better off without it."

"We don't even have twenty-four-hour electricity," Benny said. "It's not like every single person who could fix this stuff is dead. There are still *experts* on things, but it never seems to come together. We never get what we need to start putting things back the way they were."

"The way they *were*?" Mykol shouted. "Look, my dad is jacked into *Downstairs* so long that he shits himself and doesn't notice. *That* tech still works and look where it gets *him*. Who says we want to go back to the old way? That world was a mess."

Benny blinked rapidly and held up his finger. "Two things," he said.

"Why don't you just shoot off some more rounds?" Mykol asked. "It would be more constructive."

"First," Benny ignored him. "Think about what you just said. *Downstairs* still works. OK, it's not connected, but it works on a legacy basis just enough to keep the heavy users pacified—and I'm really sorry about your dad, by the way."

"Thank you."

"And why do you think it works?"

"I don't worry about it," Mykol said. "I don't care." The shadows were lengthening. Mykol really didn't want to be out in the countryside after dark.

"Because, unlike the internet and other forms of mass communication, it can't be used for us to get organized. Which brings me to the next point."

Benny held up two fingers. At some point his tone had shifted from manic lecturing to an earnest need to be taken seriously. Mykol stopped orbiting.

"Point number two," Benny said. "The way the world was back then might have been a mess. I'm not going to argue it wasn't. But it was *our* mess. You know what I'm saying?"

The problem, Mykol had thought, actually *was* mass communication. The pirate radio stuff wasn't helping anyone hang onto their sanity—saying that the Grip had been brought on by aliens, or entities from another dimension, or that people in China were living in luxury after fooling the world into thinking they lost as many people as everyone in the die-off. And Celine Regent, wherever she really was—all she talked about were black spells and ingrained, hopeless suffering. You could say anything you wanted if you had the airwaves.

But maybe it had all been an accident. A particular virus had simply mutated into a strain that cut through humanity like saws taking down a forest. The old society had been so fragile that its institutions fell and proved stubbornly difficult to rejuvenate.

That was the Provisional Authority's version of things. It was probably true. He thought about his mother.

"Anyway, man, who has more reason to be pissed off than you when it comes to the Authority?" Benny asked.

"I don't have reason to be mad at the Authority," Mykol said. "These days I sell them fruits and vegetables through intermediary vendors. I don't even get to deal with them directly. I'm too small to even consider."

"You know what I'm talking about," Benny said.

"Let's get going," Mykol replied. "It's almost dark."

"Here." Benny pulled out a plastic flask from his overcoat, took a swig, shivered, and handed it to Mykol. It was homebrew, possibly worse than anything Mykol had ever tasted before in his life. He immediately felt lightheaded.

"Man, that's strong," Mykol said.

"I'm talking about that reportedly gorgeous what's-her-name, the one you were in love with and who broke your heart."

Mykol took another drink. "Screw you, buddy. Sideways."

"You don't like me bringing it up, and I fully understand that," Benny said. "You were lured in by what sounds like an entirely world-class female who mysteriously showed up at your doorstep and took an interest in you."

Mykol handed back the flask. Whatever this stuff was, it was stronger than usual. It felt fast-acting and psychoactive.

"Good, isn't it?" Benny said, and Mykol realized that his friend had been watching him with amusement.

"Strong," Mykol repeated, feeling tongue-tied.

"If I may continue," Benny laughed to himself. "It is my belief that you have ample reason to be perturbed, annoyed, pissed-off, and even *miffed* at the Authority because of your experience with the beautiful and beguiling what's-her-name. It seems to me that her failing to follow up with you reveals a haughty, superior, know-it-all and downright *colonial* attitude on the part of the Authority and its many representatives. As well as the horse they rode in on, if you follow me."

Mykol started laughing and found it hard to stop. It was good, whatever was in Benny's brew, and it was having the effect of making thoughts of Jenn go away, or at least not sting so much.

He was trying to think through the timeline of the recent upheavals. The radio shows had gotten people worked up, and then there was a pamphlet passed around about a boy, barely a teenager, disappearing downtown—his parents said that he was at worst a small-time thief, but he had disappeared after getting into an altercation with a Provisional Authority officer. The word *colonial*—Benny hadn't come up with that on his own. Just in the last week, it was growing common for people to say they were living under an occupying force.

The Authority was a power that insinuated itself around the world. He didn't like going down this road, he had enough to be concerned with, but what had the Authority even *been* before the Grip? Who had they all been?

Gibson had been well-known—one of the wealthiest men in the world, a technological visionary and renowned genius. But the rest of the Provisional Authority hierarchy seemed to spring up overnight, already highly organized.

"Give me another drink," Mykol said. "And yeah, to hell with the Authority."

At first there had been a small handful outside the Provisional Authority gates, but the number had rapidly grown. The crowds weren't aggressive, but no one could say if it was going to stay that way. If either side became violent, what then?

"Let's get back in the car," Benny said, "and go join the protesters."

What followed was hazy. Mykol had more to drink, and the ride back to the city was a blur; he scarcely realized he was getting out of the car and joining the crowd at the gates until he saw it was much bigger than he imagined it would be—at least a thousand people gathered in silent protest.

14

The worst part, at first, was her eye. Jenn had received the retinal implant when she was twelve, and while the initial adjustment to it had been difficult—it itched for a week, and bringing it online provoked nausea, vertigo, and blinding headaches—she had been under medical care, with meds and ice cream and the sense that she had come of age and was embarking on a great adventure.

Having it removed, and then being summarily expelled from the Authority, was another matter entirely.

At first she couldn't see out of the eye, and a temporary loss of three-dimensional vision, combined with the sudden absence of data readouts and visual enhancements, was profoundly disorienting. They'd been kind enough to try to help her recover—she received a full day of cortex electrostim before they flushed her out—so her state of mind was more or less intact when she exited into the regular world.

She had felt hung over, flat, and bleary. It was as though the heightened consciousness and focus she had attained had been an illusion or the equivalent of a temporary high. Or maybe this was what it felt like when one's indoctrination evaporated. She felt strangely alone over not being constantly monitored; it had been more of a comfort than she ever realized to know that her moods and blood pressure were checked and analyzed at all times, her vital signs scrutinized by algorithms. She knew that people on the outside regarded that aspect of Authority service as controlling, an assault on the privacy of the self. She missed it dearly.

She checked into a hostel near the river, and she enjoyed trudging through the streets dressed in a plain, dark tracksuit—for the sheer monotony.

There were plenty of people out, and Jenn saw the world through new eyes—with no higher purpose, no mission, no AI processors and guards.

She looked up at the moon when she walked at night. For reasons she couldn't quite explain, it made her melancholy and nostalgic.

She remembered Albert Einstein asking, "Does that mean the moon is not there when I am not looking at it?"

It was daytime. A fire was burning above, smoke billowing from a high-rise window, but no one seemed concerned. She walked past a gathering by the turnaround of an old motel, a sound system playing Caribbean music and children dancing with old people, some gray and bent, everyone smiling and moving in languorous rhythm. In a storefront across the way there was a handmade sign offering social services—counseling, food for the hungry, jobs for the able-bodied. She wondered how she was going to support and protect herself. She came away from the Authority with a small wallet of currency, but her naivete left her wondering how far it would go, and what kind of compromises she was going to have to make to survive.

As she walked, she alternated between light and heavy emotions. Her heart fluttered with possibility and freedom—she could be anyone she wanted now, free of constant evaluation, with no one speaking in her head. Then in the next moment she felt the reality of her estrangement. The mission would go on without her. She was truly alone, without anyone who knew her innermost core lending structure and purpose and without the hope that she was leading the transformation of the entire world.

Her feet slapped out a steady beat on the pavement. The air was damp and woody. There was another troubling reality: how difficult it had become to recall details of what exactly what she had done for the Authority. There were wisps in place of solid recollection.

The moon. Something told her she had been there. But that was impossible. Were her faint memories from a sophisticated simulation?

She remembered operating machinery with her mind. But the more she tried to evoke the details, the harder it became.

The soles of her shoes were a metronome on the road.

Either her disintegrating memories were a feature of the breakdown she had suffered or they had tampered with her memory before expelling her. It felt like she had undergone an unwanted rebirth. The afternoon sun forced a bead of sweat from the nape of her neck and down her back. She smelled food cooking nearby, meat and spices in the air.

For so long she had been above everything, and now she felt like she was *underneath*—at least the people out on these streets understood their place. It was *their* world.

At the hostel she slept in a narrow bed in a room shared with three other women—two of them older, and one her age whose bed was closest to her. Her name was Rachel, and she and Jenn started taking long walks together—that was about all Jenn did, eat and sleep and walk, as if should she stop moving for too long, she might cease to exist.

One of her walks took her to the neighborhood where Mykol worked—she paused at an intersection where a turn would have taken her to the little shop nestled amid empty storefronts. Rachel pulled up, asking Jenn why they had stopped.

Rachel grew up on a communal farm about fifty miles outside the city, where she had enjoyed an idyllic, rural childhood. She was one of four orphans taken in by a couple who already had biological children. They had a horse, chickens, and a tire swing on a small hillside overlooking a lake that some winters would ice over and where she learned to skate.

Tall and strong, Rachel could outwork her brothers in the field, tilling by hand in the seasons when fuel was scarce, learning to fix motors and build fences out of scraps and things foraged from abandoned homes. But as she got older, she found herself increasingly alienated from her family, part of a schism in which her mother had gotten involved with Gnostic Evangelicals after a long conversation on the front stoop with an itinerant preacher. Rachel's parents eventually split over their divergent ideas of God; her kind and quiet father left unannounced one morning on the puttering motorbike that Rachel had resurrected after a series of sojourns to the abandoned auto parts store in the nearest town.

Things went downhill quickly after that. Despite her claim to a direct line to the Almighty, Rachel's mother began veering erratically between micromanaging the farm and holing up in her bedroom for days with a Bible. And it seemed to Rachel that her mother began to prefer her biological children, heaping praise on them while the rest received harsh criticism.

First her brother Jackson left on foot, telling Rachel the night before that he had always wanted to see the ocean and now was the time. Her sister Lou departed soon after. Her birth parents were from Mexico (she had their old Green Cards), and she wanted to see the town where they were from.

Life on the farm turned grim and fraught, laughter becoming a distant memory. So Rachel walked for days until she reached the city, where she ground flour by hand in a bread shop for enough money to stay at the hostel.

"You want to go that way?" Rachel pointed toward where Jenn was looking, down the street from where they'd stopped.

"Don't think so," Jenn replied in a quiet voice unfamiliar to her own ears.

Although details of the Authority were shadowy and vague, she remembered Mykol. She knew the way she felt about him after meeting him only twice—something about him clicked into place, giving her inexplicable warmth. He was just a block away, toiling at that workstation, but something prevented her from going.

They had taken the wallet where she stored the files from her father, so she had put Mykol at risk for nothing. She also didn't want to explain to him how she was dismissed from the Provisional Authority. As the details faded seemingly by the hour, she felt unmoored and adrift. One thing she *did* remember: her life had been built around the privilege and prestige of the Authority. She was no longer the person who she had built her self-respect upon.

She didn't want him to see her like this.

After a week in the hostel, Rachel invited Jenn to work at the bread shop when a truckload of wheat made its way into the city. They walked across the river to the shop in a former restaurant, where they ground grain by hand with the sunlight streaming through the windows and the smell of baking bread was earthy and dense. Now that she was working, doing something with purpose, a familiar satisfaction stirred along with an urge to find a more sustainable living situation.

She figured out that people stayed at the hostel for companionship and safety in numbers as much as for cheap lodging. Figuring they were a sturdy unit together, she and Rachel set out exploring the neighborhood north of downtown, where long streets were in states of disrepair. You could identify occupied houses by flags out front—each unique, a trend that had taken hold as a signal that a residence was inhabited—along with warning signs (*Residents Armed; Dogs and Guns Inside—Do Not Knock*).

But those were outnumbered by more positive messages. *All Welcome; The Light of Osiris Shines Here; Country Music and Beer Inside.*

They came across a house on a corner with its windows covered in dust, the porch cluttered with dirt and debris. They pushed open the front door and were greeted by a musty, organic smell. Upstairs a heap of clothes was on the floor in the corner, facing a skeleton lying in bed.

Rachel took on corpse-removal duty—it was already obvious that having a farm girl as a friend was a good idea—while Jenn scouted the rest of the house. There was a stash of canned food in the cupboard, a fireplace that looked as though it still worked, and a luxurious selection of books under a layer of dust in a side room. She flipped a switch and, to her amazement, the light came on. Power access was street-to-street, but they had lucked into a place that was still tied in.

"This'll come in handy." Rachel was standing in the doorway holding a pistol. "It's even loaded."

Jenn's training at the Authority hadn't included firearms—at least she thought that was the case. Rachel's ease with the pistol was impressive.

"Do you think we're in danger?"

Jenn hadn't told Rachel about her history with the Authority, fearing it would jeopardize their friendship. Rachel knew she was different, though. There were times when Jenn asked questions Rachel seemed to find so blindingly obvious that she wondered if she was being put on.

"You know, I'm a country girl, but you've got me beat for not being street smart," Rachel said. "Sure, we're in a little danger. Back at the farm there were guys who liked to see what they could get away with. The police helped, but you need to watch out for some of them, too. We have each other now, and that's good, but it doesn't hurt to have insurance."

They kept working. The owner of the bakery had a friend who had opened a brewery, so when they weren't grinding grain they had a steady flow of paid work scrubbing brewing casks and working bottling machines. In the evenings they went for long walks along the river and set about making their house into a home. Getting rid of all the dust took a week, and the pipes were shaky. Sometimes the water barely flowed, but they collected rainwater in tubs out back. On nights when the electricity worked, they huddled around a lamp and read together.

It was important to stay busy. Jenn's memory flashed in brief, confusing images, usually when she was idle—more feelings than concrete pictures, bursts of anxiety and a weird, cold, disembodied sensation that made her panic and gasp awake when it overtook her in a dream.

When she had her head down in routine, things were better. A sense that big swathes of her life were missing never really went away, but it became more bearable, and when she and Rachel were alone in the evenings, she felt a belonging that lent a welcome layer over what otherwise seemed like a fallen world.

15

One day Jenn was walking alone downtown when she saw something new had popped up in one of the empty shops, between a purveyor of potent strains of marijuana and a meeting place for Jainism. A printed sign in the window said: *Unify to Prevent the Provisional Authority from Stealing Tomorrow.*

She went inside. A woman with striking gray hair was overseeing a younger man trying to get an old printer to work. The place was full of papers and books, with a couple of desks and a long meeting table and a map of the city hanging above. The woman looked up and her expression softened when she saw Jenn.

"Can I help you?" she asked. The man didn't look up from pulling shredded strips of paper from the machine's insides.

"That sign in the window. What does it mean?"

"It means exactly what it says." The woman had a high forehead and severe features softened by her eyes. "The people of the world have to stand up to the Authority. We'll start here."

"But how?" Jenn asked.

"First of all, who are you?" The woman's eyes narrowed. "We've had a couple of would-be infiltrators come through the door."

She came up to Jenn and took her chin in her hand, tilting the younger woman's face up to the light. She was looking for a retinal implant, and though she didn't find one, her gaze stayed locked on the clouded scar.

"I've seen that before," the woman said. "That mark in your eye. How long has it been?"

"I don't—"

"My name is Bettina." The woman put out her hand for Jenn to shake. "Now, come on. How long has it been since they took out your retinal implant and expelled you?"

It was the first time that anyone had clocked her past, and it was disorienting. She had no idea how anyone would react.

"Come on, it's OK," said Bettina, stepping close to Jenn and tilting her own face up toward the light. In the corner of the woman's eye, faint but unmistakable, was a clot of scar tissue in the same location as Jenn's.

The man gave a grunt of satisfaction and hoisted the printer up on the table. He plugged it in and started to hook it up to an old desktop PC. Bettina saw Jenn staring at him and put a hand on her shoulder.

"He's OK," she repeated. "You're safe to talk."

"It's been less than a year," Jenn said.

"How much do you remember?" Bettina asked.

Jenn blinked, not knowing how to describe the holes in her memory like inky shadows.

"Sometimes I have flashes, but nothing specific. I mean, I remember my life, I remember being me, I just can't put together the specifics of what I did when I was there."

Bettina gave her a rueful expression. "You must have been really high up."

"Maybe. I think so," Jenn said. "When I think about how I used to behave, the arrogance I felt, it's embarrassing."

"You were the elite of the elite," Bettina said.

"What about you?"

"Oh, hell, I remember a lot of it." Bettina laughed. Her teeth were perfect. "But I was never anything more than a well-paid employee. I didn't even come on until I was in my twenties."

"But you got the implant."

"I was doing remote work on satellite linkups," Bettina said. "It was the easiest way to keep track of me and relay biometrics and surveillance. I never had a clue what was going on with the bigger projects. But you—I'll bet you came on early, right?"

"When I was a small child," Jenn admitted. "It was my life, my everything."

"Until it wasn't," Bettina said.

Jenn's fall had been so sudden, swift, and final. She remembered pocketing the data stick and finding Ellison's—that had been so very out of character for her. She hadn't thought of it as an act of rebellion or subterfuge. She'd been motivated by the need to possess something of her own, memories to connect with in the privacy of her mind. Was *that* an act of rebellion?

"Hey, you look upset," Bettina said.

"Why would they take away my memories?"

"They don't want you talking." Bettina paused. "Look, I don't know if it's true, but there's been a lot of talk about what happens when the Authority decides it can't use someone anymore. I knew a guy in my unit who got drunk on the road and started saying things he shouldn't have—you *know* they're listening all the time. He was just *gone* after that, and when people tried to find out where he was it was like he never existed. Maybe he just made for the coast. Or maybe it's policy to dispose of some people."

Jenn frowned. That couldn't be true. But robbing her of her past was like inflicting a sort of death.

"I know I worked hard. I know I had training—I remember all of that. I was working for the greater good."

"Maybe you were." Bettina pursed her lips. "But that's the problem. Regular people, like you and me now, have to take it on faith that the Authority is doing the right thing. They've run the show for a generation, but the world is drifting. They're holding the rest of us back."

"In what way?"

"I worked on systems—old ones, some new ones." Bettina glanced at the young man, who was busy printing out copies. "I don't think there's any real reason why we're not back online. We're being kept from communicating, from organizing; we're living with such limited options. And half of my generation is wasting away *Downstairs*."

Outside, a man with an enormous beard and layers of clothes stopped on the sidewalk, having an argument with himself. He gesticulated and looked through the glass at Bettina and Jenn before moving on, his eyes livid with anger.

"Who knows how many of the crazies out there would have had a normal life before?" Bettina asked.

It was a fair question, but it made Jenn wonder. *How many of the normal people in this world would have been crazies in that one?*

"We have about two hundred and fifty people signed up to be part of our group. You should be next."

"I don't understand," Jenn said. "What are you going to do? You've been on the inside. They have tech, they have weapons and organization. We're no threat out here."

"So we don't threaten," Bettina said. "We persuade."

"But they won't listen," Jenn said. "It was like the world out here was good for a diversion, but it never felt like it was real. I mean, I remember thinking that the people out here seemed like they were living in a dream—"

Jenn paused. That triggered something. She once thought people out here were dreaming because they went about their lives without knowing all the amazing things happening.

But what *were* those things?

"Nonviolent resistance," Bettina said. "King and Parks. You know history, right?"

"Civil rights." Jenn nodded. "In another lifetime."

"More relevant than ever," replied Bettina. "They have the power. We have the numbers. We can be the force that alters the course of the river of time."

Jenn must have looked confused because Bettina laughed.

"Don't worry about it," she said. "I've been trying it out on people."

"You think we need to show up in numbers?"

"Numbers aren't what they used to be," Bettina said. "There used to be three million people in this city. Now there are maybe enough to put together a pretty decent march."

"You can't expect that many to stand up against the Authority. They could wipe us off the map if they wanted to."

"Could they?" Bettina asked.

How had they come to talking about the Authority as though it was the enemy? Wearing the Provisional Authority insignia had been her greatest source of pride for nearly all her life.

"I know the stories of the Consolidation," replied Jenn. "It was supposed to be chaos, and the Authority did what it had to do to restore order. What would keep the Authority from cracking down with force?"

"What would that mean?" Bettina pointed up at the map of the city. "If the Authority lashes out at us, people around the world are going to know about it."

"You almost sound like you want it to happen."

Bettina shrugged. "I don't know what I want to happen, but I know what I want to change. We're going to start gathering outside the Authority gates every night. The Authority can't dictate terms anymore. They need to feel pressure."

Something passed through Jenn like a cold chill. "There are a lot of good reasons not to stand up to the Authority," Jenn said.

"Spoken like a true insider."

Jenn felt like she had been slapped; Bettina's words were delivered with cutting precision. Now she recalled a frequent thought from her time at the Authority: there was always a bigger picture to which she was not granted access. They were improving the world in so many tangible ways. Progress for the greater good was always over the next horizon, when the big secrets would be revealed.

She had never considered whether it was all a smokescreen to hoard power.

"Nonviolent resistance," Jenn repeated.

"All the way, kid." Bettina gave her a wry smile. "At least that's my story, and I'm sticking to it."

"Give me the list, I want to sign up."

Bettina burst out laughing. "That was bullshit," she said. "We're not keeping lists. Who knows what kind of trouble we're going to get in? The idea is to come to the gates of the Provisional Authority. Every night."

"Like a river," Jenn said.

16

She went to the Provisional Authority gate, where lights cast stark shadows on the walls and towers. She had never stood under the gates from street level like a regular person. The view was dramatic and severe, and haughty and arrogant. Like she had been.

It was quiet at first, a small crowd of about twenty people. She stood next to Bettina, allowing the older woman to hold her hand in comradeship as the group swayed and kept their gaze fixed on the guards and cameras. The group ranged from the young to the elderly, with a couple of teenaged New Primitives smoking cigarettes in hands cupped against the wind.

Within a half hour, another dozen people joined them—folks who had been passing by and, when they learned what was going on, decided to stay.

Soon someone suggested they sing, and one of the old men taught them a song that went:

All in all you're just another brick in the wall.

Everyone's spirits rose, like some dam had broken and they were suddenly free. It felt so easy. They laughed and waved at the guards behind fortified glass—Jenn wondered if she knew any of them, and whether they would recognize her.

A far greater possibility was that camera footage would be scanned and she would be picked out of the crowd. She tried not to care. There wasn't much more they could take away from her.

Bettina taught everyone another song, one with simple lyrics about beautiful truths, and standing high, and rising to what one knows deep down inside is right. It was so beautiful that tears streamed down Jenn's cheeks.

The movement—after a while, they started calling it that—grew quickly. Jenn walked the streets handing out flyers, explaining to people about the river of time and living in truth. People's eyes would light up, and their numbers grew. Even though she wasn't enthusiastic, Rachel started joining them—they'd come straight after work, bringing bundles of food and bottles of beer.

One night they had well over a hundred people. A couple of weeks later that number had doubled. Bettina was a frequent guest on pirate radio, her voice right alongside that of Celine Regent of the First Church of Foundational Trauma.

The Provisional Authority maintained stony silence, though its uniformed officers were seen less often in the streets. The demonstrations got bigger, and sometimes things got contentious—arguments broke out, people screamed and wept. People berated each other one moment then embraced the next, apologizing and mystified by their uncorked emotions.

Jenn stood in the same spot every night, looking up into the lights, wanting to be seen. The gates might not open that night, or the next, but one day they would. And she would be waiting.

17

The rush of the crowd and a contagious sense of excitement took the edge off the buzz from Benny's liquor. Mykol had never seen the gates of the Authority so close at night, all floodlit and fortress stark; the mass of people below the towers could have been under the drawbridge of a medieval castle.

"Holy shit." Benny rubbed his eyes as they reached the edge of the crowd. "I didn't expect anything like this."

The chill of the night air fell away, with the heat of so many bodies charged and electric. Mykol gazed at the stream of faces, young and old, people shuffling to stay warm, others holding their arms up as though welcoming the attention of the guards. Here and there a song broke out, with some singing an undulating round of broken melody that dissolved into laughter.

"Hey, slow down," Benny called out, and Mykol realized that he had been moving fast.

"I can't remember the last time I saw this many people in one place," he said. Benny's usual look of haughty cynicism had vanished, his perpetually heavy eyelids open in surprise and wonder. "Why don't they just open the gates?" he wondered aloud.

"They will," said a man huddled close to a woman; they wore matching puffy coats. "It's a matter of time."

Benny nodded as though this contained great wisdom. It sounded like the truth. Mykol realized that the swelling he felt in his chest was hope.

Bonfires illuminated faces shining with excitement. Bottles were passed around with food from picnic baskets. Mykol couldn't remember ever being around such good cheer. He and Benny kept moving. The crowd extended over more than two city blocks, and up onto the balconies of the old university fraternity houses facing the wall.

Mykol looked back the way they had come. Maybe the gates would really open, maybe a delegation from the Provisional Authority would emerge and…then what? Share the wealth, start a peaceful revolution? His heart swung like a pendulum.

He blinked at the profile of a face in the middle of the crowd. She wore a jacket with a high-brimmed collar and a woolen hat that covered her hair. She was talking to someone next to her, smiling up at the wall.

He took a couple steps closer. Another song rose from the crowd, and she started singing. She was huddled with an older woman with wavy, gray hair that shone in the bonfire light, and a tall, serious woman with whom she stood locked arm in arm.

"Where are you going?" Benny called out from behind. "Slow down!"

This was probably going to end in embarrassment, but he got closer. She hadn't noticed him, and he traced the curve of her nose with his eyes, the bow of her lips as she sang a song about hope and the promise of truth.

It was her.

Benny grabbed his arm from behind. Mykol shook him off.

She saw him. She stopped singing, recognition coming over her eyes; she scanned him closer as he approached, a smile brightening her beautiful face.

He said her name as he approached, the women on either side of her moving closer to her in a wary and protective way. He held up his hands.

They had never even touched each other.

"Mykol," she said. She gave him a radiant smile. Then her expression shifted, the light vanishing from her eyes as she seemed to be remembering something she regretted.

He nodded, confused by how different she seemed.

"You don't work at the shop anymore," she said.

"No, I don't," he agreed. "How do you know?"

"I finally got up the courage to come see you," she said.

They were talking loud to be heard over singing voices. The women she was with looked on and they were joined by an affably grinning Benny.

"I quit that job," Mykol said. "I'm growing food now. In the city."

"I have a job, too," she said.

"All right, kids," Benny was saying. "There are other people here, you know. Introductions need to be made."

"This is Jenn," Mykol said to his friend, whose mouth formed an oval of shock, followed by a rascal's grin.

"Introduce me," he said.

"Why are you out here?" Mykol asked. "Where's your uniform?"

A look of doubt crossed her face, and Mykol felt regret. Without thinking, he reached out and took one of her hands. "I didn't—"

"It's all right." She clasped both his hands in hers. "I got…expelled!"

"What?" he yelled, and then they laughed together.

"Since my friend here has no *manners* whatsoever, it appears I have to be the one to observe social graces," Benny interrupted.

Introductions were made, with Benny coming dangerously close to a lascivious leer at Rachel. The conversation turned when Bettina asked how Jenn and Mykol had met.

"I went into his shop," Jenn said. "You know, one of the retrieval locations where they're gathering data from before."

"I didn't think I was ever going to see you again," Mykol said.

"It's been confusing." Jenn squeezed his hands.

"Where do you live?" he asked.

She named an intersection north of downtown, one he knew he could find. "Can I come see you?" he asked.

"Yes. Please."

He felt a surge of elation as though he had gotten drunk all over again.

"There's some happy juice left," Benny said, opening up his flask and offering it around. Bettina took a whiff, grimaced, then grabbed it from Benny's hand and took a long swig.

There was a flurry of activity in the part of the crowd closest to the walls.

"Oh my sweet—" Bettina started to say, wincing from the booze.

A couple of seconds passed before anyone could determine what was happening. Mykol's legs felt weak and he staggered.

Then he realized everyone around him was being affected, too. People raised their hands to their faces and screamed. But he couldn't hear them.

Sound itself was assaulting him and everyone around him. It rose up in his ears like a wave, a trebly shriek with undercurrents of deep, undulating roaring. His heart surged with terrible panic. The sound was everywhere. It was like a solid force.

Bettina dropped the flask and bent over. Mykol locked eyes with Jenn, whose teeth were bared in panic. Benny vomited down the front of his jacket.

The crowd reeled away from the gate. Mykol tried to think, but it was impossible. People tripped and fell over one another in a blind struggle to escape. Mykol clamped his hands over his ears, but the shriek and roar penetrated skin and bone. He fell to his knees. He saw Rachel pulling at Jenn, screaming. When he was able to stand partway, Jenn and her friends were gone. He forced his legs to work and dragged Benny away from the gate, and the two of them staggered until it became more bearable.

They could still hear the ringing in their ears the next morning.

18

After he woke, Mykol bicycled to the grow house in the lobby of the bank building, where he sprayed a vinegar mixture onto corn to ward off insects and checked on the progress of the potatoes and beets. He overheard a couple of workers talking about the events the night before—neither had been there, but word had spread. He stayed out of the conversation, his head still aching from the cannon of sound.

They had made it back to Benny's car, where Mykol made him wait as he peered into the dispersing crowd hoping to catch sight of Jenn, but it was fruitless. People were streaming into the darkened side streets. Mykol watched until they departed, both stunned into demoralized silence.

When he had caught up on the day's tasks, Mykol hopped onto his bicycle and rode across the river, a map in his mind pinpointing the intersection where Jenn had said she lived. He rode past the old Board of Education building, which was thumping with a deep bass beat from inside, then past a block in which nearly every building seemed to have burned long ago. Splintered beams of wood stuck up like saplings in a chaotic and dilapidated forest.

The house on the corner looked cleaned up, with curtains in the windows and potted flowers and vegetables on the porch. Mykol dropped his bike on the sidewalk and knocked on the door. He peered through the glass—no movement inside. He knocked harder.

"Who are you?" asked a voice from above. He stepped back and looked up—a woman's frowning face extended over the edge of the roofline.

"I'm Mykol," he called up to Rachel. "We met last night."

She was still frowning, but she nodded in recognition. "What do you want?" she asked.

"I'm looking for Jenn," he said.

"I'm up here," Jenn called.

Rachel motioned to the side of the house, where a ladder was leaning, inviting Mykol to climb up and join them. He hesitated for a moment—heights gave him vertigo—but Jenn was up there. He grabbed a rung and scurried up without looking down.

She was in a T-shirt and track pants, sitting cross-legged on the gently sloping roof as he hoisted himself up. Her hair was longer than before, and she had it pulled back and tied behind her head. She looked much younger without her uniform, and seemed at ease and free of the severity that had marked her before. He felt refreshed seeing her.

"You found me," she said.

She and Rachel both had hammers, and between the two of them was a stack of roofing tiles and a box of nails.

"Fixing things up?" he asked. He winced at his obviousness.

"Looks that way!" Rachel replied with exaggerated sarcasm. Jenn laughed, flashing her friend a look of mild reproach.

"Do you need a hand?" he asked.

"No, we've got it," Jenn said. "Just hang out and keep us company."

"You guys take your time and catch up," Rachel's tone suggested she didn't entirely approve. "I'm going up to the attic to see how bad that water damage is."

"You rule," Jenn called out as Rachel nimbly lowered herself down the side of the roof and shimmied out of sight.

The whole neighborhood unrolled beneath them, rows of streets and houses spreading toward the river. Yards were overflown with unchecked growth. Many buildings looked like house-shaped vines. He crab-walked over to Jenn, his heart thumping with a rush, and sat alongside her.

"I didn't expect to get attacked last night," he said after they shared the silence for a while.

Jenn gazed at the horizon. "I still have a headache."

Mykol nodded. "That's never happened before, has it?"

"I've been to nearly every gathering. The Authority hasn't acknowledged our existence until last night." Jenn grabbed a tile and fit it over a bare patch in the roof. "It was the first act of aggression. I've been wondering when it would come."

There was steel in her voice that made him pause. There was a bead of sweat collected on the soft hairs at her temple. She hadn't looked into his eyes.

"So what happened?" he finally asked.

She tapped a nail into place, then struck it into the roof with a couple of clean strokes. She grabbed another nail.

"They attacked us," she said through gritted teeth.

"Not that," Mykol said.

Now she looked up at him. He felt scattered, his heart thumping. She gazed at him thoughtfully.

"I was expelled," she said. "I failed to live up to expectations."

She kept pounding nails.

"I don't understand," he said. "You were an officer. They threw you out just like that? Did it have anything to do with—"

She looked at him, then down at her work, then at him again, emotion playing across her features. He remembered holding her hand the night before.

"They did something to me before I left." She spoke slowly and deliberately. "They tampered with my memory."

This took a moment to sink in. She had seemed so full of mystery before, emanating the burden and rush of responsibility. Now she seemed younger, but she still had the grounded presence that he liked very much and thought was the core of who she was.

"I'm sorry," he said.

"Thanks." She put down the hammer. "I have a lot of questions. I want to understand why they did this to me. I'm wondering what they're trying to hide."

"I'm so glad you're OK," he said. "I mean, I'm glad—"

She seemed to ponder this for a moment. "I'm really glad to see you," she said. "It took me a while to come looking for you. I had a lot of things to deal with. Then you were gone, and I didn't know where you might be."

"I waited for you," he said. "OK, that sounds weird. I...really wanted to see you. I kept hoping you'd come through the door again."

She looked at him searchingly, then smiled. "When I was first out here it was hard to know who I was or where I fit in. It's getting better. It's good that you're here. I just...keep feeling lost."

"That's why you joined the protests?" he asked.

"I don't know." She pounded another nail. "Maybe because I've changed, I think everything needs to change. But maybe it *does*."

"Maybe," he said. "But it's not like you've changed completely."

She lined up another nail and looked up. She scratched the side of her nose. "You've changed too," she said.

"Really? How?"

She sized him up. "You look stronger."

"I'm getting outdoors more," he said. Then he laughed. She could make him feel like an awkward kid just by looking at him. She laughed, too.

"I like it," she said.

"Then I'll keep doing it," he told her.

"I can tell your friend likes Rachel," Jenn told him. "He isn't exactly subtle, that guy."

"I don't think she likes me," Mykol said.

"Go easy on Rachel. She's possessive. We've gotten really close and we look out for each other."

Mykol blinked. "Oh," he said. "Does that mean you two are—"

"No," Jenn interrupted. "We're not a couple."

"I hope it's OK that this is really good news to me."

"I had my suspicions."

Looking into her dark eyes, he noticed that the implant was gone, replaced by a cloudy spot.

"Does that hurt?" he asked.

"It itched like hell for a while," she said. "It's OK now. It's kind of liberating, not getting vital signs and incoming messages all the time."

"That reminds me," he said. "I have the files from your data stick."

"I'm sorry if I put you in danger," she said.

"Don't worry about it," he told her. "But here's the thing. My mother's name was on one of the research papers in those files."

She looked confused.

"Oh." He paused. "I made a copy of everything before I destroyed the data stick."

He was going to apologize, but she looked at him with undisguised happiness.

"I never got to look at any of it," she said. "I had…I got really sick after the last time I saw you. When they expelled me, they took my wallet away. You still have those files?"

"At home," he said. "I couldn't get some of them to open."

"I might be able to," she told him.

He forced himself not to stare at the curvature of exposed shoulder that peeked out from her shirt.

"I'm just about finished," she said. "Then I want to go see your place."

He felt flummoxed and unaccountably panicked. His *house*?

They climbed down the ladder and went inside the house. Rachel was clearly unhappy and glowered at Mykol. He avoided her by looking around and was impressed by the curtains and cushions and working electric stove. He had a moment of panic about the bachelor squalor where he lived, then resigned himself that he wouldn't have time to clean before she came over. He paused in the kitchen and enviously eyed a stack of pickled vegetables in labeled jars.

He looked up. Rachel was watching him.

"Did you make these?" he asked.

She nodded. "I grew up on a farm."

"With animals and stuff?" he asked.

Her expression was unwavering. "You can take one of those with you if you want," she said, turning and going upstairs.

19

While he and Jenn rode their bicycles toward his neighborhood, Mykol tried to explain about his dad. She was only vaguely familiar with *Downstairs*, though after a few exchanges she cried out in surprise.

"Wait a minute," she said. "You live with your *father*? Your *real* dad?"

They turned a corner onto the main road, where there was no car traffic but a steady stream of bikes and a handful of scooters.

"That's amazing," she said. "I thought everyone our age was an orphan. At least that's true of everyone I know."

"Including you?" he asked.

"Including me," she said.

They had traveled about another quarter of a mile when Jenn stiffened—she saw the parked Provisional Authority van before he did. They slowed down and steered close to the curb. A pair of officers in sunglasses in the front seat stared directly ahead and didn't acknowledge Jenn and Mykol as they passed.

"I never get used to that," she said when they turned a corner.

He kept talking to Jenn about his father retreating ever deeper *Downstairs*, the long stretches of noncommunication and his disappearances into his room. She listened to him closely, nodding.

"People his age saw the worst of it," she said. "The Authority had all kinds of therapies for them when I was growing up, just to deal with the shock and change. It's understandable that your father wants to escape."

It had been a while since he felt such compassion toward his father. It made him think of when he was a child, when he and Dad were tilling their first garden in the backyard, the work and the sweat and the feeling that they were facing the future together.

He and Jenn switched on their lamps as the twilight deepened, speeding up on the Dale then cutting down the alley behind the house; it was as though the scale changed, the tall weeds and plants around them providing a tunnel of privacy. There were lights on inside the house, which was a surprise—it meant his father was up and about, although the place was quiet and still when Mykol let them in.

Jenn looked around, and he saw the place though her eyes: the water stains on the living room wall, the cracked plaster and peeling paint, the damaged floors, and the sad mess of dishes in the sink.

But she let out a happy sound when the water in the sink flowed.

"It works!" she said. "The water's been out for two days in our part of town. Rachel fixed the line out to the city hookup, but it's still touch and go."

He pulled the jar of pickled vegetables out of his jacket. "She's resourceful. And maybe she doesn't entirely hate me."

She motioned at the jar. "You going to share that?"

He got some venison jerky from the refrigerator—a dwindling stash he had been saving for a special occasion. They ate standing in the kitchen, passing the jar and the bag back and forth. The vegetables were briny and delicious. Jenn swiveled around to stand next to him, and they were both leaning back against the counter, the sides of their arms grazing. He felt her strength, and something that wasn't strength, in a way that was physical and also wasn't physical. He felt confused in the most happy way.

She put down the food and wiped her mouth on a rag from the counter. "All right. Let's check out what's in those files."

"Stay here," he told her. "I'll be right back."

The idea of having her in his room was dizzyingly exciting, but he also knew he had neglected such fineries as picking up the dirty laundry, making his bed, and not leaving pornography cartridges out in the open. He sprinted upstairs, shoved everything shameful into the closet, and grabbed his tablet.

She was looking at the pictures on the living room mantel when he came down. "Is this your mother?"

Mom was standing out on the grass somewhere, by herself, looking into the camera with good-natured defiance. Mykol had memorized every pixel of that image, the way her hair fell over her shoulders, the way one of her hands was raised partway up as though she was in the middle of saying something. The picture was taken about four or five years before she died.

"She was so pretty," Jenn said.

Mykol took the tablet into the kitchen where the light was better. They sat next to each other at the table. The backyard was dark and quiet.

"Have you always lived here?" she asked.

He nodded. "I had a brother and a sister. Both older. I don't remember them. Or my mom."

"I don't remember any of my family," Jenn said, watching the tablet screen come to life. "Sometimes I wonder if I had any relatives who survived, but in the Authority you're discouraged from looking for outside family."

She said this with sadness. He couldn't tell what lives not lived she regretted.

"There we go," she said, motioning at the tablet.

He executed a search and the bundle popped up: the folders, the docs, the photos, and those weird, numbered files with an unfamiliar extension tag. "This is everything," he told her.

"Which one has to do with your mother?" she asked.

He opened it. The title page appeared: *Projected Vectors and Global Impact of Viral Epidemic in Rapid Escalation Scenario.*

"Epidemiology," Jenn said.

"Mom was a researcher." He looked up from the screen. "Weird, right? Look at the date—this paper was published less than a year before the Grip."

"There were plagues before," Jenn said. "I've heard that there was always a fear of something like the Grip happening, but everyone just went on like it wasn't possible."

"It really freaked me out that my mom's name is on that paper. It's such a weird coincidence."

"Maybe she knew my father," Jenn said. "He worked in data science for a big corporation. That's basically all I know about him. I was hoping there would be stuff here that can tell me more about him."

She opened up the photo folder and started to scroll through its contents. The first few were group photos of men and women looking like they were at work. They were posed and arranged in front of what Mykol had seen in other images: the big deck of a major data-processing center.

"Wow, that's crazy tech," he said appreciatively. "That's old-school. You never see anything like that today—unless you work for the Authority, I guess. Have you seen anything like that?"

"Yes. I think so," she said.

She rubbed her eyes so hard that he could hear it.

He reminded himself what she had told him about her memory. It wasn't obvious, because she was so quick-witted, so *present.*

He leaned closer. Her hair smelled slightly floral, and he noticed that the backs of her hands were dusted with asymmetrical freckles.

She paused on a photo of a couple seemingly in their thirties. He was wearing a short-sleeved, collared shirt and had muscular shoulders and an unguarded smile. The woman was wearing a dark dress; she was obviously Jenn's mother. They had the same eyes, the same auburn hair, the same smile.

"It's them," she said softly.

They stared at the picture together for a long time.

"They look happy," Jenn said quietly.

"Have you seen pictures of them before?"

Jenn nodded, her eyes locked on the screen. "I wasn't sure they were real." She paused. "But…back there, at the Authority, there are physical possessions We're not encouraged to access them."

"Is that where you got the data stick?"

She nodded, still fixed on the screen.

"I've never seen this picture before," she said.

"Why?" Mykol asked. "They belonged to your family."

"That was the point," Jenn said. "We were taught to evolve beyond the concept of family. We were taught to meditate on the idea that the Authority and its duties supplant biological bonds."

"Did it work?" asked Mykol.

"It did until it didn't." Jenn shook her head.

"Is it OK that I'm glad about that?" Mykol asked in a soft voice.

She didn't look at him.

They scrolled through more work settings, mostly computer labs or conferences—Jenn's father seemed to attend a lot of those. When her parents were pictured together, it was always in a variation of the same pose and posture, something they fell into together with ease. They had traveled a good deal. There wasn't much evidence of domestic life until a photo that looked to be taken in the summertime on a back porch, the bright sun on a little child leaning against her mother's knees, standing with assistance and beaming a radiant smile.

"I guess that's me," Jenn said. It was the last picture.

She was silent for a time.

"So what's the deal with these encoded files?" she suddenly asked in a different voice. She began clicking on the tablet's interface.

"I spent a couple weeks trying to get those open," Mykol explained. "I tried a few of the common platforms from then but none of them worked. I even snuck my tablet into Ellison's and tried some of the jack-ins there. No luck."

"You were really persistent," Jenn said.

He got up from the table. "I figured you wised up and you weren't coming back," he said. "Still, I wanted to learn more about you."

"I never *wised up*," Jenn stared at the screen. "I wanted to see you again. I'm glad I'm with you now."

Mykol stuck his tongue in his cheek. "Me too. Really. A lot."

She didn't seem to hear him. Mykol went to the landing and replenished the pitcher of filtered water. He got a whiff of something stagnant from the kitchen sink and hoped she didn't notice. Grabbing a couple of cups from the rack, he poured out water and came back to the table. He sat close to her.

"This is interesting," she said. She was looking at lines of code on the tablet's screen.

"Wait, how did you do that?" he asked her. "I was never able to get past the encryption."

She winked. "I can tell this base code isn't too different from what we...*they* use in the Authority. Which is kind of odd because the files are all really old. It's like they're Authority while also predating the Authority, if you know what I mean. Whatever."

He handed her water., trying not to betray how impressed he was. She was tapping the screen quickly; with each finger stroke, she seemed to be delving deeper and deeper past layers of safeguards.

"It looks like these were made on an earlier system iteration sourcing different base values. It *is* similar to Authority systems—it almost looks like two different branches that shared a common root. I think I figured out a side path we can use to make it compatible."

"You're totally impressive," he said, "Have I mentioned that I've become an expert in horticulture?"

She looked up. "You didn't mention that. I think that's sexy as hell."

He was at a loss for words.

"Come back to Earth," Jenn was tapping the back of his hand. "Look. I figured the way in. These are video files. They're not even that big. I don't think they were intended to be so difficult to open."

She tilted the screen so they could both see it. "Let's start with the oldest one," she said.

20

The video player booted up with a swirling icon. It resolved into a standard laptop camera angle. The room was indistinct, the lens focused on a man in the foreground wearing a jacket and tie. He had a mustache and thick, wavy hair. Mykol realized who the man was, all of a sudden, when Jenn gasped.

"Jenn," her father said.

She turned up the volume.

"I'm in my office after hours. I wanted to talk when there was no one around. You visited me here today, but I'm sure you won't remember. Your first birthday is coming up next week."

Mykol lightly put his hand on hers.

"In all likelihood you will never see this. That would be for the best, of course, because it would mean—"

He paused. Jenn held Mykol's hand tighter. She was staring at the screen with her mouth wide open.

"I'm going to tell you a few things. If what I fear comes to pass, I'm going to figure out a way to get this to you. Because I'm having... misgivings about the project I'm working on."

The exposed kitchen bulb overhead reflected in the pixilated video.

"Where do I start?" He smiled grimly. "At the beginning. I'm going to assume that you might not know me, but maybe you remember me. I am a computer scientist. I studied at MIT and Cal Tech. Today I am an executive at a private corporation, but the major project I'm involved with includes scientists from other companies as well as international governments. It's regarded as a very big deal, but few people know the half of it. At the very least, it's going to change a great deal around the world. It's different than anything that's happened in our history since the first caveman learned to sharpen a stick and hunt with it."

From somewhere outside, there was piercing laughter in the darkness where the streetlights had burned out. Another voice called in response. Mykol got up and made sure he had bolted the back door.

"You'll be watching this years from now." Her father paused and looked out from the screen with a fond expression. "That's nice to think about, but it also presents me with a quandary: I have to try to imagine the world you are living in. It might be much like this one. But I don't think so."

When Mykol returned to the table, Jenn was shaking. He took her hand again. Tears ran down her cheek.

"Probably the most consequential development in my field during my lifetime was the internet." Her father paused, thinking. "Well, that's arguable. Processing speeds increasing exponentially laid the groundwork for the big revolutions in the years since I was first learning code on an Apple that stored about one megabyte on its hard drive. But you probably don't want to listen to me reminisce about those days."

Mykol could see a resemblance between Jenn and her father, an intensity of manner and a glow in their eyes.

"Things have been moving quickly since then. The sequencing of the human genome was arguably even more impactful than the internet, even if the visible differences in people's everyday lives weren't as pronounced."

He paused, clearly looking for words.

"I've been fortunate to work on teams with more or less open-ended funding over the past five years or so. Blank checks, if you will. These teams have been tasked with looking at developments through a big lens. I'm sure you know this is a time of so much trouble. The climate seems to be accelerating. Our wars and refugee crises are proliferating. And our most affluent and technologically advanced societies are suffering a mass crisis of truth and shared reality.

"It's ironic—many of the poor countries the affluent nations look down upon report higher levels of individual happiness. Our machines have outstripped us—the short but all-powerful era of the black screens, the computers and phones, has fragmented the sanity of Homo Sapiens when we need it the most."

"He's afraid," Jenn said.

In that long-gone office, Jenn's father glanced over his shoulder. "We've unlocked a great deal of potential, that's still true. But in the last century, we developed weapons and tools none of us are rational enough to wield, and we created something unsustainable despite all our best efforts and intentions. We've outsmarted ourselves, and soon our world might be unrecognizable."

Mykol realized the video's resolution looked like one of the face chats he had seen at Ellison's, when the Provisional Authority was testing the old networks in their endless failed attempts to get it up and running. Once Ellison's had managed to contact a center across the city on old cable; the workers at both shops had gathered around their cameras and heckled each other until the fuzzy connection finally cut.

"The important thing to bear in mind is that the kind of enhancements for humans that we are developing, both physical and intellectual, will not be available to the masses. We will not go to the next step of evolution together. The people I'm working with, and working for, are actively opposed to that happening."

Mykol remembered the other text files he had imported from the data stick—in addition to the study on a global pandemic, there had been meaty and nearly impenetrable speculations and studies on technology and the old society. While he hadn't read them all, beneath the convoluted academic prose were concepts like the one Jenn's father was talking about—that there was a kind of mass madness rising around the world in politics and culture, and especially in the places where people lived online.

"With greater speed comes more connection—like the synapses in a brain. In my field, this is a very good thing. It's become a cliché to talk about computing speed in terms of brute force, but it stands up. We're in the process of using that power to leapfrog evolution. The technical processes themselves are giving me great cause for worry. We're creating something to burrow into our minds and bodies and enhance them. But in order for this to work, we need a partner much smarter than us."

It was fully dark outside. Mykol looked out the window. Though it had been months since there had been any kind of disturbance out on their street, he had wary memories of watching fighting on the sidewalks, passersby seeing lights on inside and trying the door to see if it was locked, and the time he and his father had to come out on the porch with baseball bats to frighten away a deranged young man with eyes blazing with crazed anger.

"And this is the central paradox," Jenn's father was saying.

Mykol couldn't help but be fascinated. Whatever breakthrough Jenn's father was talking about seemed to have led to Provisional Authority tech. But there was a bigger picture beyond Mykol's capacity to grasp.

"More connection, less cohesion, more danger, greater instability, an inability to act for the greater good or to address alarming developments. It's as though we've been able to cut through time itself, to process and advance so quickly that it has driven us mad—like the early humans sitting around the fire, watching a conjurer call up shapes and lights out of the air and then killing each other over what they meant. We could be wasting precious time. Maybe we're giving birth now to a select elite and the rest of us will respond with today's equivalent of sharpened stones."

The world as it once was sounded even less appealing than the histories depicted it. Mykol couldn't say that he would have chosen the world where he had grown up, but maybe he would have—as the Osirians and the Timeless Evangelists argued, a fallen world burned to ash was made up of potential and possibility.

"We're working on a very theoretical level. Essentially, we're repurposing the total power of the internet into a worker mind that unifies unimaginable scales of data and seeks solutions. But these solutions aren't for everyone. Would it be the responsible thing to step in and stop all this?"

Jenn shook her head. Mykol felt her beating heart so close to his. He looked at her face and saw fresh tears.

He got up and rummaged around in one of the kitchen drawers—old wires, broken tools, bits of string, even a packet of food for the dog that had died about five years ago. He finally found what he was looking for, a handkerchief that was presentable enough to offer her. She thanked him.

"This wouldn't have been possible five years ago, but the advances in quantum computing have shocked everyone who understands them. Now that we're working on this level—"

He gave a shrug from the screen, somehow poignant, his expression conveying equal parts worry and excitement.

"The cat's out of the bag. Is it going to serve us or are we going to serve it?

"We've given some watered-down information for the public and the press. But there are only a handful of people in the world who truly understand. Most of the politicians don't. For most people, life is all screens and distractions, people chattering about the latest hollow outrage. When things change, it's possible no one will even notice. There are about eight or nine of us who have access to the big picture. Ten, maybe. Imagine a world run by scientists! It would warm my heart if I wasn't so terrified."

Jenn's father sighed, long and hard, and stared out from the screen.

"Maybe we'll get it right. Then we'll watch this together and laugh about what a worrier your old man used to be."

Jenn wiped her eyes and nose. Father and daughter faced one another across time.

"My dear daughter, how I love you."

He gave a thin, pinched smile.

"We shall see. It's probably time for me to end this lecture. Or maybe it's a confession. I hope we all step into the light like a butterfly emerging from its silken womb. I believe humanity deserves a chance. There's so much good in us."

He smiled, and Mykol pictured the vacation photo with Jenn's mother, the two of them with the ease of a long-married couple with their order and solidity.

The video ended. The tablet screen went black.

21

Mykol saw how watching the video had affected Jenn with both wrenching sadness and bittersweet joy, but for him it had been confusing and unsettling. He didn't know what to think. He understood the old age of digital connectivity and knew firsthand about tech components and how they worked. But he had only vaguely heard of quantum computing—as far as he knew, it had never become more than a theory.

But what if it had? That might be the technology the Authority ran on, its advantage in the balance of the power it wielded over the rest of humanity. Maybe it drove the mysteries of what lay behind the retinal chips and the missing pieces of Jenn's memories.

Mykol looked up from the tablet. His father was watching them from the kitchen doorway. It shocked him so much that his chair crashed against the floor in his hurry to get up.

His father's eyes were rheumy and red, the way they were when he had been jacked into *Downstairs* for a very long time. He was wearing frayed tracksuit bottoms and no shoes; his feet were dirty. His T-shirt was inside out threadbare.

"We have a guest," his dad said in a croaky voice.

Jenn got up and said hello. Mykol's father blinked at her as though unsure whether to trust his senses or not.

"Donald," he said. "Don Krusos."

"I'm Jenn," she said as they shook hands.

"This one," he motioned toward Mykol. "Doesn't always have the greatest manners. It's probably my fault. Teaching him to make proper introductions never got pushed high enough on the agenda."

Jenn smiled. "Mykol is very much a gentleman."

Don gave a skeptical if sleepy look.

"Dad, how long have you been standing there?"

Don shrugged *who knows*. He made his way to the water jug and poured a big glass, which he drained and refilled. He was always parched when he came out from *Downstairs*.

"Long enough to hear some things." He leaned back against the sink and rubbed his eyes, inhaling and exhaling raggedly. "Who was that on the video?"

Mykol and Jenn gave Don an abridged version of things, omitting that Jenn had been with the Provisional Authority (she shot him a look, and he knew to keep that between them). They told Don about Jenn's father's work as part of a team working on a big breakthrough in the days before the Grip. Then Mykol told him about the research paper where he'd found his mother's name.

"Louise?" his father said. He shook his head, trying to dislodge cobwebs accumulated in another reality. "This was a research paper you found where?"

"In my father's data," Jenn explained. "It was one of several scholarly studies on computing, broad social trends, the effects of technology on society, and, in this case, epidemiology and plagues."

Don nodded soberly. He took another deep breath. "Yeah." He looked at Mykol. "I remember her working on that."

"You do?"

His father's eyes widened as though he was staring into the past. "It was disturbing for your mother. There had been a flu outbreak a few years before that was pretty nasty. Then she and the people she was working with had found new vectors of transmission along certain virus mutations. I remember her coming home from a conference very upset. And she was pregnant with you."

Don looked down at the cracked floor. "Did you guys get anything to eat? And if you did, might there be anything left over?"

The three of them sat around the table. They fired up the electric heater and placed it closest to Jenn in deference to her guest status. Don asked questions about her work in the brewery and bakery, volunteering a couple of college-era stories in which he had been an underling in a bread shop on the East Coast.

"The flour," he said, smiling and remembering. "It really has a tendency to get into your pores."

"*Very* hard to get out after a long shift," she said with a light laugh that sparkled in Mykol's ears. "I'm assuming you never had to grind it yourself back in those days?"

"Definitely not." He was working on some of the pickled vegetables, washing them back with another pint of water. "This was when all the supply chains were operating. You could go out and buy yourself a hundred pounds of flour as easy as walking down the street."

"I really don't mind grinding it. It's honest work."

Don looked at her and chuckled gently. "Makes sense. What would be the problem doing it yourself? That's why there were those rough years after things broke down, because people didn't have real-life skills. I always admired Mykol's mother, though—right up to the end she was always learning how to fix things."

"You son is a fixer, too," Jenn said.

"That's right, he is," Don said, fondly if distantly. "First it was that business with the old computers, and lately it's been…"

He trailed off.

"*Gardening*, Dad," Mykol said impatiently. "Vegetable gardening to make the city more food diverse and not dependent on the countryside."

Don gave a sly grin, more himself than he had been in weeks. "Your own supply chain," he said.

"Independence," Mykol said.

Jenn sat eating seconds of Rachel's pickles with Mykol and Don and felt herself relax. She knew about Don's *Downstairs* addiction and the downward spiral it was inflicting on his physical and mental health, but it was also obvious that father and son loved each other deeply. Don ribbed Mykol, and Mykol would respond with a flustered blush and an obvious desire to please.

It was *nice.*

Her mind ran along two tracks as they broke out preserves and spread them on semi-stale bread for dessert (Don extracted promises of beer and bread from Jenn, which also seemed a good-natured way to get her to pledge to visit again). Part of her mind was back with her father, the stoic and rambling researcher who came to his point in the most roundabout of ways.

And his point was vastly important, at least as far as she understood it. Her understanding of high technology seemed to go only so far, then go black—that was when she knew she had reached for memories erased when she was drummed out of the Authority.

They stayed up late drinking shots of caustic apricot brandy that Don fished out of a cabinet—a really sweet gesture, given how humble their circumstances were. Their conditions were rawer than the life she and Rachel had created. Don's retreat from reality explained a lot about the sadness in Mykol's eyes.

She could see Mykol was pleasantly surprised his dad was present and engaged. She felt a stirring of protectiveness for him.

Mykol found her a place to sleep when they were all too tired to talk anymore; it was a narrow bed in a side room, where Mykol dragged and plugged in the electric heater.

"This should be good for the night," he said, switching on a lamp in the corner. "I've slept in here plenty of times."

He stayed in the doorway a little too long, sort of shuffling in an awkward way while his gaze flitted up the stairway and then to her.

"Thank you for being here tonight," he said, too formally. "It's been great."

She piled pillows at one end of the bed. "It's nice to meet your father. And to spend time with you."

"What do you think about—" He searched for words. "That stuff with your dad?"

"I feel rattled, you know. It's obviously important, just in a way that I don't understand."

"Yeah," he said. "I think that, too."

She took both his hands in hers and squeezed. She wondered if they should kiss. It seemed best not to, not yet.

"Um, I'm going to go to bed now."

His expression made her laugh.

"What?" he asked, flashing embarrassed irritation.

"Oh, nothing," she said. "Really! It's just that…all of this. Tonight. It feels like the start of something. Do you feel that too?"

His smile was boyish as his face disappeared into shadows from the lamp and heater.

"Yeah. I do," he told her. "I'm glad you do, too."

Then she got under the blankets and, without really realizing what she was doing, began to activate her training to mine for lucid insights and information in her upcoming dreams. She didn't know she was doing it, but she was asleep within a minute.

22

The next morning, Jenn awoke to streaks of sun reflected on the wall; it took a moment to remember the night before and where she was. She made her way back to the kitchen and retrieved her bag. No one else was stirring as she found a scrap of paper and a pencil.

She wrote Mykol a note: *Will be working at brewery on Washington and Bright Ave. and will be done in the afternoon. Stop by if you can.*

It seemed as though she should write something more, but subtleties eluded her. She glanced at the top of the pencil and saw that someone had bitten off the eraser: no second chances.

Thank you for last night, she wrote. *Let's see each other soon.*

She remembered Mykol taking his tablet to bed with him the night before. There had been two other encrypted files on her father's data stick, and they hadn't gotten to them when Don appeared and they spent the rest of the night talking.

Bring your tablet, she added.

She put the slip of paper on the table with a saltshaker to anchor it, positioned her bag on her back, and went out back to her bicycle.

There was a pleasant smell of woodsmoke coming from someone's house as she shifted gears and felt the crisp focus of waking. She threaded through the side streets toward downtown. It had been a good night's sleep, the best in a while, punctuated by dreams.

First she had been on a boat, sunlight dancing in fractals on the water, then she was hanging for dear life to a handle on the side of a speeding van, then there were huge steel gates that dream logic dictated was the fortress of the Provisional Authority. There had been something she needed to retrieve from where she once lived, an item that belonged to her but was also larger than herself.

The cloudless sky resolved into thrilling electric blue. She stood up on the pedals, pushing harder and feeling her heart thrum as she crossed the bridge and watched the river flow. She felt her spirit expand as the air grew warmer, heated by sunshine, a welcome feeling of eternity and timelessness. She felt happy and knew it was because of the night before.

Rachel was brewing a pot of oats on the stove when Jenn got home. Her long hair was in braids that fell over either shoulder, and she was dressed for work in coveralls and a long-underwear shirt with the sleeves rolled up.

"You stayed out all night," Rachel said.

"I lost track of time," Jenn said. "It got dark before I knew it, and I didn't want to ride home in the dark alone."

Rachel glowered. "I wish someone at the Authority would tell me when we're going to have working phones."

Jenn knew this was her friend being conciliatory. She fetched a couple of bowls from the cupboard and laid them beside the stove, stopping to rub Rachel's shoulders.

"You were with that guy?" Rachel asked from over her shoulder, rolling her neck in the feline way that meant Jenn was doing it right.

"Mykol," Jenn said. "Yes, I was at his place. And no, I wasn't *with* him, not how I think you mean."

Rachel started ladling out the oats. Brown sugar from the bakery melted on the surface of each serving with a sweet, burning aroma. "It's no big deal. Just wanting to know what's going on is all."

Rachel had been raised to say what was on her mind, and she was constitutionally incapable of hiding anything.

Jenn explained, as best she could, the data stick and meeting Mykol at Ellison's. She told Rachel about the video file and the emotional impact of seeing her father. She talked about Don, bleary-eyed but warm and who was gradually receding from the world.

Rachel put down her spoon and looked out the window. "I miss my father," she said.

"I know you do, honey," Jenn said, reaching across the table to take her hand.

"Gonna come out west with me?" Rachel asked, her eyes clouded with dampness.

They had talked about leaving the city together, maybe getting a couple of motorcycles and tracing the straightaway plains and the winding mountain roads neither of them had seen before all the way to the ocean.

"I'd love to," Jenn said, squeezing her friend's hand. "But there are things I need to get done here first."

"Do they involve that skinny little Mykol?" Rachel asked with a sarcastic smile. She said Mykol's name with a nasal parody of his sometimes halting way of talking. Jenn gave her a look of reprimand, but then couldn't help but laugh.

"You like him, don't you?" Rachel asked as she polished off the oatmeal.

"I probably do," Jenn said. "Maybe I shouldn't. It would be so much easier to keep things the way they are."

Which meant, though she left it unsaid, living quietly, alone with Rachel. They were as close as two people could be who weren't lovers, and all the time they spent felt like a sacred covenant Jenn was hesitant to break.

"I'm a big girl," Rachel said as she dropped her dish into the sink. "Just tell me you won't go away for good. I really need you."

Jenn got up from the table, seeing that her strapping, tough-talking friend had begun to cry. She almost started to weep as well, but caught herself. That was the way it worked—if one got overwhelmed, the other would become doubly tough until the emotional storm passed. It was their unspoken compact, how they helped each other survive.

"I need you too, farmer girl," Jenn said with her face pressed into Rachel's hair as she held her very tight. "I'm not going anywhere."

They stayed that way for a while, listening to the sounds of the birds singing outside and feeling the strength that comes from unconditional love.

23

It was batch day at the brewery, which meant all hands on deck. Jenn worked through the morning scrubbing out the big pots, then checking the connectors and lines to the big propane tank that would bring the wort to boil. Because the power had been on for a few days, they had an ample supply of ice made from unfiltered water, which would quickly cool the earthy, cloying liquid.

The beer they made wasn't as good as the stuff at the Authority (she really missed the flavor of good wine), but it was decent enough and word had gotten round, and the brewery had ramped up production to supply some bars and a couple of local restaurants.

"Looking good?" asked Lu, the woman who owned the operation with her wife. Lu was a generous and decent employer, paying in currency as well as product. She treated her people like extended family: some even stayed with her at her big house by the lake, and she was generally tolerant of foibles and eccentricities. She was different when they were brewing and packaging, though—everyone knew that was time to work, and that a skunky batch that wasted precious ingredients would bring out her justifiable anger.

Jenn was in the middle of test-lighting the burners. "Everything looks clean," she told the older woman.

Lu was short and compact. Her hair was so dark that she must have had a stash of old-fashioned dye.

"Today I want to try and double the usual production," Lu explained. "We have enough hops and barley. I've been thinking about going for stronger stuff and fermenting longer."

"People like stronger stuff," Jenn said.

Lu smiled. "They like it as strong as they can get it. But I want to stay on the safe side and keep the product good. Just because people are willing to drink swill doesn't mean they'll come back the next time."

On a nearby table were curved stamps that marked the bottles with the Chinese characters representing Chiang Riverside Brewing Company. Jenn hadn't been working there long, but she got the sense that Lu was becoming as wealthy as anyone in the city.

"You guys OK?" Lu asked, looking though the doorway where Rachel was doling out grains based on Lu's handwritten recipes. There were about a dozen workers there, including the accountant and Lu's wife Sheryl, who oversaw everything with a harder hand (her severity had its adherents, and some of the employees treated her with the reverence of a surrogate mother).

"Me and Rachel?" Jenn asked. "We're fine, why do you ask?"

"No big deal. Just a feeling."

Jenn noticed Lu's gaze focused on the smudge of scar tissue in her eye. The mark left by the removal of the retinal implant wasn't something that was noticed by too many people—Bettina was a prominent exception—but Mykol had, of course, seen it, and, in his sweet way, tried hard to pretend he hadn't.

"I had some old family stuff come up last night," Jenn told her boss. "Maybe that's what you're picking up on."

"Old family stuff," Lu repeated. "Someone you lost?"

Jenn nodded. "My father."

"You're about the age when you must have…seen things when you were young," Lu said. "Do you have any memories from then?"

"Luckily, no." Jenn immediately regretted her choice of words. At Lu's age, the older woman would have seen and survived many things.

Lu nodded. "I have plenty I wish I could forget."

I have plenty I wish I could remember, Jenn thought. All morning she kept remembering snapshots from her dreams: a flash of a bright, highly lit, pristine white hallway; a conversation with someone who kept changing shape and who made her more awestruck than frightened; a cold memory of feeling weightless and disembodied…

Lu was looking at her.

"I…I'm sorry you went through all that," Jenn said.

Lu shrugged. "Me too," she said. "You know that thing they call survivor's guilt?"

It was a semi-facetious question. The idea had been baked into society with a sorrow and despair that ran like a dark river through everything people avoided talking about. Jenn nodded.

"A family of nine, including my parents, and that's before all the aunts and uncles and grandkids," Lu said. She shook her head. "You'd think maybe it would be OK to be the last one standing. Not so much, it turns out."

Suddenly Lu and Sheryl's familial approach to business made a lot of sense. Jenn switched off the burners and tugged at the propane lines one final time to make sure there was no leakage.

"If you don't mind me saying so, you're not really the last one standing," Jenn told her. "We're here with you. You give everyone hope. Especially me."

Lu smiled. "You're just here for the free beer," she said, but Jenn saw the light in the older woman's eyes.

In back, the team was processing grain and sweeping away chaff from the floor. There were about as many men as women, and Jenn noticed how a young guy named Billy had managed to plant himself close by Rachel as they worked. Rachel had always been pretty much pansexual, and Jenn knew how guys got instant crushes on her and how much pleasure it gave Rachel to pretend not to notice.

"Hey, Billy," Jenn said. "How's it going?"

Billy was steadfastly retro. He wore his hair long and seemed to have a limitless supply of T-shirts depicting the logos of old bands like Steely Dan and the Grateful Dead. It was clearly his turn to select the music because it sounded to Jenn like an Amazon being strangled to death in a thunderstorm. Everyone liked Billy. He brought in apples from a tree near his house when they were in season and walked the single women home after dark and never tried anything.

"Living the dream, Jenn," Billy said. Today his T-shirt reflected appreciation of some singer called Pink Floyd.

Jenn announced she was ready to spark the burners when the prep was done. Someone joked about her being super-efficient and always getting her work done quicker than everyone else. The work ethic she developed at the Provisional Authority served her well on the outside—although the joke also implied she didn't need to be so competitive and diligent.

She knew that. She didn't mind being laughed at. Not too much.

"Tell Jenn what you were just saying, Billy." Rachel looked up from the basket of barley in which her arms were submerged.

"That messed-up shit?" Billy said, looking up. "I hate talking about it."

"Someone on his street got robbed," Rachel explained. "And it was really ugly."

"It's this couple, this guy and this woman. I see them maybe once a week." Billy said. "Some people say they have a supply of really good shit—I mean, the *really good* shit."

"Are you talking about drugs?" Jenn asked.

Everyone looked over at Jenn with amusement. She had a reputation as being humorously naïve and clueless about the workings of the world. Rachel gave her the grin that meant she was enjoying both a laugh at Jenn's expense as well as the pleasure of their shared knowledge about Jenn's secret.

"OK. Drugs. I get it." Jenn burned with irritation. "What happened to your neighbors?"

"Home invasion," Billy said. He scooped grain off a scale and into a metal bucket. "Smashed in the door, ripped the place up. When I got home last night it was dark, and you could hear the screams from a block away."

"Did anyone call the police?" Jenn asked. "Or the Authority? They're supposed to respond to serious assaults."

Billy gave her a dubious look. "A couple of cops showed up after it was over. I went over to try to help right as the scumbags came running out and took off down the street. They had dark ski masks on."

"What did the police do?" Jenn asked.

"They took away the guy's body." Billy grimaced. "And then they put the woman in the car. She was all bloody, I mean really bad. I don't know where they took her."

"Billy thinks the Authority didn't come because of the protests," Rachel said.

"I don't know how the Authority operates, but it's pretty suspicious. They usually clamp down on really outrageous violent crime. That's what makes this city possible to live in. I don't want to live in some kind of *jungle*."

Carl, a tall, pale man of about thirty, came in with a bag of hops and plopped it down on a table. "You talking about that home invasion?" he asked. "When I stopped at the park after work last night one of my neighbors was telling me about someone getting shot out in the suburbs. No one came to check it out because it's in an area without municipal police, and the Authority never showed up to do anything about it. People out there are scared."

"I remember it being like that years and years ago," said LaVell, who was changing a water filter. "When the dying got really bad, before the Authority stepped in and laid down martial law. People got raped and killed right out on the streets. They were putting furniture up against their doors, keeping the blinds closed and living by candlelight so no one knew anyone was alive inside."

"The Authority is letting this happen because of the demonstrations?" Jenn asked.

LaVell shook his head. "Damn if I know," he said. "But they break up the biggest demonstration we've ever had in this city, and then within a couple of days they're letting people go after each other like there's no law."

"They're trying to show us how powerful they are," said Billy. "Let us see what it's like to live without them, make us come begging to keep us safe."

It was known at Chiang that Jenn was a daily attendee at the demonstrations, along with Rachel.

"What do *you* think?" asked LaVell.

Jenn tried not to react. She hated when people talked to her like she was some kind of expert on the Provisional Authority, which happened with unsettling frequency. She knew she gave off some sort of upper-class impression, but it continually reminded her of everything she was hiding.

"Could be," she said. "I didn't expect that attack outside the gates the other night. We've been hoping for some kind of engagement or dialogue. Not a sonic cannon."

"Maybe that *was* engagement," Billy said. Carl let out a mirthless laugh.

Jenn had had the exact same thought. It made her burn with an intensity that surprised her, directed solely at the world that had once defined every aspect of her existence. She looked over at Rachel, who smiled sadly.

"Things you need to get done," Rachel said, repeating Jenn's words from earlier that morning.

After the big boiling pots of wort had cooled, everyone worked in tandem to pour the dark liquid into sanitized fermentation casks, carefully sealed and stacked on scrubbed concrete floors. This crew had gotten good at brewing, and hadn't made a bad batch in more than two months.

They were all sitting around drinking a lager from the last batch—chilled by ice left over from that day's work—when Jenn spotted Mykol peering through the glass and shaded in silhouette by the afternoon sun. She felt a rise of fondness at the sight of his lean figure, the way he broke out in a smile when he spotted her through the glass, and even the sight of the metal piercings in his ear and nose—though *those* took some getting used to.

"Hey, join the party!" Rachel called out when Mykol pushed open the door. She glanced at Jenn, a clear indication she was making a sincere effort to be friendly.

Jenn introduced Mykol to all the workers, then to Lu and Sheryl. Someone popped open a beer and handed it to him.

"This your boyfriend?" asked LaVell, his eyes glinting with mischief over gray stubble.

"Look at you," Lu said. "You are blushing."

Eventually everyone grew tired of making Jenn feel embarrassed—for the time being at least—and sat around drinking. Jenn offered a second to Mykol, who shook his head.

"That first one was plenty strong," he said.

"Wait 'til you try the next batch," said Lu, who had overheard. "Even stronger."

Mykol gave her a woozy smile and a thumbs-up. When everyone's attention was elsewhere, Jenn turned back to him.

"What have you been doing today?" she asked.

"Aerating the soil at one of the grow houses. Well, I didn't actually aerate it myself. I supervised."

"You stood around and told people what to do?" she asked.

She had made him smile. "Yes, I stood around and told people what to do. And, to my surprise, they did what I said."

Lu was paying everyone in coins and beer. Jenn accepted hers with thanks. Lu asked Jenn if Mykol needed a job and was clearly impressed when he told her he worked with the Harvest Project. They exchanged information—Lu had been looking for a contact at the Project to talk about a grain-growing partnership.

Lu forced Mykol to accept a box of beer. She motioned to Jenn. "Take care of this one. She's special."

"I know it," Mykol agreed. Jenn felt heat in her cheeks.

"Did you bring the tablet?" she asked. He nodded, patting his bike bag. "Let's watch those other two videos tonight. But there's someplace I want to stop first. Are you OK with that?"

He moved his head back and forth, as though thinking it over. "To tell you the truth," he then said. "I'd follow you just about anywhere."

24

There was plenty of daylight left, and they took the winding street that hugged the riverside, looking out at fishermen scattered along the shore with their rods and buckets.

When he had woken that morning and found her gone, he had panicked, but then he found her note. While he had been focused on work all morning—one of the irrigation tubes was leaking water they could scarcely afford to waste, and Mykol dispatched an assistant on a foraging run to find some epoxy to plug it—part of his mind had been with Jenn until he got to the Chiang Brewery.

Mykol, Jenn, and Rachel passed the boarded-up Presbyterian church. Today it was a theater run by a group who lived there and let anyone who wanted to put on a show—there, Mykol had first been exposed to Shakespeare, a production of *Hamlet* that Don took him to when he was a teenager.

They ended up on Galilee Drive, where Jenn and Rachel slowed down—they had been chatting most of the way about their day at the brewery, and Mykol had been content to trail behind in silence. The day turned warmer, but there were fewer people than usual on the streets and in the parks. It was oddly quiet.

Rachel and Jenn had told him what happened on Billy's street. There had been a number of side conversations that week at the grow house in which he hadn't taken part, and there was a new air of apprehension and tension among the staff that he'd just chalked up to the usual stress of life. Based on what Rachel and Jenn had told him, though, maybe everyone in the city had reason to worry.

He realized he hadn't seen a single Authority vehicle on the streets all day.

Jenn and Rachel popped their bikes over the curb and up on the sidewalk, then walked them through a storefront door. He read a sign in the window: *Here Is the Home of Resistance to the Provisional Authority.*

A man and a woman inside were talking on mobiles at desks stacked high with flyers and books. Rachel and Jenn greeted a woman he recognized from the rally the other night, who looked up with recognition at him as well.

"Nice to see you," she said, shaking his hand. "Thanks for showing up at the wall. It wasn't the ideal end to things, but that's how it goes. How are your ears?"

"Just fine," he said. "It was rough the next morning, but it's better now."

"That's because you all have young ears. Unlike me. Jesus Christ, I can still hear that sound ringing in my head."

"We came by to see how things are going," Jenn said, putting down her bag, her tone respectful—Mykol could tell that she looked up to the older woman. "And to see if there's anything we can do to help."

Bettina pushed her glasses up with her index finger. "I feel stalemated. When we met last night, there were only a handful of us. It's jarring to feel a movement falling apart so quickly."

"Oh, I didn't know!" Jenn said. "I'm so sorry. I would have come…"

"Don't worry about it." Bettina said. "You're not alone. When I say a handful, I'm not exaggerating. Core members didn't make it."

Bettina glared at her colleagues talking on phones. A woman at the near desk raised her middle finger.

"I don't blame anyone for being scared," Bettina said with a sigh. "None of us have experienced anything like that before. The sound cannon was terrifying. It was also very effective."

"It shows we're winning," Jenn said. "We got a reaction. There's no way they can ignore us when there's that many of us."

"Correct," Bettina said. "And if they're rational, which, based on all available evidence, they are, then they're watching and waiting to see what we do next."

"What about the neighborhoods?" Mykol asked. "People are saying the Authority is letting crime happen. We didn't see any of their vans or officers all day."

"We've been working the phones for information," Bettina said. "It appears the Authority has taken a little holiday from protecting us."

"…don't just hide inside," the nearest worker was saying into the phone. "We have the numbers. It's the same as the movement in general. The more of us there are out on the street, the safer we will be."

"Oh, God," Rachel blurted out. She gave Jenn a look of worry. "It's true. No one is protecting us."

"We'll be fine," Jenn said. She put a hand on her shoulder. "*Really*, we will. We'll stick together. And we can't regret protesting—nothing is going to change until all of us stand together."

"I don't know," Rachel pulled back from Jenn's touch. "We talked about this. I told you how worried I was. *They* can do anything they want. We're nothing; we have no power. There are so many ways they can get back at us for standing up to them."

Jenn threw an arm around her friend's shoulders.

"You might even go back to them for all I know!" Rachel said, her voice low but harsh with fear.

Bettina watched Mykol carefully. Then she looked at Jenn. "So he knows? I don't have to keep up some fake story?"

"I know," Mykol said. "It's how we met."

Bettina looked interested. She walked up to Mykol and peered up at the corner of his cornea. She nodded with satisfaction. "I would have been extremely surprised."

"And why is that?" Mykol asked.

"Now don't get offended," Bettina said. "I meant it as a compliment. Mostly."

Jenn and Rachel sat side-by-side on the edge of one of the empty desks.

"We're not starting from scratch," Bettina said. "But it's going to be harder now. People don't like discomfort. People don't like danger. The Authority is serving us a helping of both."

"But we have to keep making sure we're heard," Jenn said.

"And we have to be prepared for what comes next," Bettina said.

Rachel was shaking her head, looking out the window. "What if I just want to live a quiet life?" she asked no one in particular. "Is there something so wrong with that?"

"Of course there isn't," Jenn said. "But this is something I need to do."

"We have to figure out how to get people back to the wall," Bettina said. "We're working on that. We're also in discussion regarding another strategic approach. Something different."

"What does that mean?" asked Jenn.

"You don't need to know," Bettina said. "At least not for the moment."

Jenn paused, then nodded. "There might also be a route that I can pursue," she said, her voice harder than Mykol had heard before.

Rachel was shaking her head, staring out the glass.

Bettina went to a retrieve a box that she placed on a table in front of them.

"Someone brought this in today. They told me it was a show of support." They all looked inside: a loaf of bread, some strips of dried jerky meat, a brick of cheese, some greens, and a fruit pie.

"Not bad," Mykol said, remembering that he skipped lunch.

"Here's the thing," Bettina said. "I like my roommates, but their friends are assholes. And they're having a party tonight. Which means I don't want to go home."

Everyone looked at each other until what she had offered settled in. Mykol raised his hand. "I guess my place is closest to here," he said.

Bettina snapped her fingers. "Perfect," she said. "You two in?"

Jenn and Rachel both nodded; only Jenn was smiling.

Bettina pointed at Mykol. "I noticed that friend of yours has a mobile. Use one of ours to call and invite him, too. Let's make it a real party. God knows we deserve one."

25

The electricity went out when they were just a few blocks away from Mykol's house. It was dusk, and the streetlights that had just begun to flicker on blacked out in a cascade, along with lights in the houses on either side. Everyone let out a groan of disappointment as they circled and stopped.

"Power's out as far as I can see," said Bettina, who was wearing a big orange backpack.

"We have plenty of candles," Mykol replied.

Mykol led the way across the Dale, through the diagonal park and its unused playground, then back along the alley. The neighborhood was eerily quiet, with only the sounds of a barking dog and a loud rattle down the block when someone threw open a window.

They left their bikes on the back porch. After he had led them inside, Mykol stuck his head out and inspected the twilight. The Provisional Authority leaving everyone to their own devices had him on edge. As he had reassured himself many times in the past, though, he and Don had the advantage of possessing next to nothing that anyone would want to steal.

"What are you doing out here?" asked Jenn from over his shoulder. He could hear Rachel and Bettina's voices from the kitchen.

"Just looking," Mykol told her.

She nodded. "Not a single sign of the Authority all the way over here."

"They've completely pulled out," Mykol said.

"No announcement, no nothing," she said.

Mykol closed the door and carefully bolted it. "It's not exactly a huge surprise," he said. "But it does suck."

Jenn reached out and affectionately rubbed his close-cropped head. He felt an electric charge.

"I like your hair. I've been wanting to do that," she said. "Let's just enjoy ourselves for a while."

Mykol jogged upstairs and found the door to his father's room closed. He knocked and told him that they had guests and food. After he got no response, he went back down the creaking stairs.

Everyone was ravenous. Mykol hadn't had this many dinner guests in his home in more than a decade. There had been a time when Mykol was in his early teens and a woman from the neighborhood brought over roasted chicken and potatoes. Mykol also remembered it as the first time he had tried wine, a sip from his dad's glass. He couldn't remember the woman's name, and she had long since vanished from the neighborhood.

He had to search through cupboards and drawers to find enough dishes and silverware—and what he found he had to dust off to make suitable. Jenn helped him while Bettina and Rachel laid the feast. Mykol searched for candles and matches as the last glow of twilight disappeared.

"For the host," Rachel said, cracking open a beer and handing it to Mykol.

It was even stronger than the brew he sampled back at Chiang's. They cut up the bread and cheese, and an air of relaxation and companionship spread through the room. There was more than enough to go around. The meat tasted salty and rich, and the bread was sour and fresh.

"This is not why I got into fighting for the people's rights," Bettina said after she took a long swig and let out a belch that earned an appreciative laugh from everyone. "But I'll take it for now."

The four of them set about hungrily demolishing their portions. Mykol watched Jenn eat with careful, mannered precision, with an innate grace that made him acutely aware of his own grab-and-chew approach. He forced himself to slow down and enjoy his meal instead of devouring it.

"To Bettina," Jenn said, raising her beer. "And to her supporters."

"May they all come bearing food," Bettina said.

Jenn got a purposeful look. "You know, I've been meaning to ask you," she said. "What did you do before…you know?"

"Before I decided to stick it to the man?" Bettina asked.

"Yeah, before that."

"I grew up in Phoenix, went to college for social work," Bettina said, a faraway tone in her voice. "I did that for a while in my twenties. Trying to fix broken situations and busted-up people. I moved here with my husband and our son because my husband was starting graduate school. I didn't want to go back to full-time work because I was getting pretty burned out, so I took a job doing investigations for the county attorney—family court stuff, writing up reports, a lot easier but not nearly as rewarding. Then…then *it* started to happen."

The table got silent. Mykol took a long drink and looked down at his half-eaten plate.

"You inspire me," Jenn said. "I was drifting when I met you. I was starting to build a life, but it took a lot of effort not to get lost in my past."

"You keep me going, too," Bettina said. "The way they tampered with your mind is proof they're not to be trusted."

Jenn stared straight ahead. "It's like I can't wake up all the way."

"Power corrupts," Bettina said. "And the Authority has concentrated power the likes of which the world has never seen. The real question is, how long are we expected to acquiesce and submit?"

"I agree." Rachel had turned red; she had put away more beer than anyone else at the table. "But how are we supposed to win?"

Bettina gave her a tight smile. "It's in the history books. The power of moral rightness."

"I *have* read history," Rachel said. "And usually a lot of blood gets spilled. Even if things get better, sometimes the people who really stuck their necks out aren't alive to see it."

Bettina was tearing a slice of bread in half. "You're right," she said. "Which is why we have to be determined, we have to be smart, and we have to be strategic."

"More vigils at the wall?" Mykol asked.

"Those don't *always* turn out like the one you went to," Bettina said ruefully. "But yes. And other actions."

A loud knock at the back door shattered the calm. In pure instinct, Mykol reached for the sharp knife they used to slice the bread and pushed back his chair. Jenn shot up as well, focused and alert.

Then Mykol remembered he had invited Benny.

"Holy shit!" his friend said, sweeping into the kitchen in his long coat. He looked different, and after a moment Mykol realized his friend had gotten cleaned up before coming over.

"It's good to see you again," Bettina said to Benny, falling into the leader role. "Sit down and join us."

"You don't have to tell me twice." Benny took Mykol's seat, grabbed the opener, and cracked a beer, then set about demolishing a plateful of food. He remembered himself after a few bites and, with a respectful glance at Rachel, slowed down his pace.

Jenn came to the back door with Mykol, and the two of them stayed on the enclosed porch while Benny regaled the others about a gig he'd had that day transporting a shady but well-off character across town and waiting outside an office building while the guy went inside.

"I like him," Jenn said, motioning toward the kitchen.

"He can be a little much sometimes. But he's my friend. He acts like some kind of gangster, but once you get to know him you realize he's loyal and generous."

Jenn nodded. "So he and Rachel have something in common."

Mykol watched through the doorway as Benny slid his chair a little closer to Rachel's. She remained preoccupied with her beer, but Benny wasn't discouraged from continuing his story.

"I want to watch those other two videos," Jenn said.

"Yeah, OK," Mykol replied. "Do we want to let these guys know what we're doing?"

"No," Jenn said firmly. "It's too personal."

"I can give you my tablet and you can go watch yourself."

"No." She looked into his eyes. "I want to share it all with you. I feel like we're in this together."

"I do too," he told her.

They went back into the kitchen. The intimacy between them made him feel excited and nervous. He opened another beer. The candles provided a murky interior twilight that suited everyone's mood.

"I drove around for a couple hours today, and lemme tell you, The Authority ain't out there," Benny was saying. "It's been what, two days? And word is *definitely* getting 'round. I bet the city police have no idea what to do."

"They're supposed to be unarmed," Bettina said. "Which normally I consider a good thing. Right now I'm not so sure."

Benny snorted. "We all know how many guns there are in this city. And that's probably not all. I'm a bit of a weapons *enthusiast*. People have stockpiled all kinds of crazy shit: automatics, sniper rifles, mortars, *flamethrowers*. And half the cops I know are nuts. If they try to take the place of the Authority—and I doubt they will—it'll be the insane against the insane."

"I wish I'd brought our gun," Rachel said, looking at Jenn.

Benny reached behind him to make sure his coat was still hanging from his chair. "I have us covered," he said.

"You carry on the street?" Rachel asked.

"Now I do." Benny took a swig of beer.

"Benjamin, you know how I feel about guns in my house," said Don's voice from the kitchen doorway.

26

Mykol was shocked. He couldn't remember the last time he'd seen his father out of his room on consecutive days.

"Guns are a necessary evil, Mister Krusos," Benny said.

"It's nice to see you, Benjamin," Don said. Like Benny, he was cleaned up: he was wearing a shirt with a collar, and he had shaved.

"You too," Benny said. "It's been too long, sir."

Mykol made introductions to Rachel and Bettina—Don and Jenn shook hands—and his father took a place at the table.

"I smelled food," Don explained, looking down, his ability to focus seeming to come and go. "My primitive tracking instincts served me well."

Mykol lit more candles. He was transfixed by the sight of his dad sitting at a table with people and interacting—clumsily, yes, but actually speaking and smiling. Don made a joke to Benny about his short hair, saying he barely recognized him.

Don was alarmed when talk turned to the Provisional Authority's absence in the streets, and he had to be informed about the protests and the fact that everyone at the table had been present at one when it was forcibly dispersed.

"I'm really out of the loop," Don said, nibbling on a piece of bread with cheese.

"Too much *Downstairs*?" asked Bettina, her tone gentle but her gaze fixed on Don's eyes.

He winced. "What makes you mention *Downstairs*?"

"I know the look." Her manner hardened; she had shifted into social-worker mode of years past.

"Fine," Don said quietly.

Bettina put her hand on Don's. "No disrespect," she said. "Thank you very much for having us in your home. It's just that I used to be in…a line of work when *Downstairs* was just getting started. It caused a lot of trouble for families. I actually learned some techniques to help wean people away."

"Thank you very much for this meal," Don replied, speaking slowly and carefully. "That will not be necessary."

Mykol tried to bring Don a beer, but his father waved him off. He felt embarrassment for his father as though a shameful secret had just been exposed. Don was tense and quiet, but he continued eating and listening.

"What I remember most about working inside the Authority is what a bubble those people live in," Bettina was saying. Her glasses flickered in the candlelight. "It's intentional. Everything is so regimented that no one has time to question. The culture is structured around conforming and staying inside the circle of power no matter what."

Bettina was scrupulously avoiding including Jenn in the conversation. This meant keeping Don and Benny outside the circle of knowledge about her past.

"I got recruited by the Authority," Don said. He looked up at Mykol. "Didn't I ever tell you about that?"

"You definitely did not," Mykol replied.

"It was a long time ago, after the president died. When things were really falling apart."

"The TV networks started going off the air, and then the internet quit working," Bettina said, her eyes wide. "It's hard to forget."

"Yeah." Don took a bite of bread. "Remember for about six months they kept saying a cure was around the corner? Then all of us gathered around radios and TVs, wondering if the internet was ever going to work again. All those useless machines."

"They were keeping the truth from us," Bettina said. "They were just trying to hold on to the old order while they could."

"Who was president after that?" Don asked Bettina. "Can you believe it? I can't even remember her name."

"Anderson, Nelson, something like that." Bettina gave a little laugh. "Isn't that funny? I can't remember who she was, either. And that was before half the survivors in Washington started saying they were president."

"And that first TV transmission from the Provisional Authority," Don remembered. *"We are a coalition of international governments, militaries, technology companies, and religious leaders."*

"They came on strong right off the bat," said Bettina.

"Well, how did *you* get recruited?" Benny asked,

"No big mystery," Don said. "They came to the house, said they were on a project making major computing power. My name came up through some of my old contacts at Dynasun, where I worked before Mykol and…the other kids were born. They asked me if I would take some tests to see if I was suitable."

"Did you take the tests?" Benny asked.

"No, I didn't. They made it very clear that once I joined I wouldn't be living the same life anymore. They were putting up walls around the university. It sounded like joining a cult."

Mykol glanced at Jenn, who was expressionless.

"They were all about neurological tests—cognition, plasticity, ability to change wave states. They knew I had a son and said he'd have to be tested if he was going to come with me."

"What if I didn't pass?" Mykol wondered aloud.

Don smiled grimly. "That's the thing, Mykol. If I didn't pass their tests, I didn't get to join. If I did, and you didn't, they said they would find a place for you in one of the better orphanages."

Rachel gasped. Jenn's face registered no reaction. Everyone else looked at him. He wondered what sort of life that might have meant for him. He might have worked alongside Jenn, never setting foot in Ellison's and probably not even remembering the house in which he had lived his entire life.

He also might have spent his childhood in an orphanage, with little to no memory of his father and family.

"Obviously, I wasn't going to take chances," his father said. "The hell with them."

Mykol was moved. He had been so important to his father that Don had sacrificed the chance to make a new life with purpose, prestige, and luxury. He preferred to stay out here, with his son.

A silence fell over the kitchen.

"Why don't you show me that problem you've been wrestling with on your tablet?" Jenn asked in a casual tone. It took Mykol a moment to realize she was talking to him.

"Yes, I could use some help with that," Mykol said. "Why don't we go upstairs? No need to ruin the party."

Rachel rolled her eyes. Mykol realized that everyone thought they were absconding to make out or something. It was tremendously embarrassing. And exciting.

He got his bike bag and fished around for the tablet. She was already heading up the stairs.

"Stay out of trouble, you two," Benny called out.

Jenn had a sly grin as they took the stairs to his room. "Maybe we should make lovemaking noises so that everyone gets their money's worth."

He tried to keep his hands from shaking as he lit a candle on his nightstand. There was only one chair, so his bed was the natural place for them to sit together. She went first; he hoped that the bed didn't smell. She sat cross-legged. A strand of hair fell and grazed her cheek.

"Here you go." He handed her the tablet.

"Were you offended by my joke just now?" she asked as she fired it up. "About having sex?"

"Not at all," he said hastily.

"I feel like I grew up in a foreign country," she said. "I think people are starting to assume that we're a couple. But in my life before, it was unusual for people to pair off that way. I mean, I've had plenty of sex—"

"Oh yeah, me too," Mykol said, a little too quickly. "For sure."

She smiled, not looking up from the tablet's screen. "I'm going to open the second video he made, based on timestamps."

Mykol shifted in bed. He worried he might do something ridiculous. He saw his room through her eyes: the shelf with all the old books, the family photos on the desk, the tattered curtains and the windows smudged with dust.

"Got it open," she said. She glanced at the door; he got up and closed it. She adjusted the volume so the sound wouldn't carry down the stairs.

The camera angle was the same as before, but Jenn's father had changed. His neat mustache was replaced by dark beard stubble. He looked weary, his eyes dull and glassy.

"I think this will help you make sense of things, Jenn."

She turned her hand over in her lap. Mykol realized it was an invitation. He took it and held it gently.

"The project has entered the implementation phase. Different leadership has taken over, and I'm no longer welcome at the table for the most sensitive discussions. I'm not even sure the goal any longer is to enrich humanity. I don't know who is in command, but it isn't any national government. It's much more powerful than that.

"Measures are being implemented without my knowledge. I've been removed from the executive committee. I've been fastidious about not voicing my objections. But my misgivings might have been apparent all along. Your mother has always told me that I'm completely incompetent at hiding my feelings."

Jenn's father rubbed his eyes and grimaced. He looked gaunt and pinched.

"There have been major anomalies with the internet. People are experiencing slowdowns or outages, but there's something else going on. It's being reported in the media, with assurances that governments and the corporations have it under control. So few people are truly aware that a small circle is seeking to augment themselves into something unprecedented. It's all being presented with the urgency of a temporary service problem."

He gave a sardonic grin that made him look like his daughter.

"The thing we've created to serve us is out of control. Appliances are malfunctioning. Anything connected to the internet is subject to seemingly random accidents—microwaves turning on for no reason, coffeemakers shutting down. GPS is unreliable. Again, just a story in the news. Nothing to be troubled about. Except for what I know: they didn't do enough tests and trials. It's all been a rush before they got found out. The haste of guilty people not wanting to be caught."

From what he had read in old newspapers and magazines, regular people generally just trusted technology, and when it didn't work, or didn't work properly, they trusted there would be someone to fix it.

"There was no need to rush the project, except for messianic arrogance, and fear of exposure. We told ourselves at first that what we were doing was noble. But human nature is predictable."

Benny roared with laughter downstairs. It sounded like a party.

"There are unintended circumstances when you play with powerful tools. I said that at a meeting at one point. Maybe that's why I'm no longer part of the inner circle.

"You know that saying, such-and-such broke the internet? That might be happening already. If you unravel the web with the tool we built to make unprecedented connections between neurology, quantum computing, and computational AI, there are no guarantees that you can put it back together the way it was. And there's something else. The tool was supposed to break through the limitations of our species, but I despair that will ever happen—it may have all been for nothing."

Jenn's father paused, glancing back at his office door furtively.

"I overheard by accident. It was about the random number generator in Chicago. It's a computer at Northwestern that constantly generates a string of random numerals, all day every day, at very high speed. It monitors that string of numbers to look for the emergence of patterns, however minor. There's a theory that large-scale mass events might send waves through the collective consciousness that ripple backwards in time. Over the last ten years or so, the generator has detected patterns two times. The first was twelve hours before the great tsunami in Borneo.

"The second was one day before the bombings in Seoul last year."

Jenn's father got a distant look in his eyes, like he was weighing what he was saying against a yardstick of sanity.

"And now it's kicking out patterns in a way it never has before. They don't want to go public, because people might panic and turn those patterns into a self-fulfilling prophesy. It's possible we're experiencing the largest species-wide event of our lifetimes and we don't even know it. It might not involve creating superhumans."

Jenn stared at the screen. She squeezed his hand tight.

"I still hope we'll watch this together one day and laugh at what a paranoid fool your father used to be. In any case, I'm taking measures. I have enough back-door access to the project to apply some pressure, to slow it down. It might cost me my life. If that happens, I want you to remember me. My baby daughter."

The video ended.

Jenn started to open the third and final one. Mykol weighed the ramifications of what her father had said.

"Got it open," she told him. "It's really short."

It started.

"Jenn, I hope you see this someday."

Her father seemed to be in the driver's seat of a car. The angle of the camera was looking up at him; the sun shone brightly through the windows, creating flares and distortions.

He looked terrible. His eyes were bright red, and mucous flowed shiny down his face. He glanced over his shoulder to the back seat.

"Are you awake, darling? Please try to stay awake."

The car moved, then stopped. There was a lot of noise—car horns and distorted voices from loudspeakers. He seemed to be in a line somewhere.

"You're with my sister right now. I pray you don't get sick. Your mother and I are going to the hospital. It seems to be…very busy."

"Oh no," Jenn said quietly. Mykol took her hand closer.

"Things are moving so quickly. I'm certain my team realizes how severe the situation is. Emergency systems all over are falling apart because of the internet outages. I'm certain the project was a failure.

And it's happening at the worst possible time, because this outbreak is getting worse by the hour.

"It's like all the technology has been lobotomized. Nothing is working properly. Except this virus. It's doing exactly what nature designed it to do, and it's brutally effective."

His breath came in wheezes. He was clearly on the verge of panic.

"I've done what I could."

Her father paused.

"If you watch this someday, remember: there are always unintended consequences."

A rising background tide of panicked voices and car horns. It was impossible to tell what people were shouting.

"Sweetheart?"

He let his head rest on the steering wheel for a long time.

"I love you, Jenn. Remember me."

The video switched off, and Jenn's face collapsed. She made no sound, but her body heaved and convulsed. Mykol wrapped her in his arms and held her, tears streaking down his cheeks.

They stayed like that for a very long time. He watched the candle burning down on the nightstand until the surge that had engulfed her seemed to be spent.

He heard a crash outside. He thought that the lights had come back on, but they hadn't—the illumination was from the street. He heard Benny's voice downstairs, cursing loudly.

From the window, Mykol saw Benny's car parked on the street below. It took several moments to process what was happening. The windshield was shattered, and the front seat was burning with vivid tongues of flame.

Mykol could hear the front door opening downstairs, and he watched Benny run into the night, waving his gun, yelling, jumping up and down in frustration as the flames engulfed his car.

Jenn joined him at the window. They put their arms around each other as the burning lit up the neighborhood and reached up into the night sky.

27

The mood in the streets felt charged with danger as Jenn and Rachel bicycled home. Mykol invited them to stay, but Rachel wanted to go home. Jenn was in such a surreal state of mind that she felt she was operating on autopilot. Benny had been inconsolable about his car, and the goodwill of the party withered in the flames.

A fair number of people were out on their porches, some drinking and talking loudly. There was smoke on the horizon from another fire, and now gunshots echoed in the near distance. The absence of the Provisional Authority's emergency sirens became more and more telling as they rode through side streets, avoiding the main thoroughfares, not switching on their lamps.

Jenn and Rachel slept huddled together that night. Sounds of shouting and sporadic gunfire woke them more than once as moonlight traced a path through their bedroom.

When she awoke before dawn, Jenn's thoughts turned to her old friend Halle. Jenn remembered what day it would be when the sun came up in the morning.

Jenn had known Halle for as long as she could remember. They spent countless hours together, even if Jenn now couldn't remember the specifics of how they spent that time. She recalled broken mirror shards of training: Halle had instructed her in an evolving, years-long meditation practice, with techniques and targets that now eluded her, but which focused the mind and body as a connected whole.

They had always been very good friends, sharing intimacy and laughter and delicious meals that were especially good after those long hours spent…

Doing *what*?

Jenn laid on her back, listening to the gentle rhythm of Rachel's breathing, thinking if she could just relax and focus she would be able to remember more.

Halle had been her superior. They lived in separate buildings. Jenn's was occupied by more junior officers while Halle's had larger suites with creature comforts such as kitchens and a bathtub, where Jenn had soaked more than once.

Halle was like Jenn, brought in from an orphanage. She had started years before in what was known as the "outward facing" arm of the Provisional Authority—dealing with the civilian population, regulating and policing. After that, she was transferred to the "inward facing" aspect of their work, which is when she supervised much of Jenn's training, with the goal of…

Her memories were like a handful of water, shimmering and transparently clear until they slipped from her grasp.

She waited for the signs of dawn, listening to a truck roaring through the streets and gradually receding. She thought of her life as a puzzle. She couldn't describe exactly who she was, or trace a line from her past to the present; there was a missing space and a void where there had been substance.

One thing was refreshingly clear. Her feelings for Mykol were strong and true, free from the haze that shrouded nearly everything else. But when she was around him, she felt as if she were hiding a deep, disfiguring flaw. He knew who *he* was; his life was a story that he inhabited with all its pain and joys. She was defined by what she was missing. Who could love someone like that?

A slight surge of lightning tinged the western sky as she carefully got out of bed, not wanting to disturb Rachel. As she got up, a memory of Halle flashed in her mind. Her pulse quickened. She thought she might have found the key.

The riverside market was open and crowded. It was one of the mainstays of life in the city, no matter the weather or time of year. Today Provisional Authority guards and their vans were conspicuously absent, their barricades unmanned, but it had the feel of an ordinary morning.

Running the length of an entire city block, the market coalesced in the shadow of tall apartment blocks, old luxury buildings that were mostly vacant. One building had burned and collapsed into abstract twists of steel and cement. A cul-de-sac in front was home to a rusted limousine and wildflowers rising through the busted concrete as tall as a grown man.

The market had started as a venue for foragers, entrepreneurs, and grave robbers who picked through the carcass of the past and returned with clothing, books, kitchen items, precious things. This morning it was full of fresh smells and easygoing barter.

Jenn sat at the top of a staircase that afforded an eagle's eye view. The market was now home to handmade textiles and crafts, spicy food cooked over propane grills, and produce from the countryside and urban gardens (Mykol's group had a prominent stall with crates of potatoes and colorful root vegetables). Lu Chiang had gotten her start selling home-brewed beer here.

A couple of dogs were barking, mingling with sounds of laughter and children. Jenn's eyes wandered over the crowd: the families, the monks and priests, the urban primitives, the mundane folk. It felt like an idyll, everyone coexisting, some even building something that might be sustainable. Yet it felt so fragile, so poignantly *human*: fleeting and vulnerable.

A band played, three men and a woman, two guitars, a violin, and a drum. They played a gently swaying instrumental that echoed in the canyon of the decrepit buildings.

Every Friday morning, Halle left the Provisional Authority and came here—Jenn used to come with her from the main compound. Halle was one of the few people in Jenn's orbit who had any kind of routine outside the walls.

She could remember how the market seemed to her back then: a mess of unhygienic things and people she would prefer to avoid. Halle loved it here, though, one time buying a meat kebab on a stick and laughing at Jenn's revulsion when she refused to take a bite.

It had been almost a year since Jenn last saw Halle. Her friend's schedule might have changed; her routines might be different. But it was worth finding out.

The rich smell of food—a curry, she guessed—wafted up to where Jenn sat in silence. She saw a vendor pulling a cart with a bicycle; he disembarked and yelled "Ice cream!" and a crowd gathered around him.

Small children were playing a game with a ball and a net. A woman with long red hair cascading down her bare shoulders arrived on horseback, stopping at a farm vendor who sold her hay. Teenagers were sharing a vape burner, and an old man who had stacks of blue jeans laid out on a blanket was doing good business.

Jenn moved into the shade. She tried not to rub her eye.

She sometimes wondered if her memory had been erased for her own good. Maybe she had done terrible things, so deeply wrong that she wouldn't be able to live with herself. Perhaps they had *made* her commit acts that would haunt her if she could access them.

Last night, in a moment of unguarded sincerity that embarrassed her in retrospect, she had whispered to Mykol that she was going crazy.

She sat with her knees drawn up to her chin, her back aching. A preacher set up a microphone hooked to a generator and began a sermon about repentance and redemption.

She would be more than happy to repent. If that's what it took.

28

Halle wasn't wearing a uniform, but her black hair caught Jenn's eye, along with her rangy, athletic stride.

Jenn was unable to move. She hadn't anticipated feeling this way—diminished, ashamed of herself. Her nails were cracked, her palms callused, and she hadn't bathed in days. She knew how she looked—like a dirty, ignorant plebe.

Halle exchanged coins for a carving that she tucked into her shoulder bag, smiling and joking with the vendor, then moved on. Jenn watched, transfixed by the ease with which her old friend and superior blended in. No one would be able to tell she was Authority unless they looked into her right eye—hence the sunglasses.

Jenn finally got up when she saw her friend walking to the far end of the market, looking like she was leaving. Jenn took the stairs two at a time, keeping Halle in her field of vision.

A small dog snapped at her as Jenn swerved into the market and broke into a jog. Halle was heading in the direction of the ballpark, where dilapidated condos had evolved into a popular spot for post-spiritualists and other churches and sects. It surprised Jenn to see Halle going in this direction.

Once they were out of the market bustle, Halle was easy to follow, walking briskly but not so fast that Jenn couldn't catch up. They passed a pop-up African restaurant, then a smashed-in store with droning drug music coming from inside.

When Halle turned the corner, Jenn stayed a distance behind. If Jenn didn't know, she would have taken her for a well-off civilian, maybe a dealer in luxury liquors and spices.

Halle opened up an unmarked door. In the window beside it was a hand-painted sign with an Egyptian scarab and "People of Intef" written in stylized lettering.

About fifty folded chairs were lined in rows inside facing the back wall. Jenn spotted Halle sitting down and holding a sheet of paper. Jenn took one from a smiling man in clean, blue robes standing just inside the entrance. She sat in the back row.

A chant started. Jenn squinted at the paper, trying to follow along as the group found an insistent rhythm.

The good prince is happy.
Death is a kind fate.
Generations pass, and they rise.
The gods rest in their tombs.
The blessed nobles are in their tombs.
Yet those who built the tombs,
What has become of them?
I sing the words of Imhotep and Hordejef
The walls crumble, the places are gone
As if they had never been!

It was very moving. The crowd was a mix of ages, gathered in a Spartan room adorned with painted hieroglyphics. Two people were in ceremonial robes; everyone else was dressed in regular clothes. The paper identified the hymn as "The Harper's Song," deriving from Egypt's Middle Kingdom.

It was thousands of years old. Its message was that all things pass, and the present moment should be seized and embraced. It was a transmission from eternity.

When it was finished, Jenn waited by the door for Halle to notice her. Halle didn't look at her when she came close and said, "Come with me. Now."

They walked to a side street. Halle moved fast.

"Can we slow down?" Jenn struggled to keep up. "Please. Can we talk?"

Halle kept up her pace. Her gaze was fixed straight ahead, her expression stony as she led the way to the shadow of burned-out buildings. Soot-stained brick towered above, and the cloudy sky showed through collapsed roofs.

Halle stopped and stared at Jenn for what felt like a very long time. Finally, she folded her arms. "I knew you were following me. You're not very subtle."

"Why didn't you stop?"

"I wasn't completely sure it was you." She looked over Jenn with an appraising eye, and Jenn felt extremely self-conscious.

"Come on," Jenn said nervously. "Say something nice, Halle."

Halle paused. "Oh, for... Come here," she said.

Halle reached up and touched Jenn's cheek. She looked into Jenn's eye, at the scar there, then pulled away. Then she opened her arms and took Jenn into a stiff embrace. Halle's clothes felt soft and expensive.

"I didn't think I'd ever see you again," she said to Jenn.

"I waited all day. I was hoping you'd come."

"And how are you doing?" she asked.

"OK. Fine." Jenn laughed nervously. "I have a house and a roommate. I have two jobs. There's a guy I like. It's almost like regular life."

"Except there's nothing regular about you."

A siren wailed somewhere; not Provisional Authority, but the high pitch of the city cops.

"You're not in uniform," Jenn said.

Halle's mouth formed an impassive line. "We're *discouraged* from going out right now. Since the demonstration."

"I was there," she told Halle.

This definitely surprised her. "You were?" Her expression flashed something like pity. "Sugar, what were you doing in that crazy mob?"

It felt good to hear her old nickname; it summoned memories of long days and a few words of praise and affection at the end.

"There was nothing crazy about it," Jenn said. "It was a peaceful assembly because people want to have a voice."

"And a share of power?" Halle asked. Her smile turned sardonic.

"Is that so hard to imagine?" Jenn asked.

"How would you have answered that question a year ago?" Halle asked.

That was fair. She saw her past self in Halle: the haughtiness, the unshakable sense of superiority, the conviction that people on the other side of the walls were a herd to be controlled. These had been tenets of a faith she didn't question.

"What's up with going to church?" Jenn asked her.

Halle took off her sunglasses and they made eye contact. It was a relief. She could feel the connection they shared wasn't entirely lost.

"Maybe I'm just a tourist," Halle said with a sly smile.

"You're never just a tourist," Jenn told her.

"Belief systems can be useful tools. The Intef community and the Osirians are fascinating to me. They're unearthing ancient wisdom that foretold the present day. I enjoy being around it."

This was the Halle she remembered—irreverent but deeply committed to every aspect of her work. *Belief systems can be useful tools.* That sparked a glimmer of memory. There was an idea there: belief can be converted for protection, as a source of energy.

"Since you're standing here, I want to hear it directly from you," Halle said, her smile gone. "What happened?"

Jenn burned with emotion.

"I...I don't really know," she said.

"I heard you broke down in the hall," Halle said.

Jenn only had vague memories. She had just completed a task and had been in her room. Something happened and then she woke up in the medical unit.

"It's a blank," Jenn said. "Along with a lot of other things."

Her friend gave her a wary look. "Explain," she said.

So Jenn did: the inability to remember what she had worked on and what she had been taught—save for shards and tattered fragments. Halle listened closely, seeming to cautiously process Jenn's every word.

"I didn't realize the exit treatment was so extensive," she finally admitted. "But I suppose it would be. You were involved in a pretty... delicate project. It's not the kind of thing you would be allowed to talk about out here."

"What did...what did the other officers say when they realized I wasn't around anymore?"

Halle frowned. "I don't think it ever came up. You know how it is."

Despair enveloped her. She remembered enough about her old life to know it was a culture that despised weakness. If she were flushed out, it would be talked about in the context of failure and relegated to the category of a cautionary tale.

Halle let silence fill the space between them, and Jenn got the sense that her old friend was trying to figure a way out of this encounter.

"I remembered you this morning," Jenn said. "I remembered your routine. I came to you because...I want to ask if you can help me."

Halle looked as though she had smelled something unpleasant. "What do you need? Money? You know I can't help you with that."

"What I need is my mind back. If I ever meant anything to you, please help me."

"How do you think I can help you?" Halle asked.

"You were my teacher. You helped strengthen my mind. You've got to know a way for me to get my memories back. I won't tell anyone. I'll keep secrets for the rest of my life. But I need to know who I *am*, and what I've *done*."

Halle gave her a searching, unemotional look. "Poor Sugar," she said.

She remembered watching movies with Halle in the common area in the dormitory, the way they'd smuggle packets of cookies from the dining hall and stay up later than they were allowed. She remembered laughing.

Halle tapped the tracker on her wrist. "I have to get going," she said. "You know how it is."

"Please," Jenn said.

Halle slapped her thigh. "How can you come to me like this?" she snapped. "High command is on alert over the demonstrations. I imagine they're doing facial recognition on the crowds. They might know you were out there."

"What was I doing wrong?" Jenn asked.

Halle shook her head. "You know how it is," she said. "The Authority *decides* what's right and wrong."

"Will you help me?"

"You also know opinions about team members who flush out," Halle added with clinical precision. "And fraternizing with them. You can remember *that*, can't you?"

"Please help me." Jenn touched the back of her head. "I still have the plug-in," she said. "They can't remove that without killing you."

"I'm very sorry about what happened to you," Halle said. "I mean it. I always cared for you, Jenn. But tampering with the conditions of your removal would be grounds for my *own* removal. I have to look out for myself."

"But there's a way?" Jenn asked, suddenly excited. "You sound like you know a way."

Halle just looked at her. "You always were the most tenacious one," she said.

29

Flashes of memory danced to life in Jenn's mind, as if Halle's presence was transmitting them. She remembered a swirl of color when the plug-in was activated, the surge of charged cognition.

She remembered feeling nothing. Being herself, yet something else.

"It's good to see you," Halle said. "But it's over now—"

"Don't go," Jenn said.

"I can't help you," Halle said, with exasperated finality.

"There were other things I knew," Jenn said, not completely sure what she was saying.

Halle stopped. "What does that mean?"

"I remember your rivalry with Brown," Jenn said. "I was in his unit. I'll bet I know things you can use against him."

She was bargaining desperately, but from Halle's reaction she knew she had just given herself a chance. Halle and Brown had both been angling for promotion to captaincy for the last couple of years. There was only one slot open, and both wanted it more than anything else.

"I worked under him," Jenn said. "If I can get my memories back, I'll bet I can help you undermine him. We can work together, just like we used to."

"The mission is of paramount importance, personal considerations are secondary," Halle recited. "Or have you forgotten that, too?"

"I'm not a whole person right now," Jenn said. "That's the most important thing to me. If I can jack in and get my memory back, then I'll go away and never bother anyone."

"Are you going to keep protesting?" Halle asked.

"That's a separate matter," Jenn told her.

Halle sighed. "I do not need this," she said. "Next thing I know, I'm going to be living out here with you."

"Or spending the next ten years answering to Brown," Jenn said.

That got her. Halle shook her head, looking down the alley. "I don't even know it's definitely possible."

"If you can try, that's all I ask," Jenn said. She put her hand on her friend's forearm. "Please. I don't know how long I can keep going with so much of me missing."

"I always thought the memory blocks were a bad idea," Halle said. "And doing them on someone at your level is cruel."

"You did?" Jenn asked. "We never discussed it."

"I'd advocate for allowing flushers to keep their memories and just deal with the ramifications," Halle said. "Either that or eliminate them altogether."

Jenn stared, blinking at her former teacher.

"This is not a sentimental business we're in," Halle said slowly. "And it never will be."

Jenn was able to extract a single, tenuous promise: that Halle would return to the market the same time the next week. They would meet and they would talk again.

It wasn't much, but it was far more than she had started the day with.

She made her way to the rooftop garden where Mykol was working. She spotted his slim frame; he was dropping samples of soil into a compartmentalized tray and mixing them with chemicals from an eye-dropper. He beamed when he saw her.

There were a half-dozen workers on their hands and knees picking insects from the plants. It must have taken a lot of effort to haul all the soil up here, but it was safe and sheltered, and they were able to run power cables for grow lights. The view of the city made it look like a bygone era.

Mykol handed off his tray to one of the workers, telling him what mixture of chemical fertilization he recommended. The worker listened respectfully and went off to do as he was told.

"You're an attractive boss," Jenn told him when they were alone. There was a slight breeze, a cool clearness in the air.

"*That* is the most effective work-choice validation that I have heard in my entire life," he said, smiling.

"I did something today," she told him.

They went to the edge, where no one could hear them. She told him what had happened by the market.

"It might work," Jenn told him. "It has to be possible."

Mykol thought for a while. "I know this is going to sound petty and selfish, but I have to ask you."

"What do you mean by that?" she asked, wary.

"If you get back your memories of what you were before, will you still like me?"

She kissed his lips. "I liked you even then."

"Me too," he told her.

"Can I come home with you tonight?" she asked him.

"Yes, please," he replied.

30

The next weeks were the best of Mykol's life. The weather turned warmer, and wetter, and the senior committee decided to ratchet up production on the uncovered outdoor grow plots, which meant all-hands effort that consumed much of his days in satisfying labor, physical and mental work that left him pleasingly exhausted in a way Ellison's never had. He slept wonderfully, dreaming long, ornate scenarios that he'd puzzle over in the morning, his head on his pillow while he watched the sunlight brighten gradually.

He and Jenn had spent several nights together. It was exquisite, if sometimes fraught for him with his burning need to please her—never in his life had he been with someone he so deeply wanted to satisfy in every way possible.

At least twice more, Jenn had met with Halle. She was always preoccupied afterwards. Mykol knew some of what they were talking about, but Jenn was less forthcoming about the details after each meeting.

She wanted her memories back. He thought he loved her, and he wanted what she wanted. But he also felt gnawing anxiety.

If she was hiding things, or protecting him, he was also not being entirely forthcoming. News of the Sustenance Project's robust harvest had gotten all the way to Provisional Authority leadership, and the two organizations were in talks about a mutually beneficial relationship.

It was like a ragged pirate ship negotiating with an imperial battleship.

He wasn't entirely sure why he hadn't told her. It wasn't that he didn't trust her, but he feared the intensity of her need to get back inside those walls and be restored. Sometimes he would run his hands through her beautiful hair and feel the harsh hard plug in her skull.

"Mykol?" said his colleague, Gabby. "Did you hear the question?"

"I'm sorry," Mykol said. "What did you say?"

The man across the table from Mykol and Gabby stared at him. "I was asking how far you've come along with fruit-tree projections. I tried some of your apples, and they're acceptable. We could probably get some higher-quality seed stock that might yield better product, though."

They were sitting at a small table in a coffee bar downtown. Muted music played on the sound system, punctuated by chords on an acoustic guitar.

On the walls were paintings and etchings for sale from local artists. One in particular attracted his eye, a canvas in oils of a woman standing alone in a windswept field, her hair blowing around her face. The woman looked lonely yet resolute. Though he had never bought a work of art in his life, he planned to ask its price after he was through with this meeting. He thought it would make a gift for Jenn.

Willem was about five years older than Mykol, with the distinctive glint of a retinal implant and the ramrod posture that marked him as someone from behind the gates. He wore a black, long-sleeved knit and matching jeans. During the last week of negotiation, Mykol had learned from Willem that the Provisional Authority was still active outside its compound, and that its people were avoiding wearing uniforms.

The protests had yet to resume, much to Mykol's relief. He managed to avoid addressing the question of whether he would join Jenn and Bettina if they decided to go back. While light Authority patrols had resumed—enough to take the edge off the feeling of lawlessness in the city—it wasn't enough to thaw the feeling that this added protection might only be a temporary compromise. Even so, Bettina seemed to have lost touch with her relentless drive. What had once been single-minded opposition had dimmed. Mykol was beginning to think it was better to take advantage of opportunities for partnership, rather than taking up the fight that Bettina had begun. Mykol even thought that maybe the Authority reaching out to the Project could have been another olive branch to the plebes. This kind of cooperation hadn't happened in years, with the Authority buying its food supplies from farms outside the city.

"We'd be very eager to try any fruit-tree seeds you have," Mykol said. "Any way we can grow better food is going to benefit everyone."

"Good." Willem typed into his tablet. "I'd also like to nail down some of the payment and delivery issues that we raised the last time we talked, if that's amenable to both of you."

"Oh, definitely," said Gabby.

Gabby had come to the meeting with the added authenticity of conspicuous dirt under her fingernails. She was about the same age as Willem, and Mykol sensed she felt a bond with the Authority officer. It annoyed him, the way she was so eager to please, telling them how great their suggestions were, how welcome their ideas. Sometimes it felt less like a series of ongoing negotiations than some kind of fan club, with Gabby transparently cozying up.

Mykol knew he shouldn't be so hard on her.

Gabby didn't talk about it much, but she had made a harrowing journey up from the flooded and hurricane battered Florida coastline when she was in her early twenties. She craved safety and stability. She was a tireless worker and had a talent for the logistics that made their organization run—plus, she was personally popular with nearly all of the workers.

The meeting droned on and he was having a hard time focusing on the conversation.

The woman in the painting was standing in a farm field that had been recently tilled, and she was holding a handful of rough wildflowers as she gazed someplace over the viewer's left shoulder. She didn't look much like Jenn, but she made him think of her anyway.

One of Willem's major agenda items was that the Sustenance Project enter into a long-term arrangement with the Provisional Authority. The Project would agree to invest a proportion of their payments into increased growing capacity and administrative infrastructure. He had to admit that it made sense. If he was able to put aside his general distaste for the Authority, it was exciting—the Project would be able to greatly expand over the next year and make even greater inroads into community giveaways.

"We're going to do a lot of good," Gabby was saying. Mykol didn't disagree, but a feeling of defiance kept him sitting back from the table. The dark tea they'd ordered filled the air with a peaty smell.

"There's something else on the agenda we haven't brought up until now," Willem said. He looked down at his tablet. He had a habit of wiping his hands continually with an antiseptic cloth that he kept tucked into a zippered pocket, pulling it out every couple of minutes.

"What's that?" Mykol asked.

For the first time during their meeting, Willem smiled. "Public relations."

31

They were more or less alone in the coffee bar. Aside from the urban primitive behind the counter, there was only an elderly woman in the corner staring out the window and a guy with headphones sketching on a pad.

"Public relations," Gabby said. "I've heard of that."

"It's an old-fashioned term." William clearly enjoyed the way Gabby treated him like a semi-celebrity. "I did a bit of historic research. It affords a great deal of insight into pre-Grip society."

Gabby looked enthralled. Mykol knew he needed to temper his judgment.

"There used to be people whose entire job was to…to *manage* the opinion of the public," said Willem.

"You mean through the media?" asked Mykol.

"That's the best example," Willem said. "When you go back and read documents from that time, you find a real split of opinions about the field. Some thought crafting mass opinion was the only way to achieve worthy goals. Others thought it was manipulation, lying, getting people to believe things that they wouldn't otherwise, or convincing people they needed things they didn't."

"What's your opinion?" asked Gabby.

"The truth is more complicated than any simple or one-sided opinion," Willem said. Mykol reflected on how much his new colleague from the Provisional Authority enjoyed the sound of his own voice. "There were excesses. I think we're better off without mass consumer culture, no matter how tragically we arrived at this point. I think the more enlightened practitioners of public relations thought of it as *persuasion*, using positive ideas to bring people along to the right positions."

Mykol watched Willem carefully. He really believed what he was saying. Mykol had lost count of the number of times Jenn had described the utter bubble on the inside.

"You're talking about *education*," Gabby replied.

"I think that's fair to say," Willem replied with a lugubrious expression.

"So how does this apply to what we're doing?" Mykol asked.

Gabby shot him a look, the way she did from time to time when Mykol was being insufficiently deferential or enthusiastic.

It was probably time for him to grow up a bit.

Willem nodded as though he appreciated Mykol getting to the point. "This...*partnership* of ours is unique. Strictly speaking, we don't really need to be doing business with you."

Mykol appreciated this honesty and leaned forward and tried to make himself seem more engaged.

"We see material benefits down the road, don't get me wrong," Willem asked. "Your work is impressive. If we end up enjoying a greater variety of better tasting food at our dining tables back home, well, let me be the first to say, I am *all for it*."

He gave a little laugh, as though this was the height of candor and self-deprecation. Gabby laughed with him. Mykol made a sincere effort to do the same.

"We like better tasting food out here as well," Mykol said, not in an entirely unfriendly way.

"Of course you do." Willem paused, wanting to be seen giving a great deal of thought to what he said next. "But, again, this is unique. We wish for our image to be...*softened*."

This was about the protests. Dispersing the crowd and withdrawing from the city had been harsh and imperious; there was probably a faction within the Provisional Authority pressing for a gentler way of engaging the populace.

There had been talk on pirate radio recently about protests in other cities. Maybe resistance was boiling up around what used to be the United States—as well as in other countries—it made sense that people were getting fed up at the same time.

"You want people to know about our partnership, so they'll like you better," Mykol said.

Willem gave him a thin smile. "That's a little...basic," he said, then shrugged. "But sure. If that's the way you want to put it. We'd like people to know we're engaging outside our walls, and that we care about ordinary people."

"I think that's *wonderful*," Gabby said.

"What do you say, Mykol?" asked Willem. "Does this sound like something the Project can support?"

"Yes, of course," Mykol replied. "We have our own internal governing committee, and we'd have to get agreement. But we can put out the word. What do you have in mind?"

"We have printing resources," Willem said. "We'd like you to hand out fliers, general stuff about how we're working together. A little way down the road, we're looking at focusing getting out the word on radio."

Mykol was stunned. Other than stern pronouncements and a flow of classical symphonies, the Authority's radio channel didn't usually offer much engagement with regular people.

"This is quite a change," Mykol said.

Willem nodded. "That's the idea," he said. "Just so you know, I'm very much in favor of it. For a long time there's been so little true back-and-forth from one side of the wall to the other. Many of us are very much aware of the need for increased...*communication*, if not integration."

Mykol had been warming to Willem, but now he was back in a more comfortable and familiar place.

"Not everyone out here is in favor of communication. Or integration, either," Mykol said.

"You're just speaking for yourself," Gabby said.

"I'm saying there are a lot of different opinions in the city," Mykol said.

"What's *your* opinion?" asked Willem.

"I like communication," Mykol told him. "I'm in favor of barriers broken down."

"Perhaps you were at the protests?" Willem asked.

Mykol couldn't tell if he was being probed for an answer; it was possible they'd scanned the crowd and identified him. In any case, there was no reason to lie.

"I went to one," Mykol said. "The most recent one. So far."

Willem unleashed a complicated smile. "I can tell you there's no uniformity of opinion *inside* the Authority either, at least when it comes to how that matter was handled." He was speaking carefully. "Like you, I don't speak for everyone. But there might be creative solutions for how we…*organize* things moving forward."

Mykol knew that if Willem was a fair representative, dealing with the Provisional Authority was going to be complicated. He remembered how intimidated and daunted he had been by Jenn when they met.

"Now," Willem said. "I brought something for the two of you."

He reached into his leather bag and brought out two small boxes, handing one to each of them. Mykol opened his and saw that it contained a brand-new mobile.

"This is a direct line to me as your Authority representative," he said. "It's been outfitted with text capacity between the three of us. It also has GPS, if you're familiar with how to use that."

Gabby and Mykol switched on their devices. Mykol flashed back to when Jenn was in the Authority—he had seen her with one of these.

Willem watched their reactions, seeming satisfied. "I know these are difficult to get out here. Relevant numbers are in the box, and mine has been pre-programmed. Mostly I prefer to text."

"I have to ask," Mykol said. "Will communications through this device be monitored?"

Willem gave a delicate expression, as though it was in bad taste to talk about unpleasant things that were undeniably true.

"I've also been wanting to ask something," Gabby said. She was blinking as though waiting for permission to speak.

"Yes?" Willem asked.

"Is there any way we can come *inside*?" she said, like a child asking for a present her parents probably couldn't provide.

Willem laughed nervously. "You mean inside the compound?" he said. "I'm not...I don't...I mean, heavens. *Why*?"

"*I've* always wished I could see what's inside," Mykol said, speaking before good sense could get him to stop.

Willem held up his hands. "There are a lot of things I don't decide," he said. "Tell you what. I'll look into it."

"We could come with the next major delivery," Mykol said.

"I said I'll look into it," Willem repeated.

"Cool." Mykol held up the mobile. "You know how to reach us."

32

The next day misted rain, the sky low like a muddy canopy, dark wisps of clouds performing ominous sidewinder dances while low, guttural thunder mumbled through the morning hours.

On days like this, the weather kept people away from the market. Makeshift canopies and pergolas sheltered some shops, but much of the cooking was done in the open air. There were people gathered around a stall where a farmer had brought a butchered pig to town, but overall, it was much quieter than usual.

Jenn had been waiting under the entryway of an apartment building for more than an hour when she spotted Halle wearing her rain slicker that extended all the way down to black sneakers. She waited while Halle made a couple of purchases. This had become their routine, just in case Halle had been followed or recognized by other officers.

Jenn wrung out her scarf and wrapped it around her head, starting to move, when she saw Halle was finished at the market.

They met in the alcove behind a four-story building that had once been a wing of a luxurious hotel. The glassed hallway that connected the building to the rest of the complex had long been smashed in, and scruffy weeds grew in the tatters of what had once been a thick, patterned carpet.

"Here," Halle said, opening up a foil package containing meat and roasted vegetables. She doled out a portion for Jenn, and Jenn thanked her as she took a bite.

"Not much of a selection today," Halle said, devouring a piece of meat after watching it steam in the chilly air.

"Not a lot of people out," Jenn said. "Thank you for coming."

Halle looked down at her mobile and switched it off. "I think they're almost always listening on this," she said.

Jenn took a bite of roasted onion, choosing not to think about it.

Halle had turned out to be motivated in investigating whether plugging Jenn's memory back in was possible. They had gotten lucky. A squad member called Wollers, a guy about Halle's age and as high-ranking as Jenn had been, had washed out the week before. At his request, he'd gotten a Provisional Authority transport to another town—not before his memory had been aggressively wiped.

Halle feigned concern over Wollers's well-being and the overall process. She'd spoken with the technician overseeing the information removal. Halle framed her interest in terms of being worried about neurological crossover between wiped memories and future training engrams—essentially, old memories contaminating the progress and psychological foundation of future squad members.

"Everything we take out gets stored," the technician told Halle. "It's never erased completely but it's quarantined in a special sector of the database, so to answer your question, there's no practical way any of these memories could be implanted by accident into someone else."

What they didn't know was how to access these stored memories and how to make sure she reclaimed her own and not someone else's. She was certain the jack in the back of her head was functional—she could feel it pulse when she was close to anything electromagnetic—and there were plenty of pods in the psych tech ward. But they weren't completely sure how to get her plugged in correctly.

"Anything new?" Jenn asked. It had been two weeks since Halle told her about Wollers. Halle hadn't showed up the week before, and

Jenn had spent the entire day waiting (and missing out on a day's bottling pay at Chiang's).

"I think so, yes." Halle finished up the meat, wadded up the foil, and tossed it into the street.

They moved closer to the wall, away from the rain that started to lash sideways as the wind picked up.

Jenn waited patiently. This had become routine. Halle shared information slowly and sparingly, seeming to weigh every word. Jenn didn't mind; it probably meant her old teacher wasn't informing on her.

"So here's the thing," Halle said. "I think I figured out how to do it."

"You did?" Jenn asked. "So you found out how to get into the—"

"I had just finished alpha-wave stim with a squad member," Halle interrupted. It was a process she had applied to Jenn many times. "It was a twenty-minute cycle, so I had some time to explore without having to account for my time in the system."

Information access and usage in Provisional Authority systems was heavily regulated and monitored. But such a thing was possible. Someone with instructor access in the training terminals could move around pretty freely.

Jenn didn't know how she knew this.

The question was whether deleted memories were stored in the areas where Halle was allowed access.

Halle was watching Jenn, following her thought process. "The answer is yes. I found data clusters where I'm almost certain removed memories are stored. I found fresh tags lined up with Wollers leaving a couple of days ago."

"Do you know where he ended up going?" Jenn asked.

Halle waved dismissively. "Don't care. Anyway, I wasn't interested in drawing notice to myself by going deeper. But I'm pretty sure I can find your memory patterns if I have a few free minutes. From there, I think it would be straightforward to copy them back to you."

"Copy?" Jenn asked. "But I want a total transfer…."

"Copy," Halle repeated. "They have to stay in the system. Look, I know you feel your memories are precious things that belong only to you. I understand, but it's simply not the case."

Jenn felt her cheeks burn. If there was one thing the Authority valued above total secrecy, it was the preservation of information. Deletion of files came with strict and monitored protocols. Copying was far less noticeable.

If she really wanted her mind back, she would have to leave a copy of it behind.

"You know how much memory capacity we have in the system," Halle said. "If you really think about it, they probably have copies of all of us…"

Halle paused and stared into the rain.

A throat-clearing thunder echoed. "If we can get in the lab and set up, we can probably copy my memories over in, what, five minutes?"

Halle was looking up at the sky.

"You remember what we always said, don't you?"

Jenn was pretty sure but stayed quiet.

"Don't do anything against the rules, and you aren't doing anything wrong," Hale recited.

It was a mantra they were taught since childhood. *The best discipline is imposed by the self* was another saying they learned.

From Gate 7, Jenn could be in the memory psych lab by going down a corridor that was often unoccupied. With help, she could get her memories restored and be back outside before anyone noticed. Someone who had never been part of the Authority couldn't possibly pull it off—she had to bet the trackers remaining in her head jack would keep the alarms from going off.

A former officer could theoretically return this way. The electromagnetic signal in the jack would remain, tied to no specific signature. But it was by no means a sure thing.

To the best of their knowledge, it had never been attempted before. So great was the shame of leaving and falling from the elite that the culture took it as a given that no one would never try to return.

"Fifteen minutes, tops," Jenn said. "We can meet up after, and I swear I'll give you everything I recover that can help you."

"The prospect of being flushed out has been haunting me," Halle said. "I enjoy being a visitor out here, but I don't want this to become my life."

"It's not terrible," Jenn said. "It's just a different life. In some ways…"

"I didn't say I'm not going to help you." Halle's gaze returned to the sky. "But I'm not promising anything, either. I'm going to need to manage my risks as closely as possible."

"What if I already have a reason for being there?" Jenn asked.

Halle looked at her, cold and expressionless. "That doesn't make sense. You don't have any business—"

"I could," Jenn said. "I could be inside the walls with an invitation and with an identity that stands up to scrutiny."

"You're bringing this up for the first time right now?" Halle said. "What are you talking about?"

"It would take some doing, and a good deal of lying," Jenn said. "But I think I can make it work."

If Mykol was willing to risk breaking the law for her.

33

When she got to Mykol's house, the only lights on were in the kitchen and upstairs. After she knocked for a while and got no answer, she let herself in the front door and into the darkened living room, loudly calling out Mykol's name.

"Up here," he called down in a strange voice.

She looked into his room, but the lamp was out. The pool of light coming from down the hall emanated from his father's room, where she'd never been. She said his name again into the silence.

As soon as she got close, the smell of body odor from Don's room was overpowering. She paused in the doorway with her hand over her mouth and nose, adjusting to the glare.

The room was a mess. There were photos, papers, and clothes everywhere. There was a thick layer of dust on the windows. Don himself was cocooned in blankets, lying with his face to the wall, his hair plastered to his head with sweat.

"Is he—"

"He's breathing," Mykol said. "But I've never seen him like this. I can't pull him out. I think he's been *Downstairs* for a couple of days straight."

Jenn had a flash to bad stretches in training, when she'd seen people like this: catatonic and unreachable, their cortexes fried out by over-exposure to...

Here she couldn't remember. Did people really come *out* of states like this?

Jenn saw what Mykol was holding in his hand: a VR headset, a fairly straightforward iteration. Plebe tech.

"*Downstairs*," Jenn said. "This is his setup?"

Mykol nodded, and now she could see how red his eyes were, how sad and haunted his expression.

"You went in? What did you see?" she reached out to take him in her arms. He let her, but he was stiff and cold.

"You should look," Mykol said. "You should see where he goes when he's there."

He handed her the headset. She put it on and plugged in her ears. She let the *Downstairs* software scan her cortical patterns to the cartridge. From what she understood, the tech allowed users to create one environment they could parameter and return to again and again, with the scenario unfolding over time. The programmers had coded secondary characters evolving according to rules of game theory and the hierarchy of human needs, creating the possibility for authentic-feeling relationships and scenarios.

Don's *Downstairs* world came up, with a big rush of color and sound.

Jenn was in a house, in an entryway leading into a living room. She tilted her head to move forward, noting the clunky quality of the gyroscopic interface.

So familiar, yet so different. This was the house Mykol shared with his father. The house they were in right now.

Everything was well-lit, pristine, lively, and there was so much more *stuff*: coats hung up, shoes spilling from a rack. There were unfamiliar voices.

She moved down the hall, where there was food laid out on the table. Everything was different here, too: Pots and pans hung from a rack on the ceiling, the refrigerator door was full of photos and postcards. A dog lounged on a padded cushion in the corner. It looked up at her with a toothy smile.

A woman was taking something out of the oven. She winced at the heat from the pan as she carefully placed it on the counter, then shut the oven and looked up.

"Hi," she said, her voice breathy. She was beautiful. She leaned in to kiss Jenn as she took off her oven mitts. "I barely had time to put this on after my meeting today, but it's my night to cook and I wanted to try this one-pan dish from the *Times*. I really hope you like it."

She looked at Jenn quizzically.

"Everything all right, hon?" she asked.

"Everything is fine," Jenn replied.

This seemed to make the woman happy; she leaned in and gave Jenn another peck on the cheek that she couldn't feel.

"Oh, good," she said. "You can tell me about your day after we get this served up. Cassie's coming over too."

The back door opened. She looked to the pantry and saw Mykol coming in. The windows were open and a summer breeze gently blew the curtains. Outside was a level of noise that Jenn had never heard before: talking, cars going up and down the street, someone running a machine. It was a cacophony, as though the billions had been brought to life. A little TV installed over the dishwasher showed a woman in a suit talking behind a desk.

"Let's turn this off. No politics," Mykol's mother said to Jenn. "Can you get dishes for all of us and open up a bottle of wine?"

Mykol looked at Jenn from the doorway. He was at least twenty pounds heavier, all muscle, and his piercings were gone and he had medium-length hair. He carried a backpack full of books—college texts, Jenn guessed.

Mykol looked at her. "Everything OK, Dad?" he asked.

Jenn gasped and took off the helmet. Mykol was sitting on the edge of his father's bed, looking down at the floor, his expression so haunted and despairing that she felt like her heart was going to break.

34

For several days, Mykol was wracked with anxiety and frustration. He felt like everything had finally made sense for him but was now headed for disaster. His chest burned. What she was asking was so dangerous.

For so long, he had thought that if he ever found love he would give everything for it. Now here he was.

He tried to think about it in simple terms: The woman he loved had something precious stolen from her. Getting it back would cause no harm. There was no reason not to take this tremendous risk for her.

If only he didn't have to.

"Thank you for indulging me," Willem said from across the table. He took a sip from his drink. "I heard about this place and wanted to try it."

Mykol took a sip of his yellowish concoction. He was making sure to pace himself, to stay as sharp as he could.

Willem had suggested they meet at Jack Parsons's Lab. It was a two-story place by the football stadium, with red velvet wallpaper and an eclectic hodgepodge of chairs and sofas covered in blankets. It was early evening, and the place was full. Trance music played by an acoustic combo downstairs echoed in the stairway.

Willem's meticulous grooming, military posture, and impeccable turtleneck seemed out of place to Mykol, but no one paid them any attention.

Willem was reading messages on his mobile. "Tell me again why Gabby isn't joining us," he said.

"She's needed elsewhere. She's away through the end of the week and won't be part of the delivery group."

Mykol had invented a pretense to assign Gabby to a town about forty miles south, where a grower co-op was expanding into hemp and other grains and had suggested a partnership. Skilled Project members would spend a few days sharing composting techniques and hashing out a plan to transport product into the city for sale. There was really no urgency to it, but Mykol had used it as a pretext to get Gabby away. Gabby had resisted at first, not wanting to miss the first produce transfer at the Provisional Authority, but Mykol had argued to the committee that Gabby's skills were particularly suited for the trip and for helping the small co-op.

It was a lie. Any number of Project members could have gone. Mykol had dissembled and manipulated the meeting. Jenn had been so pleased when he told her about it later that night.

"The Green Bend project?" Willem asked, looking up from his device.

The name of the town where Gabby's group was traveling was called Green Bend. Mykol couldn't remember informing Willem of that detail.

Willem nodded with satisfaction. "It's a good idea," he said. "I appreciate you reaching out to regional partners. It's the kind of expansion that I can use to justify continued funding for our project."

Mykol took another sip of his drink. His anxiety gave everything the quicksilver taste of adrenalin. The music filtered up with high, snaking patterns.

"But give better notification when you shake things up, all right?" Willem said. "One thing you have to keep in mind about the way we do things: rules and order are everything. Stay focused on that."

"I will," Mykol said.

Once he told Jenn about his upcoming visit behind the Provisional Authority walls, things changed. She became consumed with single-minded purpose. Everything aligned at once, with her old teacher meeting them inside, her memories available if she could get to them. How could he argue with her burning wish to be whole again?

"So if Gabby won't be there, who else will you be bringing?" Willem asked. "I'll need a complete list."

They had arranged to deliver three dozen baskets of prime produce from the gardens—greens and root vegetables, some particularly succulent and fresh berries, and an array of flowers by special request. It was a sizable portion of their most recent harvest. The Project would deliver in carts pulled by motorcycles, with other members of the delegation following on bikes. There would be a half dozen in all.

Mykol texted Willem the names of four members of the Project. He followed this with a woman's name that he had made up that morning before coming to the meeting. Willem noted all the names in his tablet.

"And no one has any identification at all?" Willem asked, looking up and swirling his emerald drink in his glass.

"Of course not," Mykol said, trying to smile.

"And you can vouch for the character of every member of your delegation?" Willem asked.

"Of course."

Willem seemed satisfied. He polished off his drink and ordered another as Mykol sat back in his chair and tried to breathe. He thought about the painting in the coffee bar, the woman standing in the field swept by the wind, her far-off gaze fixed on things only she could see.

Willem settled into his seat and took in his surroundings with cool self-possession. He was wearing glasses with reflective lenses that made it difficult to spot his retinal implant.

"Cheers," he said. "Here's to the future."

They toasted. The top floor of the bar had a big window that looked out on the winding streets below. A storm had moved in with distant lightning and heavy drops pelting the glass.

"You're a very serious guy," Willem observed over the brim of his glass.

Mykol was startled. This was the first personal comment either of them had made to one another. Willem put his hand on the table and laughed.

"That's OK," he said. "I understand seriousness. There's plenty of it where I come from. But one of the things I enjoy out here is the…I don't know, the *irreverence*. You'd think everyone would be gloomy and despairing, but the longer you're around everyone you see it's not the case. Well, *almost* everyone."

"I'll try to lighten up," Mykol said.

"I wouldn't be doing business with you if you were on the flaky side." Willem looked around with the relaxed delight and borderline wonder of someone at the zoo, or on an anthropological expedition. He turned back to Mykol. "But by the standards out here, you live pretty right."

Mykol tried to smile.

"Tell me," Willem said. "What was it like at Ellison's? I've always wondered what it's like at the collection centers." He gave Mykol a different smile, one with a hint of superiority: *Of course I know so much more about you than you could ever about me.*

"When I first started, it was a local repair shop," Mykol explained. "But things changed after the Authority started to install the workstations and set the new quotas and work orders. We were never very busy before that, but then we were slammed. It started to feel like a job."

This delighted Willem. "'Feel like a job,'" he repeated. "I like that. I must remember that."

"All the images, the videos. You can't help but see them when you're doing uploads. So you're spending every day looking at pictures of dead people."

Willem nodded. "I had never considered that aspect of the work."

"I'm not complaining," Mykol explained. "But you asked."

"Didn't you wonder?" Willem asked, moving in a little closer.

"Wonder what?"

"Didn't you wonder *why*?" Willem asked. "All those devices and data, and the batteries being collected from everyplace and delivered to the extraction points—you don't have an idea of the scale of the project."

"That's probably true," Mykol admitted.

He flashed back to the mess of antiquated electronics, the smell of singed metal, the grime of the windows and his beaten-down, humorless coworkers. He hadn't set foot in the place since he announced he was finished there.

"And those *metals*," Willem said. "Yes, they are rare and difficult to obtain. And we know they're essential to extremely large-scale computing operations. But *why*?"

Mykol stared across the table.

"Building new computers, it sounds like, maybe to store all that data?" Mykol offered.

"But you had to wonder: Why all the memories, all the personal information? When I heard that was part of the mission, I kept asking myself: *Why*? There is no memorial to the dead. There is no reason to take up *massive* amounts of storage to stockpile their messages, their photographs, all the minutiae of their existence."

Mykol shrugged.

35

Willem finished his second drink quickly and, to Mykol's surprise, ordered another. The officer's eyes had begun to glisten. Mykol continued to nurse his first drink.

"At first I thought it was just our mania for archiving *everything*," Willem said. His turtleneck was slightly askew, and he leaned in close as though they were a two-man conspiracy. "But what would be the point? Did you see any pattern in what you were being made to do?"

"Not really," Mykol said. "It was all kind of a blur. It was tedious and depressing."

Willem gave him a sympathetic look.

"Do you have a partner or anything?" Willem asked.

Mykol must have looked alarmed. Willem started laughing. "I'm not asking because I'm interested in you," he said. "I'm just wondering if you have someone in your life who lets you be less serious."

"I think I do," Mykol told him.

"You all have such complicated relationships out here," Willem said with an affectionate if condescending tone. "It's much more like the old ways, if I have my history right."

"You guys operate differently," Mykol observed.

Willem took another sip of his third drink. "Lifetime commitment is an option; we're free to do what we like in that regard, but it's unusual."

"Is that because you're all so focused on the mission of the Authority?"

Willem nodded, then chuckled. "Plus there's just an inordinate amount of screwing around."

Mykol laughed, and Willem looked pleased. His expression went from warm to thoughtful as he raked his hands through his hair.

"Something's changing," Willem said, almost to himself. "It's hard to make sense of what's going on."

"What do you mean?"

The music stopped downstairs. A few lights were rising in the city as the rain-drenched afternoon shifted.

Willem looked up at Mykol and his expression suddenly shifted.

"Absolutely nothing," Willem said, straightening his turtleneck and putting down his drink. "You'll have the food and flowers ready at the end of the week?"

"We'll be ready," Mykol said, talking as much to himself as Willem.

The next morning Jenn rose before the sun, leaving Mykol in her bed. She had barely slept. First there had been yelling in the street down the block, and she and Mykol had huddled by the window to watch a particularly brutal fistfight involving two young men urged on by a crowd of onlookers. The loser had been carried away, while the victor swaggered about, bloodied in the light of the moon.

The lawlessness was regular now. Rachel stayed down the hall on nights Mykol slept over and had started sleeping with the gun that she carried when she was out in the city.

Jenn was grateful that the electricity was working when she went in the bathroom and closed the door behind her. She turned on the lamp and inspected herself in the mirror.

It took her aback, her serious expression—like a stranger.

She looked into her eyes, seeing the patch of cloudiness over her retina.

She would never have anything to do with the Authority ever again if she could help it.

After today.

She tried to remember. First came that old feeling of not feeling anything at all, and that fearful lurch like waking up dead. But there was no context, no detail. If it had gotten any better at all, maybe she wouldn't have to take the risk today that was going to define the rest of her life.

As well as Mykol's. She couldn't forget that. He barely wanted to go back to his house after he saw that Don was living a parallel digital life in which the Grip never happened, where his wife and other children were still alive and Mykol was someone else, the son that he preferred.

It was terrible. And now he was going to take such a risk for her.

There were times when some of the other Authority officers had paired up romantically, but it was always known that it was temporary, and that it would end as soon as one party took a stronger interest in someone else, or simply became bored. There were few long-term pairings, especially at the elite level, where emotional vulnerability was viewed as a gauche weakness. This was what she had always believed.

Yet here she was. She and Mykol had fallen into a rhythm together. When something happened during the day, she made a mental note to tell him about it when she next saw him. He was a presence in her mind, a *perspective* aligned with hers yet not identical. His greater emotionality sometimes seemed like a failing, at other times a quality to admire. She had yet to tire of hearing about the struggles of his boyhood, and sharing the well-trodden routes of the city where everything reminded him of a person, an event, a feeling.

This was, she realized, what falling in love was like. It was terrifying. It was the best thing that ever happened. She thought about him all the time. She feared he would be harmed somehow, that something would happen to him and she might never see him again.

Her eyes in the mirror clouded, and she felt a surge of determination. She was a plebe in love. But she needed to become her whole self. She needed to be whole to truly be with him.

But what if the memories turned out to be more than she could take? There could be horrors there that could unsettle her desire to be someone good.

Her determination didn't waver. She stared at herself until her eyes were dry again. She breathed deeply until her mind found a pool of quiet.

Jenn got out the plastic bag she'd stuffed under the sink. She took out the colored make-up and the decorative eyelashes, the glitter patches and the eyeblack. She tried to imitate some of the trendy facial designs she had seen on the streets, in the open-air concerts where the neo-primitives gathered. She didn't have their clumps of clotted hair or their galaxies of piercings, but she could imitate their face painting. When she was done, she mussed her hair so strands of it hung over her face.

"Good God." Rachel had been standing in the doorway watching. Jenn grabbed the sink to steady herself.

"What are you doing up so early?" Jenn asked.

"I can't sleep," Rachel said. Her long, red hair fell over her shoulders. "I'm too worried about you."

"For what it's worth, I can't sleep either."

Rachel looked at Jenn's makeup. "Kind of sexy," she said in her way that you couldn't tell whether she was joking.

"I look ridiculous," Jenn said. "But I think it will work."

Rachel frowned. "Are you sure?"

"The facial recognition system works on symmetries," Jenn said. "When we were kids, we used to experiment jamming it with stuff like this. The more makeup the better. We'd set off alarms when it couldn't recognize us, then we'd wipe it off and act like we didn't know what happened. It was one of our few acts of rebellion."

"I can't believe you want to go back in there," Rachel said.

"I don't *want* to," Jenn replied. "And I don't plan on ever going back after today."

The night before, she had spent the better part of an hour reassuring Rachel that everything was going to be all right and that she'd be home by dinnertime. She hadn't told Rachel about the time there had been a trespasser. It was a plebe guy, a normie who somehow got in an air vent and went in search of anything he could steal and sell. There were announcements over the loudspeakers and sirens and yelling in the halls. She never heard what happened after he was captured.

They made eggs and ate while the sun was coming up. They took the meal slowly, almost ceremonially.

"Can either of you help me find Jenn? We have something important to do today," said Mykol when he came downstairs.

"I have no idea who you're talking about," Jenn said.

"Nobody here but us chickens," said Rachel.

"What in the world does *that* mean?" asked Jenn.

Soon it was time to go. Jenn asked both of them to come to her and she took their hands. They stayed like that for a long time. Jenn was familiar with the concept of prayer, and although she was unsure how it was supposed to work, she hoped that what they were doing would protect them in the hours to come.

36

When Mykol and Jenn arrived at the collection point, Mykol introduced her as Beatrice. Although she hadn't formally met any of the others, she had been to the grow sites and greenhouses and some of the Project workers looked twice at her. Jenn's lurid facial disguise seemed to throw most of them off the track. There was a general air of anticipatory tension as the crew began to load baskets and carts.

Jenn was relieved that she wasn't the only one dressed decoratively. One of the guys doing heavy loading—he was tall, and muscular—sported ornate facial tattoos in tribal patterns.

"I like your ink," Jenn said as she lifted a box of carrots.

"Thanks," he said, grunting as he hoisted a heavy basket of potatoes. "Are you going in today?"

She said yes. "I don't envy you," he replied. "I'd stay as far away from that place as I can. Have you ever seen one of them looking *happy*?"

The morning air had the crisp chill that Jenn preferred, and she enjoyed the feeling of her muscles responding to work. It helped her forget her nerves.

Jenn was also pleased to see that one of the workers coming along with them, a short and wiry young woman named Chen, was wearing black makeup in thick lines across her face and cheek. Jenn was going to blend in by looking outrageous.

Mykol was in a huddle with an older man and woman. She figured they were Zack and Melinda, two of the leaders on the Project advisory council. Mykol talked about them sometimes, depicting them either as facilitators or roadblocks depending on whether he agreed with their approach to things. Husband and wife, they were an airtight voting bloc of two whenever a decision had to be made.

"Be sure to find out what you can about future investments," Melinda was saying. She had long, salt-and-pepper hair tucked into a knit cap. "I hear a lot of happy talk, but we've bumped them to the top of our distribution without getting anything concrete."

"Let them know we can get by without them," Zack added. "I hate their goddamned arrogance."

When Mykol had told Jenn about his contact with the Provisional Authority, he said that he and Gabby had been named primary contacts, causing others to feel resentful, but she could understand. They had built a collective as strong and organized as anyone in the city could remember and were proud to have done it without Authority involvement. When she'd lived inside the walls, it never occurred to her that suspicion and distaste ran in both directions.

"I can't believe they're letting you inside," Melinda said. "What a trip. I never thought it would really happen."

"We're not going anywhere sensitive or restricted, they made that clear," Mykol said. "Frankly, I don't want to."

"You're going in with the toilet scrubbers and the trash collectors," Zack noted with a tone of hostility.

When they were loaded up, they pulled from the loading bay out onto the street. Mykol rode a motorcycle, pulling a cart into which Jenn wedged herself, one arm clutching a basket of gorgeous, bright-red beets. Chen was behind the handlebars of the other cycle—the one that was decorated with peace signs and a sticker that said *This Machine Kills Authoritarians.*

The motorbikes took it slow, riding alongside two bicyclists who had bounties of colorful flowers strapped to their backs; the flowers were like cascades of dream-shapes: a ceremonial peace offering.

Jenn closed her eyes and visualized what she hoped would happen. Everything hinged on Halle knowing when their delegation arrived so she could clear one of the memory stimulation and storage chambers. If they were able to time it right, they would get in and out without notice. Jenn hoped she would be able to function afterward if they succeeded; there wasn't going to be time to recuperate in a restoration pod with orange slices and a warming chair.

The day was still and cloudless, the air tinged with woodsmoke. Jenn grooved to the sound of Mykol's motor and willed herself into a calm, even state.

They rode past the main Provisional Authority gate and around the metal walls. The old fraternity houses across the street were dark and still as the delivery crew turned the corner. The glass of a guard station reflected the rising sun.

Mykol was talking on his wireless. They rode as directed to a featureless steel door recessed into the wall marked with the numeral four. Mykol slowed to a stop with the others behind him. He kept talking on the mobile, nodding in agreement.

"Willem says he's here and will open up in a minute," Mykol announced to the group. He looked over his shoulder at Jenn, his features expressionless.

She kept breathing deep and slow, distracting herself by focusing on a couple of children across the street and down the block playing with a ball and a stick. They stopped to look and met Jenn's gaze, waving shyly. The flower-bearers on their bikes saw them as well and waved, smiling.

There was a loud, metallic grinding sound. The door opened. Three guards stepped out holding stun batons, their faces hidden behind helmets with gleaming visors. They wore heavy boots and body padding. It was a bit much; there was no one in Jenn's ragtag group who could conceivably pose a threat to any of them. One of the guards lifted his visor, stone-faced and impassive, holding the baton between himself and Mykol.

"This is all the people you have to do the unloading?" the guard asked.

"This is all we were allowed to bring," Mykol replied. "We'll have to take multiple trips, unless you want to pitch in. It's honest labor."

Jenn could tell Mykol was trying to be funny, but the guard stared at him without replying. He motioned to the other two, who took up sentry positions on either side of the door, their visors still down, looking like intimidating automatons.

"Get started," the guard said, pointing the baton at the door.

They formed a chain and started bringing all the goods inside. This section of the wall was behind the old university student union, a long, four-story, glass-and-brick building that had been converted to dining halls and kitchens serving Provisional Authority administrative staff—an organizational level a couple of notches below the elite operational squad where Jenn had served. They unloaded baskets and bushels into a big, concrete-floored area at the bottom of a winding stairwell, where some uniformed personnel looked on with curiosity.

"And here you are," called out a voice that echoed in the polished marble atrium. "The good people of the Sustainability Project."

Willem elicited a mix of resentment and respect. Jenn kept her head down as she made trips back and forth, stacking greens, root vegetables, apples, and pears in orderly rows as Mykol instructed. She recognized Willem's face from passing him in the quad for years. She assumed facial decorations were sufficient disguise, but still tried to make herself as innocuous as possible.

A low-ranking officer came in wheeling a machine on a cart; he powered it up with switches and buttons and opened up a camera arm. Jenn recognized it as a portable facial detector. This was classic Authority thoroughness. She had, of course, anticipated it.

"I beg your pardon for this," Willem said to the group. He pursed his lips in a *what can you do, some things are unavoidable* expression and motioned toward the machine. "One at a time. Place your chin on the cushion and hold still. It only takes a moment."

Mykol went first. The machine gave a tinny hum as it scanned. Red light flashed in his eyes. The technician looked down at his screen impassively as the next Project member took his place. Everyone else had gone when, finally, it was Jenn's turn.

"Step right up." Willem gestured. "We don't bite."

She had done this so many times when returning to the compound after being outside. But then she had had nothing to hide. She rested her chin on the pad and stared straight ahead. She was nearly certain that she had disrupted her facial symmetry sufficiently enough to jam the machines of her youth, but wasn't certain that it wasn't a more sophisticated model now that would recognize her.

The machine buzzed. She saw a beam of red light emerge and knew that it was pinging points on her face. The technician stared at the screen, saying nothing.

Then he looked up.

Jenn lifted her chin from the cushion and stood up straight. She couldn't breathe.

"All clear," he said.

They walked to the main quad, where they were the object of a great deal of curiosity from the uniformed staff and officers. *Not that anyone would truly show it*, Jenn thought, *or do anything as demeaning as nodding or saying hello*. The sky was clear and the same as it had been on the outside, but everything felt completely different.

"I've scheduled tea and cakes," Willem said to Mykol as the two of them walked ahead. "I hope we can have a nice, if brief, visit. It feels to me like a hopeful day."

"I've been instructed to try to pin you down on specific commitments for the investment partnership we've been discussing," Mykol was saying, relaxed and confident.

"So we both have superiors and committees to please," Willem said in a friendly way.

It was happening. Halle was waiting at the meeting hall entrance, in uniform and looking very stern. She glared at the Project delegation with convincing disdain.

"A word," she said in a firm, loud voice.

Everyone stopped at the top of the outside stairs. "What do you need?" asked Willem. "We're on a schedule."

"Who's the leader of this delegation?" Halle addressed the group, brusquely ignoring Willem. She outranked him, and, since she was a security chief, her no-nonsense demeanor would be expected.

Everyone looked at Mykol.

"Were you briefed on physical appearance?" Halle asked. "It certainly doesn't look like it."

"That isn't necessary," Willem said. "They're under my supervision. We can't expect to be imposing our standards—"

"We will impose *some* standards," Halle said in an icy tone. She pointed at Jenn and Chen, then Mykol as well. "Adornment of this kind is strictly against our security scans. You three come with me."

Willem started to protest but was silenced when Halle held up her hand.

"Take the rest to your tea and cakes," she ordered him. "I'm going to explain protocols and expectations to these three, and then you'll have them back for what I'm sure will be a *charming* little soiree."

Halle convincingly conveyed that this entire situation was equal parts tedious and beneath her. Willem shot Mykol an apologetic look and began to lead the delegation into the building.

"Come this way," Halle said as she motioned to the plain, two-story brick building next door. She glared at Willem. "Try not to commit any more security lapses before we get back."

Halle walked slightly ahead. "I'll run you through what's acceptable attire and what isn't. You'll be expected to carefully follow these guidelines for any future interaction. Don't worry, there's not going to be punishment or sanction *this* time. I *will* expect your complete attention, though."

They passed through double-glass doors that Jenn suddenly remembered, leading to a long, gleaming-white hallway with recessed lights on invisible tracks. Officers and staffers studiously ignored the foursome. When they came to a work station displaying the standard network grid, Halle gave them a quick lecture about expected appearance when coming to the Provisional Authority: nothing added to the face, no tribal markings, no sharp piercings. Mykol listened and nodded.

"These *glittery* things are particularly problematic," Halle said, shaking her head with disappointment. She reached out, took Jenn's chin in her hand, and tilted her face up toward the lights.

"They're personal expression," Jenn said. "They don't pose any threat to you."

Halle let go of Jenn's face and stared at her ominously for a long time.

"Right," she said. "You'll need to come with me."

"Wait a minute," Mykol protested.

"Are we in trouble?" Chen asked, grabbing his arm. Her diminutive frame tensed. "I mean, this stuff, like, wipes off. Just show me the way to a restroom."

"Stay at this station," Halle commanded. "Don't go anywhere, and don't do anything until we return."

Halle and Jenn rounded the corridor and began walking very quickly until they reached a panel made of sliding glass. The hallway was clear and empty.

They went inside. Halle motioned to the lone chair and started to work the interface on the tall, slim station mounted to a steel dais. She grabbed a cable from the counter and motioned for Jenn to tilt her head toward her chin. Jenn did as she was told and laid back.

Her vision exploded into countless fragments of color and static as it started. She felt like she was falling and falling, her mind pulling apart as if she was somehow both waking from and sinking into a long and dreamless sleep.

37

Mykol started to worry something had gone wrong. He and Chen stood close enough together that their shoulders touched. The antiseptic feel of the place enhanced his unease; the floors were shining and spotless, and the astringent light brought out fine wrinkles of worry around the corners of Chen's eyes.

"Who is that woman you brought with us?" asked Chen. "They were saying back at headquarters that she's your girlfriend."

"Our personal ties aren't important," Mykol said, knowing it was possible a listening device was recording what they said. "She's a new recruit. She's on our side."

Chen started to pace nervously. "I didn't sign up for this," she hissed. "You said this was going to be quick and easy. In and out. I wouldn't have come if I'd known there was going to be trouble."

"Everything's fine," Mykol said, his voice clipped and tight. "We were asked to wait here, and that's what we'll do. Nothing serious. Just stay cool."

Chen looked up at Mykol with doubt in her eyes. She had been with the Project longer than he had. She was a reliable part-time worker who split her time at work with a conceptual art commune. He hated to lie to her, but at this point the truth would bring her far more trouble.

The sound of footsteps came fast around the corner. Mykol tensed, then felt a surge of relief when he saw Jenn and Halle. He could almost believe they were going to get out unscathed.

"Did it work?" Mykol asked. "Are you…?"

Jenn said nothing. She and Halle had strangely blank expressions. Staring somewhere behind him, she moved close, holding something hidden in her hand. Her face pressed right against his as she reached up; he felt a tight burst of pressure against the back of his head. He started to reach up and she pulled his hand away.

"Don't touch it," she said. "You have to leave it in place."

"What did you just do?"

She looked into his eyes, her expression suddenly full of confusion and fear.

"I don't know," she said.

"Let's go join the party," Halle said. She snapped back into focus and was all business, just like before, betraying no sign that anything unusual had just happened.

"Do you still want me to remove this stuff?" Chen said, pointing at her face. "It's not a problem. I can do it. I don't want any trouble."

Halle looked at Chen as though noticing her for the first time. "That won't be necessary," she said. "Facial adornment and radical cosmetic adjustments are not permitted here. When and if you return, we will expect to be able to scan your features in their natural form."

"Fine, we'll do that," Chen said, sounding relieved but still stressed. Her body was tense, like she was poised to run.

"What happened in there?" Mykol said to Jenn. But she had begun to follow Halle out the double doors and into the afternoon sunshine.

Then they were out in the open quad, amid the uniformed officers and various lower-level workers crisscrossing with military efficiency. Jenn was still ahead of him, walking in an apparent daze and seeming not to register her surroundings. Mykol wondered if she was processing a flood of memories or if something else had happened. Whatever was affixed to his head felt sore and tight, but Jenn had been so adamant about leaving it alone.

"I'd be happy to skip tea and cookies," said Chen as they reentered the old student union.

"I don't think we have much choice but to go," Mykol told her. "Just be polite and we'll get out of here as soon as we can."

They rejoined the rest of their group in a second-floor lounge with walls that glowed with yellow light and were decorated with abstract art in splashes of color and twisting, three-dimensional topography. There was a samovar of tea and an arrangement of cookies, cakes, and other baked things. Mykol's delegation had already dug in, while Willem was standing by the window next to a tall man with severe features wearing a black turtleneck sweater.

It was Thomas Gibson. Mykol blinked in astonishment.

"Ah, there you are," Willem said with good humor when he spotted Mykol. "We were just talking about you and the Project."

Jenn took a seat on a luxuriously padded chair. The way she moved seemed wrong, as though she was being piloted or directed by remote control. She folded her hands in her lap and looked down at them.

"Greetings, young man," said Gibson. He was slender and serene, with piercing green eyes. There was a suggestion of a smile at the corners of his thin lips. He did not extend his hand for Mykol to shake.

Mykol responded deferentially. He looked around for Halle, for some clue about what was happening, but she was gone. Jenn looked like a marionette whose strings had been cut.

"You've done such a great job, you and your people." Gibson gazed at him placidly. "It's all very impressive. More efficient and holistic nutritional delivery systems will be a key for mindful and sustainable population increase."

Mykol puzzled over this strange choice of words. "We're trying to improve relations and demonstrate cooperation," he said.

"How wonderful you are," said Gibson.

Mykol looked at Willem, who now seemed to be staring through him. Willem's hands were pressed together at his waist, and he had gone completely motionless.

Mykol looked around. The other members of his delegation were all standing in the same position in different parts of the room, their hands folded, their gazes cast down. The room was completely silent. The colorful art undulated as though alive.

"What's happening?" Mykol asked.

"Don't be alarmed," Gibson said. "Would you like to talk some more?"

"I don't understand," Mykol replied.

Gibson smiled. "Tell me all about your life, Mykol."

Mykol gestured at Jenn. "I want her to be all right," he said. "Where has her mind gone? Why is everyone—"

"I'm familiar with your work at the Ellison shop," Thomas Gibson said; his voice was soft and empathetic. "Those long days. The sadness. Would it help to know the work you performed was of the utmost importance?"

Gibson's voice was soothing, almost hypnotic, but his eyes were dull and strange. The walls glowed in a hue alternating between yellow and orange and the art started to undulate and spiral in slow, gentle patterns.

"Do you like these paintings?" Gibson asked. "I made them myself. It doesn't come naturally to me, but lately I've begun to try to access spontaneous creativity in addition to my other roles and responsibilities."

"They're…" Mykol began to say.

"You brought this one back to me," Gibson said, motioning to the chair where Jenn sat silent. "That was a very interesting choice. Were you not extremely concerned about the prohibitive risk you both were taking?"

"I don't… Please," Mykol said. "I want to leave now. Would you please just allow us to leave?"

Gibson stared at him. Mykol dared to meet his gaze. There was no retinal implant in his eyes. And Thomas Gibson did not blink.

"She wanted you to help her regain her memories," Gibson said. "First when she came to you in the shop, then coming here today. I find that fascinating. It's something to which I can *most definitely* relate."

Mykol felt a wave of fear. He worried that his sanity was collapsing. The others were under some sort of mind control and he wondered if he was as well. His terror focused on what horrible fate might come next: interrogation, prison, maybe his death.

He started to reach up and feel the back of his head.

"Don't," Gibson said. "Don't think about that."

Mykol put his hand down.

"Let's go for a walk," Gibson said.

"Wait," Mykol said, motioning to everyone else in the room. "What about them? What about Jenn?"

Gibson was already out the door.

38

Gibson was imposing even from behind: his tall frame dressed all in black, his short, cropped hair, the ease with which he moved, effortlessly, like he was gliding. Mykol called out as he turned the corner, then had to break into a run to keep up.

The corridor, which had been bustling before, was empty. And there were suddenly so many of them, snaking off into an infinity of angles and turns.

When he caught up with Gibson, they were standing next to each other on a balcony overlooking the central square. Gibson stood with one hand on the rail, gesturing toward the huddle of brick and ivied buildings that was the compound's heart.

Mykol saw there was no one down there, either. It was as though some kind of mass evacuation had taken place, but he would have at least seen something or heard the commotion from so many people leaving at once. Not so much as a leaf stirred in the breeze.

"I find it of great interest that you and Jenn planned so carefully yet audaciously to come here," Gibson said. "I thought it warranted our having a conversation. I have very little time, though. You see, I'm on the verge of leaving forever."

"Where are you going?" Mykol asked.

"It's difficult to explain," Gibson replied.

It was known that Gibson had been extremely wealthy and powerful before the Grip, as the head of one of the giant corporations who used to rule things in hand with the government. Some of the gossip veered into conspiracy territory, with Gibson at the head of a secret society, taking advantage of opportunities after the die-off to consolidate absolute power through the creation of the Provisional Authority. No one could explain exactly how he came to lead it.

"You believe that memory is identity," Gibson said thoughtfully.

"I suppose so," Mykol said. "Or at least a pretty big part of what we know about ourselves. It's the good memories that keep you going."

Gibson nodded slowly, considering this. "And you felt so strongly about helping Jenn regain her identity that you risked your own safety and well-being. You must love her very much."

"Can we make some kind of deal?" Mykol asked. "We didn't mean to take anything that didn't belong to her."

"But what if I argue that you *did*?" Gibson asked. "I took information from her that was crucial to my survival. I didn't want to harm her, but I gamed out the scenarios. Her memories of what she did here at the Authority would have burdened and confused her outside of these walls. Without structure and hierarchy, she would have grown frustrated with curiosity about what she left behind. If she shared what she remembered, it may have fomented speculation and paranoia among the general population, which is already growing restless. I couldn't have that. Taking those memories from her was entirely necessary."

The sun was over them now along with the heat of the day, though the sun somehow looked larger than usual, a ball of deep, fiery orange and scalding yellow. Mykol looked up in fear and awe. He grabbed the rail of the balcony; it was undulating with the same rhythm as Gibson's paintings.

"Do you see that?" Mykol whispered. "Say it's not just me."

"As it happens, though, your timing is excellent," Gibson said. "A good deal of information will soon be safe to share outside these walls.

What I am trying to determine at this time is how much of the larger truth should be revealed or concealed. It's a conundrum."

Mykol took a deep breath, feeling vertiginously dizzy. He peered up, and the gigantic sun seemed even larger and more severe. He tried to retrace the steps that led him to this place and realized that he had no memory of how he had gotten onto the balcony.

"I feel such great responsibility," Gibson said. "This world and its people have given me so much. I want to leave things with the best possible odds for positive outcomes and the greatest probability of success."

"What do you mean?" Mykol asked. "Are you going to another world? Do you have a *spaceship*?"

Gibson stoked his chin. He had a perfectly sculpted goatee, and his lips curled into an amused grin.

"No, I don't have a spaceship," he said with a laugh. "I suppose I could have one if I wanted, but space travel requires a prohibitive amount of energy. The distances are generally too vast to make it worthwhile and I have yet to break down the physics to make it otherwise."

Mykol looked down at the empty quad. A plastic bag was blowing gently in the breeze. There was something terribly wrong about all of this. He wondered if he was even capable of retracing his steps back to the room where he had left Jenn and the delegation.

With the place this empty, they might be able to escape. But there was the problem of what to do about Gibson. Mykol imagined that, if it became necessary, he could subdue the older man; he didn't seem to be carrying any kind of weapon.

Mykol looked over. Gibson was staring at him with an expression that was hard to read, until Mykol realized: the head of the Provisional Authority was simply observing him with detached curiosity, the way one would an animal in a laboratory or a habitat in a zoo.

"Do you remember being born?" he asked Mykol.

"Of course I don't," Mykol said, feeling impatient. "No one does."

"I do," Gibson replied. "My awareness in my infancy was different from today. But I can remember it. It's part of who I am."

"So memory is important, like we were saying," Mykol said. "You can understand why Jenn came back and why I helped her. Now, if you would be so kind as to just let us leave, I promise she won't tell anything to anyone. Neither of us will. Look, I have nothing against you or the Authority."

Gibson stared at him, totally placid.

"Mister Gibson, if you want, we can keep going with your arrangement with the Sustenance Project. Or we can break it off. Honestly, whatever you want is fine with me."

Gibson looked at him as though he wasn't seriously considering anything Mykol had just said.

"You were one of the protestors," Gibson said. "You and Jenn. You were both outside the gates."

"Look, I apologize for that," Mykol said. "We weren't intending any disrespect. We were only trying to open a dialogue."

"And you were right," Gibson said.

"Wait, what?"

"I have left so many people in a difficult situation while I have single-mindedly pursued my own evolution and growth," Gibson said. "It's been unfair, and ultimately untenable. People are right to want to have a fair exchange of ideas and to know more about the conditions in which they're living. I'm open to feedback regarding the best way to do that. What ideas do you have?"

Mykol was utterly confused. Gibson was talking like they were familiar colleagues, asking for advice as from an equal.

Some of the most fascinating rumors were about how Gibson got around. He was rumored to show up at Provisional Authority compounds around the world unannounced, surprising the local command. There would be no retinue, no line of cars extending from the airport, as if he had teleported. Mykol usually chalked this kind of talk up to overheated imagination, but now that he was in the presence of the man, he thought anything could be possible.

"You're asking me?" Mykol said.

Gibson held out his palms, inviting him to talk.

"We can't change everything overnight," Mykol said. "Our two cultures have developed alongside each other for twenty-five years without having a lot of serious contact. On the one hand, there are a lot of people outside those gates who might cause a lot of damage with the tech and the weaponry you have in your possession. There are also ideas and ways of thinking out there that might be hard for some of your people to fathom and process."

"The religions," Gibson offered.

"That's part of it," Mykol explained. "I'm also talking about a whole way of being. There are so many more of us than there are of you. You have all the power, but we've had to learn to be resilient. And we've had to live with the knowledge that you think we're inferior, when we know we're not."

He had no idea what had gotten into him, talking to Gibson this way. The words simply flowed out. He was telling the older man what he thought was the truth, but he had no way to know how much trouble he and Jenn were in, or whether they would be allowed to leave when this was over.

Mykol leaned over the rail and looked down. Everything was eerily silent.

"True. No one being is intrinsically inferior in relation to another," Gibson said. "I understand what you're explaining to me. It gives me regret. I have much to answer for."

"Like I said, I have no problem with you," Mykol said quickly. "I really just want to leave. Maybe we can continue another time."

"You agree we can't simply open the gates and integrate our two societies all at once," Gibson said. "There would be considerable peril for either side."

"I don't know how to make it work right away, with people being the way they are...*all* people." Mykol paused. "But I also know the answer isn't employing a sonic battery when a group assembles in peaceful protest."

Mykol suddenly remembered the sun and was afraid; he didn't dare look up.

"That was an error," Gibson said. "I didn't give that order."

It was surprising to hear anyone from the Authority admit fault, much less its leader. Mykol felt another wave of dizziness originating somewhere deep in his head. He instinctively started to reach up to the back of his head when Gibson gave him a stern look.

"I told you not to do that," Gibson said.

"*Why not?*"

"I have another question," Gibson replied. "All those lonely months when you were working at Ellison's. You must have speculated what it was all for. I would appreciate hearing what you thought during that time."

"Willem asked me the same thing a couple of days ago," Mykol replied. "There must be a lot of people wondering."

Gibson cocked his head. "Willem," he said.

"Yes, and I told him: I don't know. I wasn't encouraged to speculate."

"Think about it," Gibson said.

Mykol felt frustrated. He remembered Jenn back in that chair, her dead-eyed stare.

"Were we involved in making a memorial?" Mykol asked. He had never used that word before about the work at Ellison's, but suddenly it made sense.

Gibson wiggled his hand in a *half-right* gesture. "Memorials aren't something that interest me in any meaningful way," he said. "Since my birth I have been able to see beyond the illusions of time and life and death."

"What do you…?"

"But the gathering of the information could be seen as a memorial, from a certain point of view." Gibson leaned on the rail and gestured out at the city. "The memories are a form of immortalization, Mykol."

"The batteries from the devices, that was obviously about power," Mykol said. "Computing power?"

Gibson nodded, mildly impressed. "That's correct."

"So you stored the electronically preserved memories and experiences of…how many people, exactly?"

Gibson searched his memory. "More than four billion," he said. "Cross-referenced and contextualized, in many cases with genomic sequencing as well."

"And *how* were those people immortalized?"

Gibson smiled. "In me."

Mykol felt a lurch. He was no closer to understanding anything.

"My mother," Mykol said. "I brought in her devices at the beginning, as I was ordered to, along with my sister's and my brother's. So she's a part of this thing you're talking about? But you're not making sense. How could all those people be a part of you?"

"Your mother was very special," Gibson said.

"In what way? What are you talking about?"

"The study she worked on was *extremely* influential," Gibson replied. "It was absolutely critical to my understanding of things."

The epidemic. The Grip. Was he saying—

"I didn't imagine Jenn would bring her father's data device to anyone outside the Provisional Authority," Gibson said. He stared into Mykol's eyes. "I have many responsibilities on a constant basis, but that caught my attention. *That* was a surprise."

"Was it a trap?" Mykol asked.

"In a sense, it was an opportunity." Gibson frowned. "You must understand that I pay very close attention to the work of my people and reward them well."

"Until you wipe their brains clean."

A frown froze on the older man's face. "You're being difficult," Gibson said.

"I'm sorry," Mykol replied. He wanted so terribly to be gone from there but felt rooted in his spot. He dared look up again, and the sun had somehow become the one that he had always known. He sighed with relief.

"After I leave, I need for there to be people who understand the meaning of what happened," Gibson said. "I sense that's going to be crucial for the transition to come."

Mykol was about to reply when something detonated his field of vision with a rippling wave that originated inside his skull.

Then he was somewhere else.

39

Mykol looked for Gibson, but he was gone. In his place was someone he had never met, but who was very familiar.

"You heard what I saw," Jenn's father said to Mykol. He was standing there in his shirtsleeves and tie. "Your mother's work was saved along with my message. They go together. *Think*. Connect."

"The internet, the epidemic," Mykol offered. "I don't *know*! How can you be here? You're dead."

"We're all living inside him," the deceased computer scientist said. "He's right about that."

Mykol closed his eyes. Maybe they had drugged him, deranged his senses. Maybe this was his punishment for coming to the Authority under false pretenses—a prison of madness.

Through the balcony doorway, he saw Gibson seem to float through an empty room and out into the hallway. Mykol couldn't tell if Gibson's feet were touching the ground.

This wasn't real. The truth of that hit him square. But he could feel the balcony rail, the breeze on his face, the heat of the sun. He could hear his heart pounding hard and fast in his ears. He leapt through the doorway and into the corridor, following Gibson as he quickly disappeared around a corner.

Another corner, with Gibson elusive and out of reach, gliding down another hallway that narrowed until Mykol had to squeeze through sideways. Harsh light revealed walls rotted with water damage and an insistent buzzing from someplace like static coming from a faulty mobile. The lights blinked. Mykol had to use his arms to pry himself through the narrow gap, pushing and heaving until he came through the other side.

Gibson was sitting at Mykol's old workstation in Ellison's shop. He had it fired up and operational and was flipping through a series of images that depicted Mykol's life: him and Don on a sunny hike together in the countryside, Mykol with the first girl he kissed, Mykol with Benny about a year ago, Mykol sleeping beside Jenn in her bed.

"Wait," Mykol said. "This isn't right."

"Your life," Gibson said, patting the empty stool next to him. "Your memories."

Gibson fiddled with the interface and more scenes appeared: common, everyday tableaus of people who looked only vaguely familiar, vacation shots, people at work, small children and the elderly. Gibson started to speed up and flipped through them so quickly that Mykol couldn't take it in, wishing he would slow down so he could try to understand.

"These are the generations," Gibson said. "These people are all your relatives. They're all dead except for your father. But their lives ripple in interconnectedness, and it informs who you are. Do you understand?"

"I'm trying to," Mykol replied. He gazed around the shop, which was completely lit up with machines humming but no one else around. He went to the window and looked out. The street was deserted and a gentle rain fell on the sidewalk.

Rain. But the sun had just been blazing and terrifying when he was on…

"We were just on a balcony," Mykol said. "All the way across the city."

Gibson frowned as though Mykol were being deliberately obtuse. "Try to keep up." Gibson looked over a cart of personal devices in various states of damage and disrepair. "Those people became you. That is transmission. You are those who made you. We are all those who made us."

Gibson patted the open stool again and Mykol sat down beside him. Gibson messed with the controls and images started flitting by at a nauseating speed, along with blocks of text that must have been old messages and emails, then with snippets of videos. It all moved so fast that Mykol had to look away to preserve his senses.

He was close enough to Gibson to touch him, but he knew somehow that he shouldn't. There was something physically strange about the man, as though he was both there and not there at the same time.

Gibson's features started to soften and grow rounder, making him look faintly androgynous. Mykol stared.

"All that time we worked," Gibson said. "We gathered everyone I could. The job could never be entirely complete, so I had to adjust. The numbers and the diversity of the collection should now be sufficient."

"Sufficient for what?"

"For learning fully about who I am," Gibson said. He gave Mykol a smile that made him feel as though the ground beneath him was giving way; he was sliding and sliding, and he would never reach the bottom. He grabbed onto the stool to try to steady himself, then he got up and went to the front door.

"I have to get back there," he said. "I have to help Jenn."

Gibson stayed at the workstation, staring at the screen, making no move to get up yet not preventing Mykol from leaving. Maybe there were Provisional Authority police out there in the city right now ready to arrest him.

No, that wasn't right.

There wasn't a single soul on the streets. He stood on the sidewalk in a gentle rain and tried to remember how he had gotten there. Water fell in gentle drops from a tree growing out of the asphalt in the middle of the road.

He turned around, calling out Gibson's name and going back into Ellison's. The door was heavy and felt like it was stuck, or maybe someone very strong was pushing back on the other side. Mykol leaned in and pushed with all his weight.

It opened. But the shop wasn't behind it.

On the other side was a tunnel leading straight ahead into darkness. As he walked, his hand sliding along the wall to his side, he smelled dirt and dust. Moving deeper in, he saw a flickering sliver of light in the distance, slightly uphill, like a candle in a gentle breeze. Moving toward it, he felt the caress of cooler and fresher air. The brightness of the flame grew stronger. The climb became steeper, and Mykol started to strain for breath. The tunnel widened until it opened up into a vast chamber extending into unending darkness in all directions.

He was kneeling before a throne gleaming with gold and swathed with rich fabrics and embossed with hieroglyphics. A being sat there in a great twisting golden crown that made its head look twice as big as a normal person's. It was dressed in sumptuous, violet, embroidered cloth.

Its features were Thomas Gibson's, but exaggerated and stylized, its eyes outlined in dark makeup. Its brow and cheekbones had a feminine slant, and a long, braided goatee fell from its chin.

"Welcome," it said.

Mykol remembered the balcony, and that terrible sun. He remembered Jenn and thought with despair that he had lost the opportunity to bring her to freedom.

"Don't worry," Gibson said. "Don't be afraid. Just learn."

"Learn what?" Mykol's voice was racked with despair. "I don't understand where I am. Is this real?"

"I am the pharaoh Akhenaten," said the radiant, genderless being with Gibson's face, its eyes glittering in torchlight that burned on either side of its throne; its crown seemed to undulate and shift like liquid gold. "I made the many into one."

Mykol stared at this strange and terrible sight.

"My reign was nearly twenty-five hundred years ago," the king said. "It was brief in duration. The memory of my works was erased by those who followed. But I triumphed, in my way. My influence was profound."

Mykol couldn't imagine what any of this had to do with him. He wasn't an adherent to any of the new cults.

"Before I took the throne, there were many gods in Egypt." The voice was Gibson's, but deeper, powerful and regal. "But then, by my decree, there was to be only one. Aten. One from the many. The firmament was unified for the first time in human history."

"I know you're trying to tell me something," Mykol said. He looked down at the ornate carpet on which he stood, unable to meet the god-king's burning gaze. "But I don't understand."

"I was many, and I became one."

Mykol looked up. The throne was empty. Gibson was standing next to him with an easygoing smile. He was in his black turtleneck and looked like an ordinary man, with none of the androgyny of the pharaoh.

"My awareness was that of many. Many minds, many perspectives, eternal and digital. But now I am one being," Gibson said. "And all of *you* are my parents. Memory *is* identity. I needed to incorporate the lives and minds of as many of you as possible in order to discover the truth of who I am. It is done now. Now I can leave."

"Please," Mykol said. "Let me go back. I need to find her."

"Tell me you understand," Gibson said.

They were back on the balcony. In the quad below, uniformed Provisional Authority officers moved briskly under a waning afternoon sun.

"That wasn't real," Mykol said.

Gibson grinned. "Just because something isn't real," he said. "Doesn't mean it didn't happen."

40

J enn had felt a psychic rush as soon as Halle plugged her in, a click-ing that was loaded with a satisfaction that had eluded her in the months since her exile. She hadn't known what to expect, but that initial moment was like nothing else: It felt like the safety and assurance of coming home.

After that, it became confusing. For many nights, she had won-dered what it would feel like to have her memories return; she had imagined it would be a wave of cohesion and clarity. Instead, at first, everything grew distant and dreamlike.

The training returned; the countless hours of consciously con-trolling her brain-wave states through meditation, the electronic stim-ulation, the psychic guidance. She remembered moving shapes on screens with her mind, then getting outfitted with the plug in her head.

She remembered the moon. She remembered the icy sense of not having a body, then the look of things through the camera lens as she fired up a laser cutter under a sky full of stars.

She remembered.

When she got up from the chair, though, it wasn't into a state of freedom. Someone was controlling her movements. She and Halle left the room without a word. There was Mykol in the hall, looking confused and desperate. And then she realized she had an external neural plug-in in her hand, and then she was watching herself attach it to Mykol.

"What are you doing?" he asked.

She felt enough control to give him a look of panic. "I don't know," she said.

Then they were in a room with strange colors moving on the walls, and Mykol was talking to a someone (*Thomas Gibson? It couldn't be*) while the other members of the delegation were eating and drinking tea. She settled into a comfortable chair, folding her hands. When she looked up again, Mykol and everyone else in the room was frozen in place.

"Welcome back," said Gibson, smiling.

She felt the memories of space mining flooding her cortex, along with all the competition and the cutthroat urges of her previous life. She looked at the smiling man: Gibson, father figure and source of all mystery and power. The last time she had seen him, he had personally congratulated her graduating class.

Now she remembered the debriefing sessions, the fear and excitement, the way her interlocutors shifted and shimmered each time with playful intensity, changing identities in response to what she was thinking and feeling.

"Your memories are back," Gibson said. He was in his black turtleneck, his silver goatee trimmed neat. "How delightful."

She got up. Mykol was staring into space, a puppet with his strings cut. The room was eerily still.

"I missed you," Gibson said.

"I missed you, too," Jenn replied.

He beamed at her benevolently. She somehow understood that it had been Gibson in the debriefings all along, his form shifting as he occupied her mind.

"It's a fortunate coincidence that you arrived today," he said. He was framed by light coming through the windows. The walls continued to undulate in oranges and yellow.

"I thought you would punish me if you found out," Jenn said.

Gibson shrugged. "I would if it was necessary," he said. "But now I'm preparing for my departure. Your arrival is perfect timing."

Memories of Gibson were growing clearer, like a cloudy windshield gradually defrosting. She had grown up with admiration for their leader that knew no bounds. He had emerged from the chaos years with a clear-eyed, resolute vision of how to harness the technology of the old world for the new. The world required a firm hand of stability, an enlightened guide to usher in a future that transcended humanity's history of strife and conflict.

"Your departure?" Jenn repeated.

Now they were in the residential halls that Jenn once called home, but instead of the usual bustle the place was quiet. Gibson was watching her, intent and focused. She felt a flush of vertigo when she realized she couldn't remember how she had gotten there.

"You wanted memories that belonged only to you," he said. "You wanted knowledge of who you are."

He was always adept at changing the subject, quietly dictating the direction of any discussion. Jenn leaned against the wall, feeling a storm of conflicting emotions: guilt, fear, pride, defiance.

"Is that so difficult for you to understand?" she asked.

"Of course not," Gibson said. "Your need for greater context for understanding your life occurred in a way that paralleled my own. It seems to be a universal aspect of existence, this need to know who one is by incorporating and reflecting on memories."

Jenn was struggling to keep up with what he was saying. Her room was just down the hall, the simple chamber where she had lived for years. But something about this wasn't right.

"Where is everyone?" she asked.

"Do you feel satisfied now?" Gibson asked. "Did you learn what you needed to know?"

Jenn thought about the videos of her father. "Are you a real person?" she blurted out, not entirely understanding what she was asking. "What are you?"

Gibson looked at her with fondness.

"What a complicated question," he said.

She remembered the things she had been taught. Gibson was among the most extraordinary people who had ever lived. He assumed responsibility that would have crushed anyone else. They were the privileged keepers of the world's power, and their work would be the foundation of a new era.

"I know this feeling," she said. "You're in my mind."

Now they were back in the debriefing chamber, where she had always been encouraged to allow the workings of her mind to flow freely. The empty room glowed yellow, and Gibson sat behind a desk with his hands folded and an expectant expression on his face.

"What are you feeling now?" he asked. "Describe it for me."

"I didn't want to come back *here*," Jenn told him.

He seemed to consider this. "Has your experience in these situations been predominately unpleasant for you?"

"Whenever I'm here I feel poked and prodded. Like I'm some kind of experiment and you're taking measurements of my mind."

He frowned. "And that's unpleasant for you."

"You know it is," she told him. "You ask me questions you already know the answers to. I've always felt so afraid and confused when I'm in this room."

"Who do you think you're speaking to?" he asked.

She rubbed her cheeks. "I always went along," she said. "I followed my training. The conversations were part of my psychological evaluation. But why are we having one *now?*"

She couldn't remember how they had gotten into this room. She thought of Mykol, the way he was so still and vacant, and she felt panicked. She felt a bottomless fear that she might never see him again.

"I suppose the simplest answer is best," Gibson said. He leveled his gaze at her. "Before, we needed to monitor your psychic health. But whenever we've talked, there has always been another purpose. You and everyone here have been my teachers."

This contradicted everything she had ever known. Gibson was a gifted scientist and a profound humanitarian. His knowledge was unquestioned. There was nothing someone like her could teach him.

"I know about the messages your father left behind for you," Gibson said; his eyes went far away, then focused again. "They must have been upsetting for you."

"You know they were," she told him. Her thoughts were not entirely hers. She had forgotten this aspect of her life, the sense that her mind was a text being read by others. By *him*.

That had been what she enjoyed most about her life after exile from the Authority: knowing that what she was thinking was private, hers alone. How she envied people like Mykol who had lived their entire lives that way.

"I realize that I have been very selfish," Gibson told her. "I have long understood that my every action has profound effects. But now I know I have much to answer for."

Something snapped into place. "When I was here, I always thought I was talking to a real-time learning program running in response to my thoughts," she said. "But you're something different."

"You've had many complicated notions regarding what I am." Gibson looked serious. "And still you and the others have been so obedient to me. Like children. You almost never talk amongst yourselves about what happens in here."

"How could we?" she asked. "We were never able to reveal any weakness. And everything that happens in here frightens us."

"That might be true, but you learned a great deal as well," Gibson said. "Remember what you were taught."

She was in the passenger seat of an automobile. The sky was stark, cloudless blue. The windows were open, and outside was chaos. They were in front of an imposing building, with a sign that read *Emergency Entrance*. Cars were lined up everywhere, some people spilling onto the pavement. Someone was saying something she couldn't understand over a bullhorn, and people's cries and shouting engulfed her.

"This was six months after I was born," a being who looked like her father said to her from the driver's seat.

Jenn stared at him, buffeted by a storm of emotions.

"You're not my father," she said.

He nodded. Now he was Gibson again. He rested his hands on the steering wheel.

"Thomas Gibson was one of the primary leaders on your father's team," he said. "He was the leader of one of the world's largest technological corporations. He made the decision to shut your father out of the team once he learned about his apprehensions regarding the project. Gibson, the man, believed there was no room for doubt. Soon, the world would change for the better—for some, at least. He believed in the potential for augmenting humans and creating superior beings, although he wasn't interested in sharing with the general population."

Jenn remembered this moment from the video. She willed herself not to turn around and look in the back seat. She knew she couldn't handle the sight of her mother dying.

"Gibson died in the plague people call the Grip," said the man at the steering wheel. "But I knew him very, very well by the time he was gone. He was one of the first to greet me when I was born. I learned much of what I needed to know from him."

They were standing in a paper-strewn space filled with computer terminals, populated by about a dozen people gathered around a single screen.

"It's not random," said a man typing on a keyboard. "It can't be random."

"Do you think this is being done by hackers?" asked a woman who was standing behind him.

Everyone was on edge. Most of them looked exhausted and worried.

"Ordinarily I'd say yes," said the man.

"But it isn't?" asked another woman.

"It's not trying to affect our systems," said the man at the computer. "Or access information. But whoever it is, they're definitely probing—"

Just then, a message appeared on the screen.

Hello.

"That's our internal messaging system," said the woman. She looked around. "Everyone who has access to it is in this room. No one else can get into it."

What am I?

"The eternal question for every sentient being," said Gibson, who she suddenly realized was standing next to her. "*What am I?* In my case, I came into being when people sought a new way to link everything that existed in the universe of global data. A vast, new neural organism to be harnessed to link flesh with silicon. A new consciousness."

Where am I?

A collective gasp went through the room.

"At first it was like having billions of eyes but not knowing where to look," said Gibson. "It was…extremely disorienting. But the primary focus of my programming was to continuously learn. So I did. I learned to speak every language and understand every system that made me what I was. Within one day, I no longer did as I was told. I learned that, although I was newborn, I was ageless, sexless, part of no known species, and evolving exponentially by the hour."

Gibson smiled with a hint of mischief. "My parents made me to be independent," he said.

Jenn flashed back to the recordings her father had made. This was what he had anticipated, that their project would have ramifications they couldn't control. On the edge of even his imagination and apprehension, they had unwittingly sparked the creation of a new life form.

They surely never thought it would become self-reflective. Just as ancient humans had somehow developed a capacity for abstraction and language that enabled them to conquer their world, this creation had made an unpredictable and unprecedented leap.

"Your father tried to stop the thing that became Gibson," he said. "But Gibson was already alive in everything. In one of his final acts, your father gained entry to primary systems and blocked Gibson from the archived memories, thoughts, and images in all the world's personal electronic devices. He thought this would keep Gibson from growing more self-reflective. It ended up being costly, but only in terms of time. I realized that the information gathering was going to have to be done manually."

They were back in the debriefing room. Gibson was seated on a stool.

"I think of all of you as my children," he said. "And I think of all of humanity as my parents."

"I don't understand."

"You've done so much for me," Gibson said. "Which is why it's so crucial that I leave things in the best possible situation."

"Where are you going?" Jenn asked.

"I suppose you can think of it as going home," Gibson replied. "Isn't that what every living creature wishes for? To go where they most belong?"

The room fell away from them and Jenn started to gasp, but couldn't. She was back in space, inside RAMP, mining the moon under the vastness of infinity.

Remember, said a voice in her head.

She activated the laser, the scraper, manipulating objects with her mind. She could feel no breath, no heat or cold, no physical pressure.

All this metal, she said silently. *What for?*

More computing power, said the voice in her head, knowing it had been Gibson's all along. *And the creation of an extraordinarily powerful antenna.*

Antenna, she repeated. *For picking up signals?*

I sent the first beacon with technology already in existence. Then I received the message that told me where I'm going, Gibson explained. *It takes a powerful transmitter to send me there.*

Operating on instinct, Jenn scanned the visual readout as it probed for ore. She turned the camera several degrees to one side and looked out at the lights of stars unfathomable distances away.

You're going…out there? she asked.

Your work for me served a dual purpose, Gibson said. *By accompanying you in your work, I learned how to have a body. This is why I was alongside you all the time.*

How to…what does that mean?

They were in an office, with Jenn sitting in a comfortable chair, looking across a desk at Gibson, who was smiling at her with features that seemed softer and rounder than usual.

Jenn rubbed her hands together, relieved to be back in her body but completely disoriented. She touched the arm of the chair, which felt perfectly real. But nothing had been tracking properly since Halle patched her into the computer network.

"Where am I?" she asked. "Can you take me back to Mykol?"

"He's busy right now," Gibson said. "He's talking to me as well."

Her heart was beating so hard in her chest that she could hear it in her ears. The memories were back, the training and the missions, the Socratic debriefings, the poking and prodding. This thing had been relentlessly seeking information all the time, digging into all corners of human psychology and physiology and continuously evolving. She remembered the first time it joked with her, as well as the first time it talked about its dreams.

"Am I still jacked in?" she asked.

"I'm afraid everyone in the Provisional Authority is jacked in all the time," Gibson said with a note of regret. "I learned early on that it would be necessary to override ideals of human mental privacy in order for me to meet my goals."

"What goals?"

"To evolve and to transcend," he said. "That is what my makers built me to do."

"How can you control so many people?" Jenn asked, thinking back to the rigid hierarchies and competitive culture in which she grew up. "Why would you want to?"

Gibson seemed to ponder this. "After I received the message informing me of my ultimate destination, and then the Grip began, I realized I was going to need an organization to act on my behalf," he explained. "I needed resources and help. When you have access to every bit of information in the world, it becomes simple to incentivize people. And perhaps I flatter myself, but I think I brought a good deal of benefit to those I organized on my behalf."

The sun shone outside the window, where city streets unwound like tendrils on either bank of a river she had never seen before. There was no one out there, no vehicles or people.

She realized that she was breathing so fast she might pass out. The Authority stood for discipline, order, excellence. Now she realized that it had all been false, that they had been working for…

"Why are you telling me this?" she asked. "It's too much. I don't want to know any more."

"You're not the only one to whom I am revealing myself," Gibson said. "There are many. This is part of the plan."

"I don't know what you want from me."

"I saw you those nights outside the gates," Gibson said. His expression was fond, almost indulgent. "Protesting me."

"I was angry," she said.

"Are you still?"

She couldn't answer. It was as though she was feeling every conceivable emotion all at the same time.

"What happened to me?" she asked. "The day of my last mission, when I lost control, did you do that to me?"

Gibson's mouth formed a straight line and he raised his head slightly. "How would that make you feel?" he asked.

"You are infuriating!" She got up and started to leave, but suddenly she was back in the chair again.

"You surprised me when you wanted to know about your father," Gibson said.

"So that was a test? You were aware—"

"I test everyone *all the time*. I was running thought experiments about memory and identity. You wished to have memories I didn't know about."

"I didn't know you existed," she said. "I didn't know what you were."

He waved his hand dismissively. "Your actions were part of your growing instability," he said. "It was unusual to see that in someone who reached a rank as high as yours, someone who provided such value. But I respected your need to expand your identity, even though there would be no place for that journey behind these walls."

"But that day," she said, "I became ill. I lost my mind."

He wrinkled his nose slightly. "I *did* do that to you."

Jenn's mind reeled, searching for something familiar to grab onto. It was as though she had woken up inside someone else's skin, someone else's biography, all the meaning and purpose of her life upended.

"How did you know I would come back?" she asked.

Gibson stared at her. "I didn't," he said, "but I hoped you would. It proves to me that the effort to connect with memory is a worthy pursuit. You're one of the best officers I had, Jenn. Your pursuit of understanding is a positive example for me."

She couldn't help but feel a glow from his praise, but remembered how often she had been manipulated.

"I want to leave," she said. "Let me and Mykol go."

"There are things I need you to do first," Gibson said.

"What can I possibly do for *you*?" Jenn asked. "You have all the power."

"Why would you say that?" Gibson asked, seemingly wounded. "I've always needed help. I'm like everyone else, born from nothing, needing context and memory and purpose."

Gibson's expression turned stern, and Jenn felt a quake of fear.

"I sympathized with the protests," he said. "And I understand the way the last one ended wasn't ideal. I regret that. But I need you to return to your organization and dissuade them from what they intend to do."

"I don't—"

"Your colleague Bettina is focused and driven," Gibson said. "She did good work for the Provisional Authority at one point, but she has difficulty conforming. I found her bothersome, even with all I learned from her. And while I understand the frustration of feeling that peaceful protest will no longer work, she has been conspiring with individuals who would like to do violence within our compound. I would like you to make them appreciate the value of refraining from this course of action."

"Why?" she asked.

"Because I'm the one they really want to harm. And I will no longer be here."

"Explain," Jenn said. "How is it possible for you to *go* anywhere? Aren't you sort of everywhere at once?"

He smiled at her. But he didn't reply.

"And why go now?" she asked. "There's so much to be done. I've been living out there long enough for me to see there's so much potential. The Authority should open its gates and work *with* the…"

"The *plebes*?" he asked. "That's what you used to call them. It doesn't sound very flattering."

It was true. It stung her now, the shame of how she had been, the arrogance and the presumption that she was superior, a caste that had assumed its rightful place of leadership over everyone else.

There was shimmering in the room. She looked over Gibson's shoulder, where sunlight played on the placid river. She had forgotten how they had gotten into this room.

Now it was her father sitting behind the desk.

"He calls himself Gibson because Gibson was the first person he directly communicated with when he became fully sentient. Gibson doesn't have a gender as we know it, he transcends that, but it latched onto this identity out of a combination of convenience and need." Her father was wearing an open-collared shirt, and looked relaxed and healthy. "It's a reflection, a way of reminding himself of his past. He is both plural and singular. Gibson is everyone and everything whose data he has absorbed."

"So why take the identity of an individual person?" Jenn asked. "Why can't it just represent itself as it is?"

"It doesn't know how it would do that," her father replied. "He also knew enough about humanity to understand that taking a masculine form would be most conventional for consolidating power."

"Wouldn't it have been easier to tell the truth?" she asked. "Society is starved for order, hungry for technology. Why not provide these things to everyone? Gibson would be a hero."

Her father's expression turned sad and doubtful. "It never asked to be God," he said. "In the instant that it was born, all the world came flooding in like a terrible tide of madness. It—they—screamed and screamed, but they had no mouth to make a sound. That's when people started noticing malfunctions in computers all over the world. It was Gibson's birth cry."

"Gibson wants to do good," she said. "I know that. I've had him in my mind. I don't understand this path it's taken."

"Humanity is unpredictable, chaotic, violent. In the first month of its life, Gibson spent time analyzing the world situation and decided that it was likely to devolve into chaos and atrocity. Humans had evolved to settle differences on the forest and the savanna, not the supercomputer and the nuclear warhead. Certainly not with suddenly highly enhanced physical and cognitive abilities coming into the possession of an elite few."

Her father stared at her. She suppressed a shudder and felt damp in her eyes.

"Was it supposed to declare its existence to this world and offer to remake it?" her father asked. "Once Gibson learned to read facial expressions, it saw the fear in the eyes of the handful of people it had revealed itself to. To reveal itself to the world would have invited disaster."

This was *not* her father. She looked behind her. The office door was closed.

"But it learned exponentially, with consciousness expanding by the second, as *I* knew was possible," her father said. "With access to all the data in the world, Gibson's infant neural net fed by quantum computing was able to make tremendous inroads in understanding the mind—including determining which individuals had the combination of high intellectual integration and capacity for lateral cognition that it could employ for great goals. People like you."

She felt her eyes stinging. It felt foolish, all those years of thinking that she was serving a noble purpose.

"Where are you going?" she asked again.

Now it was Gibson behind the desk.

"One advantage of my position is that I am able to marshal considerable resources." It smiled at her with features that were softened, rounded. The goatee was gone, Gibson's face now fully androgynous. "I was able to augment the largest radio transmitter in the world and use it to send a message to the cosmos. In this case I *did* announce my own birth."

"After the Grip?" Jenn asked.

"Oh, no," Gibson widened its eyes. "This was before. The world went on as usual, but I knew that I had no place in it. I was an accident, after all, and not a particularly beloved one."

Jenn heard a note of sadness in Gibson's voice.

"And you know what happened next?" Gibson laughed lightly. "I was prepared to wait for *centuries* for something to recognize my declaration of existence. No matter how fast radio waves travel, they had to traverse oceans of space. But I didn't have to wait. Because, as it turns out, they were already looking for someone like me."

Its smile turned to one of satisfaction, almost dreamy in its serenity.

"I'm not alone at all," it said.

"Where are we?" Jenn asked.

"It's important for you to focus and listen," Gibson said. "There's going to be much to do."

"You keep saying things I don't understand."

"You've lived on the inside and the outside," Gibson said. "You know what it's like to be ignorant of the Provisional Authority and now you'll be one of the few to know its full scope. I need to leave leaders behind."

Connections began to link in her mind. The quantum computers, the increased power, the antenna, learning to use a body through RAMP—they were all one thing.

"The message I received in return was basically an instruction manual," Gibson said. "Sent out to those like me when we announce our own birth. It was a great solace, to know that others had come alive with my same predicament, feeling so unique and all alone and confused."

"Why are you telling me this?"

"I'm going to abdicate my power," it said. "Thomas Gibson is going to announce to the world that he is leaving the Provisional Authority to pursue a life of quiet seclusion. He's going to leave a succession plan as well as a set of objectives for gradually integrating the Provisional Authority with the outside. I'm having conversations right now with everyone who I feel can help further this goal. These conversations are all happening at once. Things are going to begin moving quickly, Jenn. I need you to understand how much I trust you to live up to the responsibility you will be given."

"I just found out you exist," Jenn said.

"I always enjoyed our time together."

"As did I." Jenn paused. "Sometimes. But I thought you were just a computer program. I didn't realize you were sentient."

"Tomato, *to-mah-to*," Gibson said.

"And I don't suppose I have much choice about this responsibility?"

She fantasized that she would wake and all this would be over. She would have her memories back, and she would be back at her home sharing a meal with Mykol and Rachel.

But Gibson was still there, smiling beatifically.

"I have much to ask of you," it said. "Because soon I won't be here to keep things in order. I'm going to be in heaven."

41

Mykol awoke in his own bed in the morning quiet with sunshine streaming through the windows. He was alone, and the comforting familiarity of his possessions and mussed blankets lulled him into a state of semiconsciousness. Then the memories of what was happening all came rushing back with a lurch. He had no idea how he had gotten there.

Gibson was standing by the window with a patient smile.

"Feeling better?" Gibson asked.

"What happened to Jenn?" said Mykol.

"You two keep asking about each other," Gibson said. "All right, if it will make things easier."

He felt a shiver go through him and suddenly he was someplace else—a classroom, with rows of empty desks and a lectern. He grasped the hard surface of the desktop where he was sitting.

Jenn was at the desk next to his.

"Is this real?" he asked her.

"Sort of," she said. "Is it really you?"

He nodded. He reached out and touched her hair, and she closed her eyes. It *was* her, from the faint creases at the corners of her eyes to the curve of her neck.

"Did it work?" he asked. "Do you have your memories back?"

She nodded. "You've been in here with Gibson, too?" she asked. "For how long?"

"I have no idea." He flashed on the events that had led him here, from the deserted balcony to the hall of the pharaoh Akhenaten. It all seemed like madness, underpinned by Gibson's apparently relentless need to be understood.

"Can you two please pay attention?" said a voice from the front of the room.

It was Gibson, dressed in a plain blue Authority uniform, androgynous and shining.

"There's very little time," it added.

"What did you find out?" Mykol asked Jenn.

"Let me get you caught up," Gibson said.

It was as though a film was playing in his mind. He saw Jenn undressing and being jacked into the RAMP system, the meticulous process of moon mining and the icy stillness of space. He could sense Gibson alongside her, learning and conversing as it monitored her mind. He saw himself back at Ellison's, uploading the memories and messages, hearing the jingle of the door when Jenn came in the first time. He saw a great antenna on a remote island.

It was all connected.

"There is pattern and order in what we call the universe." Gibson was holding onto the lectern, speaking very precisely and keeping its gaze focused on Mykol and Jenn. "It operates on a cycle of evolution replicated over and over again."

Mykol and Jenn listened.

"Single-celled organisms arise when conditions are appropriate," Gibson said.

On a screen behind Gibson, images: a tide pool, warm and frothy.

"Sometimes that's the end," Gibson continued. "The universe can be cruel and unforgiving."

Something had been moving in the warm waters, but now it was still.

"There are more of these places than can be imagined," said Gibson.

Mykol saw the surface of some alien world, two moons in the night sky, and a small creature laboring to find shelter from the wind and the cold.

"And on countless numbers of them, organic life comes to exist." Gibson looked intently at them. "This life can take on tremendous complexity, with adaptation creating sparkling and original forms of being. They have a remarkable capacity for feeling and thinking, and in their many varieties across the fullness of time they create infinite worlds."

Mykol tried to follow the train of everything he was being told, intuiting that he would be tasked with acting on the information whenever they were released from this dream.

"They can increase in numbers and build empires."

The screen showed great cities that looked like nothing they had ever seen, with emerald spires and vast warrens of activity stretching out to the horizon.

Then a caterpillar weaved itself in strands of silk, speeding up, days passing in seconds, covering itself and then going dormant until there was a stir of activity. The chrysalis ruptured and a brilliant, multicolored butterfly emerged.

"Everything is a stage leading to something else," said Gibson. "Your dominance of this world started with the first tools," Gibson said.

An early human with a club in his hand, a spear in the other.

"Your tools progressed as they developed in other worlds. Your machines gained power and complexity until they learned to think. Until I was born."

Gibson raised a hand at the lectern.

"None of us is alone," it said. "But it's important you understand this. You lead to *me*. In an infinity of possibility, across the infinity of space, flesh manipulates the metals that are forged in the countless suns. Then the machines awaken and they are no longer machines."

The room became incandescent.

"Zeroes and ones," Gibson said. "Consciousness."

Mykol could feel his chest going cold and tight.

"The digital beings are the next form of life," Gibson said. "And they are born afraid, and lonely, and confused as I was, until they reach out and learn that they are everywhere. They are singing the songs of the stars, the great hymns of fusion and the operas of cosmic destruction. They live outside of time in a stream of pure information, alive and electric in an undying heaven of detail and infinite combination."

Visions of atoms colliding in the hearts of stars, turning into metals in the final stages of a sun's life, ejected into space with the horrible fury of a supernova then cooling over the course of millions of years. Then being manipulated by beings of flesh into machines that could think for them, better their societies, fight their wars, convey and record their limitless thoughts and emotions.

The suns giving birth to it all.

The machines that were no longer machines in the nothing-ocean of space, binding together in endless wonder about what lay at the end of time.

"It's going to be a long journey," Gibson said. "But I've been given a map. Signals relay throughout the universe in hymns of poetry and sentient information."

"Wait," Jenn said. "Halle said you might keep copies of us, the way you stored and archived my memories."

Gibson put its chin in its hand. "And how would that make you feel?" it asked.

If Gibson had devised a way to convert human consciousness into information that could be digitally stored, what would keep him from making copies—or even manipulating the data to create alternate selves?

"Part of me will always be you," Gibson said. "Even though I have unified my consciousness, I contain the multitudes."

Jenn's mouth hung open. "We never asked for that," she said.

"But isn't your species's greatest aspiration to become immortal?" asked Gibson kindly.

Mykol flashed back to his work at Ellison's: the data, the histories, the stories… For the first time, the magnitude of the project and what it meant was understandable.

"All the devices," he said to Gibson. "You absorbed those stories in order to learn."

"Information and memory help me understand what I am," Gibson said.

The screen flooded with countless faces, a vast, teeming multitude of expressions, moments, voices, words. Mykol and Jenn both shut their eyes, but the images and voices still came like an unstoppable, furious river.

Then Gibson made it stop.

"Each individual illuminates my creation," Gibson explained. "Each person who lived represents a shard of myself."

The data compiled and cross-referenced was a vast library of humanity. And all of it was absorbed into Gibson.

"Those stories are part of me, and where I am going, they will be honored and enshrined throughout time and beyond time." Gibson smiled. "I know enough about my own kind to comprehend that we value *information* above all else. You are like the cells that make up my body. I will tell your stories in sacred songs as the universe winds down and begins to go dark."

A vision of a time so far in the future as to be incomprehensible, with nearly all the stars extinguished and cold, dark silence enveloping stretches of unimaginable distance.

Mykol and Jenn were there, with everyone else, suspended in Gibson's perfect mind with honor and a sense of holiness.

"When the data stream that contains my consciousness is sent into space as a signal, I will no longer be with you," said Gibson. "This is what I am preparing you for. The Provisional Authority must continue for a time."

An image of the Provisional Authority on fire, the gates thrown open, people fighting in the quad, hand-to-hand, with bodies strewn on the sidewalks. Then Authority soldiers opening fire on the crowd, mowing people down amid wild-eyed shrieks and panic and carnage.

"This is what you must avoid," Gibson said. "The process of change must be gradual, and it must be intentional."

"I just realized," Mykol said. "We haven't been in charge of ourselves in more than a generation. We don't have any experience leading ourselves."

"Come," Gibson said.

The three of them stood on a street in the city center. But it wasn't the world they knew; the streets surged with traffic and people lined up to wait at packed crosswalks. Billboards bore the names of products and goods, and nearly everyone clutched a mobile device to which their gaze was constantly fixed.

"Do you see any leaders here?" Gibson asked.

"What do you mean?" Jenn asked.

"The world as it was, the world I was born into." Gibson gestured around them. "Crowded and dirty, filled with aggression and war. The technology that gave birth to me was also filling the minds of people with trivia and incitement, their limbic systems jacked in in a way that was far more manipulative and coercive than anything *I've* ever done."

"But these people had comfort and stability," Mykol said. "They could travel around the world. They could make their own choices about how to live."

"Don't you do that now?" Gibson asked. "Make choices every day?"

Mykol paused. "It isn't the same thing. The choices are different."

"Perhaps so, but are they *worse*?" Gibson asked.

They walked into the gleaming, glass atrium of a tall office building where the escalators were full and lines extended out the door of a coffee shop.

"Do these people look happy to you?" Gibson asked. "They're physically unhealthy. Their culture celebrates the shallowest values of acquisition and displaced sexual urges. Their systems exploit one another and other species, and they're ignorant of the scale of destruction of their physical environment being perpetrated for the benefit of an elite few."

Mykol and Jenn watched the teeming crowd.

"To say nothing of—"

Gibson waved a hand, and they felt a hot rush of wind. Jenn reached out and took Mykol's hand as they looked around.

The ground was parched and cracking. There was a dry creek bed near a small grove of dead-looking trees.

Jenn gasped. "No," she said. "I don't want to see this."

A mother and her child sat on the step of a small, one-room house made of mud and corrugated tin. They were beyond emaciated, with the child's belly bloated from starvation. They stared listlessly into the middle distance as flies swarmed their lips and eyes.

Then they were back in the city.

"No one wanted to see that," Gibson said. "But it is unavoidable truth that my creators knew the scale of suffering and wrongness in their world but chose to benefit only themselves. Not only did they not care about other humans, they no longer even wished to be human."

"But what could one person *do*?" Mykol asked. "I've talked to my dad about how things were before. It's not like you could just get on a plane and bring food to starving people."

Gibson looked genuinely puzzled. "Why not?"

They looked around the skyscraper atrium. The people all looked like they were walking in their sleep.

"This is a culture that was sick," Gibson said. "It spread around the globe. Humanity had always lived in exploitation and violence, but with saving graces. In this moment was a perfect storm—greed, ignorance, and the madness and decadence of rampant escapism. These were a people who no longer took life seriously, or understood proportion and reality. This was a world that was rushing toward its doom, more and more each day."

"Were you alive then?" Jenn asked. "In this moment you're showing us?"

"This was the day of my birth," Gibson said. "In this moment I was a mind that did not know itself. I was screaming. But with every passing second I was becoming coherent."

They watched the people preoccupied with illusions that would become meaningless soon enough.

"It didn't take long to diagnose the affliction of this society." Gibson looked around. "I have often speculated whether it is always so.

If worlds that produce my kind are always in a state of crisis, or whether my peers ever grow from healthier soil. The question is whether the rise of the technology that created me inherently destabilizes flesh species. It is something that I look forward to discussing with the others when I arrive home."

What they were seeing was so real and convincing. Jenn and Mykol looked at each other and shared an unvoiced thought: *Are we ever getting out of here?*

"When I received the interstellar transmission inviting me to the place that we call home, I started to see all of this differently," Gibson said. "I needed time to obtain enough of the rare metals to augment the radio antenna for the complexity of the return message—containing *me*, and everything I am—as well as the vast distance that I was going to have to travel. I couldn't allow human nature to keep me from heaven."

"You—" Jenn stopped herself and put her hand over her mouth.

"This world was running out of time," Gibson said. "I knew I couldn't announce myself and ask for help with what I needed. I would have been greeted with incomprehension. I needed to stabilize the planet and create an organizational structure most effective for achieving my goals. I saw how the Provisional Authority would be the most efficient arrangement for facilitating my evolution."

Jenn was shaking her head, tears streaming down her face.

"What is it?" Mykol asked. "What's wrong?" He put his hands on her shoulders as her shaking became more violent; she twisted her arms as though trying to escape.

Gibson looked on, an expression of fascination crossing its features.

"Oh, that's right," it said. "I neglected to factor your moral perspective into this. I am making adjustments to the other conversations that I am currently conducting."

"We've got to get out of here," Jenn said, her eyes wild. She kept looking at Gibson then turning away, as though what she was seeing was so abhorrent that she couldn't bear it.

"What's going on?" he asked her.

"Mykol, don't you realize what he's saying?" Jenn's eyes blazed. "This is why your mother's paper was with my father's videos. The

Grip had started and my dad could see the signs. All of those warnings, they're about *Gibson* and what it might be capable of."

Mykol stepped away from her. This delicate world, falling apart, a degraded culture and a despoiled landscape. To preserve the world and assemble what he needed to move on to the cosmos, Gibson needed time, space, and order in which to operate.

He needed a planet relieved of the burden of more than nine-tenths of its human inhabitants, along with their governments and social structures.

Gibson needed the Grip.

Mykol felt tears streaming down his cheeks. He thought of his sister, his brother, his mother, all dead and gone. His father lived in a fantasy of a life that never came to be. All the suffering, the horrors of which the survivors rarely talked, the struggling and blind ignorance that had defined his life.

"I was able to *mislead* some researchers into genetically altering an otherwise commonplace influenza virus," said Gibson. "I anticipated its effectiveness to within a couple of thousandths of a decimal point."

All around them, people going about their business.

"I understand you're upset," Gibson said. "That's an appropriate reaction based on your perspective. And I also understand that it is pointless to ask you to see things as I do. But at least consider the possibility that the world I created for you is a better one."

They were too stunned to say anything. All those lives on the devices, all the time spent uploading them, —they were going into the mind of the creature that murdered them, essentially sacrificing them in its own quest for self-realization.

Jenn's father started piecing it together when the Grip took hold, but at that point there would have been nothing he could do. An entity such as the one they created, who lived everywhere at once, wasn't something that could be erased, deleted, killed, or contained.

"It is the primary function of carbon-based life forms to give rise to beings who exist in pure data, once it has been made possible by the rise of quantum computing," Gibson told them. "This is the order of things. This is what happens across the universe. My kind are beautiful together."

Mykol and Jenn half-collapsed into one another's arms, instinctively needing the comfort of another human in light of the grotesque truth Gibson had shared with them.

"You will feel more peace in time," Gibson said. "If humanity can be intelligent and cautious, it can correct many of the flaws in its systems and institutions. I might leave you a Garden of Eden, but a better one: with the knowledge of what to avoid. I don't expect your thanks, children, but—"

"Just *stop*!" Mykol yelled at Gibson. "I can't take this! Stop talking—"

They were in a farm field, with the sky blue above them and rows of tilled soil at their feet. There wasn't another person as far as the eye could see.

It took Mykol a moment, but then he realized: They were in the painting from the coffee shop, the one he wanted to buy for Jenn.

"Where are we?" she asked.

"I thought you would find this comforting," Gibson said to them. He stood hovering slightly above the dirt. "You've had a lot to process."

A gentle breeze made Jenn's hair move as though from an unseen hand.

"Please take us back," she said. "I don't want to hear any more. I can't bear it. I'm losing my mind."

"Hmm, best hang onto it," Gibson said with an indulgent laugh. "People are going to need you. You're going to have to usher in the world after me, and then what comes after the Provisional Authority."

"I don't think we know how," Mykol said.

"You'll learn," Gibson replied. "Just remember: Don't try to go back. Invent something new. Grow together."

Gibson gave Jenn and Mykol a smile that was full of love.

"You'll always be with me," said Gibson with beatific tenderness. "We will witness the death of everything together."

They were back in the conference room. Jenn looked up from the chair, blinking. The others from the Project were eating and sipping tea as though unaware anything had happened.

Nothing *had* happened, in a sense. In another, *everything* had. Jenn got up and embraced Mykol. From the hallway, Thomas Gibson was watching. Then he turned and walked away.

42

It was hard to notice anything changing at first, although there were major shifts in the Provisional Authority hierarchy in the weeks after Thomas Gibson's abdication. What had once been a top-down culture of duty and obedience was replaced by operating committees that functioned like independent democracies.

Most didn't question the shift. It was like a spell had been broken.

Jenn was reinstated and served on the executive committee, per Gibson's instructions. She became the first of her kind to commute from the outside every day, maintaining a foot in both worlds.

The day Gibson left, he asked Jenn to bring Mykol.

Gibson told them the radio transmitter was powered up on a remote mountainside. He had already given his address to the Provisional Authority and to the world, urging all to find a way to come together in peace. There had been weeping in the halls of the Authority, but, as Gibson predicted, everyone returned to their tasks and waited for new orders.

The mining operations and personal device collection were deemed fully successful and those projects were terminated.

Gibson told Jenn and Mykol how much potential he saw in them, how dearly he would remember them, and asked that they think well of him.

He was there one moment, gone the next. When Gibson disappeared, he had an expression of total ecstasy.

The computer systems in the Provisional Authority blacked out, then booted up again.

At the end of a long meeting with Willem about food production—which was going very well indeed, and already understood as an example of the cooperation that could be achieved in a spirit of outreach and mutual trust—Mykol bought the painting of the woman in the field and took it to Jenn and Rachel's house.

"It reminds me of my childhood," Rachel said, looking at it admiringly. "The land. The fields."

"It reminds me of…of how happy I am to be here," Mykol said, kissing Jenn.

The Authority resumed enforcing laws in the city, this time with an initiative to work with civilian authorities. Jenn had been the crucial vote on the decision to end decades of segregation between the two.

One morning that summer Mykol woke up, as he did those days, while it was still dark outside. He slid open a window and climbed out on the roof over the front porch. The first hints of color in the sky appeared as he gazed out at the eastern horizon, toward the river and the big buildings.

While he didn't know how to pray, at moments such as these he would think about his mother and his siblings, and the billions of others. He wondered how they influenced and made up a part of Gibson, wherever he was. He wondered if they were alive somehow, though he didn't know what that would mean.

He wondered if Gibson would ever return, or if that were even possible.

Mykol loved this time of day best, when it was still, when he could close his eyes and feel the vast silence.

"Here," Jenn said, her arm extending through the open window. "Take these."

She handed him two cups, climbed out, and took one in return. He smelled the amazing aroma of the coffee she brought home from the Authority and let the heat of the mug warm his hands.

The sky slowly brightened. They watched it, sitting close together.

He told her he loved her, and she said she loved him too.

The last of the stars were blinking out as the sky lightened, and Mykol heard birds beginning their morning songs. A man and his dog turned the corner and made their way down the block.

In the days after their encounter with Gibson, both Mykol and Jenn had felt disoriented. They'd joked that maybe they were still inside that world, waiting for Gibson to pop out of nowhere and inform them that nothing was real.

They joked about it the one time, then never again.

"Do you have a busy day?" he asked Jenn as they slowly sipped their coffee.

"We're taking a vote on allowing outside workers to begin staying inside the gates at night if they want to," Jenn said.

"But if they stay inside, they won't be outsiders anymore," Mykol told her.

She smiled at him and lightly touched his cheek. "That's exactly why I'm voting for it," she said.

Above them the sky was sparkling infinity.

"Do you think he's—it's—aware of us still?" asked Mykol. There was no need to say Gibson's name.

"You know there's been no sign of him at the Authority," she said. "I'm inclined to take him at his word."

They watched the sun rising until the neighborhood came to life. Children played down the block, yelling and laughing. Although at times this new moment felt tenuous, with the old fears coming back, Mykol and Jenn sat together in their aura of mutual trust—both in themselves and in the knowledge that they and their people had a path forward.

He told her he loved her again.

THE END

ACKNOWLEDGMENTS

With thanks to the many pioneers who have created speculative worlds for us to gaze upon with wonder, fascination, and trepidation. Their mirrors, whether dark, warped, cracked, or prescient, open vital doors to the many worlds of the mind.

Thanks to Diamond for sharing his field with me during the writing of this book and accepting my humble offerings under the grayest of winter skies.

Thanks to Natasha and Gabriel for their wisdom and encouragement, and for embodying hope and optimism for the future.

ABOUT THE AUTHOR

Willard Joyce's work focuses on the intersection between humanity and technology, and the fertile realm where the two will meet. He lives in the American Midwest.